A BULLET FOR THE ANGEL

Don Santina

BookLocker
Saint Petersburg, Florida

Print ISBN: 978-1-64718-980-8
Epub ISBN: 978-1-64718-981-5
Mobi ISBN: 978-1-64718-982-2

Published by BookLocker.com, Inc., St. Petersburg, Florida.

Printed on acid-free paper.

BookLocker.com, Inc.
2020

First Edition

Library of Congress Cataloging in Publication Data
Santina, Don
A Bullet For The Angel by Don Santina
Library of Congress Control Number: 2020918092

For Laura: the toughest and finest editor
a lucky writer could encounter.

ONE

North Beach, San Francisco

Saturday, December 12, 1959

"Bless me, Father, for I have sinned . . ."

Oh no, D'Angelo again.

The old priest sighed. Even in the darkness of the confessional, he recognized the profile of the bookie on the other side of the grill: the raspy voice, the telltale Sen Sen on his breath and the overpowering fragrance of Aqua Velva aftershave lotion. The priest frowned. *Aftershave at dinner time.* He shifted on his hard wooden seat.

Just about every two months, Frankie D'Angelo decided that he needed to go to confession. His sins never changed. Inside the musty cubicle, he enumerated the same offenses he had declared two months earlier: bookmaking, flirting with the young woman at the bakery, short changing the tourists at his cigar store. Sometimes he included hitting his children, but he wasn't sure that was a sin. The priest would remind him that it was only a sin if it was done in anger. D'Angelo didn't think so: he was not an angry sort of man. And so the discussion continued six times a year in the hushed whispers of the confessional booth.

"Yes, my son," the priest murmured as D'Angelo poured out his litany of familiar transgressions. Ultimately, the priest gave him his penance and absolution with a pointless admonition to sin no more. The bookie exited the confessional and turned down the center aisle of the church to the altar.

D'Angelo was a small thin man who sported a barely visible Don Ameche moustache on his upper lip. He favored dark shiny clothes, heavily starched white shirts, and flashy footwear. Tonight he wore his palomino wingtips with metal taps on the heels, so as he walked toward the altar with his hands folded and his eyes lowered in penitence, his heels clicked loudly at each step.

In the candlelit alcoves off the side aisles of Saint Peter and Paul's, old women in black coats and head scarves looked up briefly at the distraction, twitched their mouths in disapproval, and then returned to their prayers. The plaster faces on the saints above them grimaced and glowered in the flickering lights of the votive candles. Now and then a few coins dropped from arthritic fingers into the metal offering boxes, a match snapped and a new candle blazed in the alcove.

D'Angelo paid no heed to the old women. He had gotten the easy priest again. The other priests always scolded him and ordered him to make a novena. This was easy: a rosary. He knelt at the altar and began his penance. He did not have rosary beads, so he imagined a pari-mutual board with ten lights going on and off sequentially as he said each Hail Mary. Soon there were eight lights, then seven.

As D'Angelo prayed, the high-ceilinged gothic church groaned and creaked about him as a brief gust of wind whistled through the alley between the church and the grammar school. The women finished their supplications and, tightening their coats about them, began shuffling out of the church. It was Saturday night near dinner time, twelve days before Christmas Eve.

He missed a few Hail Mary's in the last decade of the rosary because his mind wandered to the business offer he had turned down several weeks ago. Should he have taken it? No, it was an offer for chumps, and Frankie D'Angelo is not a chump! Maybe his partner is kind of a chump, but he's a rich kid and they both knew that if they waited, they would make a lot more money. He didn't like his partner, but they were in for a pile of money. *That's what's important, that pile of money we'll make if we wait!* So they told that guy to stuff his chintzy offer. He smiled at the memory of telling off that chiseler.

D'Angelo's mind wandered to Serafina, who worked at the bakery. Maybe he'd see her tomorrow when he'd go to get pastries for the family after Mass. Maybe their eyes would touch for a moment. *Maybe*. Abruptly, he put her out of his mind and crossed himself. It was bad luck to think about such things while doing penance. He arose from the altar, genuflected, and clicked back up the center aisle. He stopped at a pew near the door of the church and picked up his overcoat and hat. He pulled the coat on, nodded to one of the old women who was leaving and held the door for her. Then he blessed himself from the holy water font and stepped outside, pulling his fedora down on his head.

There was no one in Washington Square Park across the street from the church and very few people on the sidewalks. An unusually heavy fog hung on the streets of San Francisco on this eighty-fourth day of the drought. The Christmas shoppers had gone home, and the night club crowd wouldn't be out for a few more hours. Even the beatniks stayed inside. A few cars hissed by on the wet pavement, their windows rolled up against the elements.

D'Angelo turned up the collar on his overcoat and walked down the steps of the church to the sidewalk. Some hardy soul had left his window open in one of the apartments next to the school. A radio was playing Christmas carols and he cocked his head to the strains of "Rudolph the Red Nosed Reindeer." He smiled and stepped into the street after quickly looking both ways. The D'Angelo family lived in a flat on Stockton Street two blocks from the church.

Down on the corner of Columbus, a dark green Buick hardtop eased out of its parking place. There were two occupants in the car. The driver flicked the headlights on and crawled slowly up the street. The electric window on the passenger side slid quietly down as the Buick moved forward.

D'Angelo had reached the sidewalk on the Washington Square side of the street when the Buick drove alongside and stopped.

"Hey, Frankie," a voice called from inside the Buick.

He turned, a smile on his face. A bookmaker never knows when business will come to him. The smile vanished when he saw the long barreled automatic pistol poking out of the car window at him.

"Merry Christmas, Frankie!" the voice laughed, and the automatic fired.

No! D'Angelo thought he said as the first bullet hit him in the chest. He staggered at the impact and grabbed at the parking meter as the automatic fired once more. His legs collapsed under him, and he slid down the meter pole. Another bullet hit him as he landed on the sidewalk.

The bookie named Frankie D'Angelo was dead when he flopped over into the gutter, his overcoat falling open and exposing his sharp pressed slacks and polished palominos to an overspray of the park's broken sprinklers. Above the lifeless body, Gene Autry continued his story about the reindeer who saved the day for Santa Claus.

"Hey, what's going on?" someone yelled from outside the restaurant on the other side of the park.

The Buick sped up the hill, turned the corner on Grant Avenue and disappeared into the night.

TWO

Fillmore, San Francisco

Saturday, December 12, 1959

He couldn't understand why his arm was on the ground and his watch was still ticking. He studied it like a biologist analyzing a new splat of something new on a glass tray under a microscope. The second hand on the Waltham continued its course around the dial, but his fingers were not moving. *That's odd.* He followed the arm up to a point just past his elbow. The cloth of his GI shirt sleeve sliced neatly, his arm a mass of butchered bone, muscle and blood no longer attached . . . he screamed.

"Johnny, Johnny, it's just a dream, baby, please, baby, it's just a dream!" Cayenne Phillips held John Maletesta in her arms, rocking him as he cried aloud. "Just a dream, baby, just a dream."

Maletesta stopped shaking, pushed his fingers through his dark curly hair and opened his eyes. He was soaking wet in perspiration.

"Cayenne, I'm sorry," he strangled the cry in his throat.

"I love you, Johnny," she whispered, holding him tighter as they slipped into an unquiet sleep.

They awoke about 5pm, and he reached over with his right arm and slowly pulled the sheet down. Cayenne's dark eyes blinked sleepily as he stroked her silken bronze skin. She flashed the smile that had so enthralled him when they first met. Her short natural hair accented her high cheek bones and full lips.

"Johnny, stop it! It's time for you to go. You'll get in trouble."

"Drink to me only with thine eyes," he murmured as he caressed her breasts.

"Corny ass professor . . ."

Shortly before seven o'clock, Maletesta slid out of bed and began putting on his clothes at the dressing table near the window. Cayenne watched him dress, studying his thin athletic body marred by the stump of his left arm.

There were some scary times when her man with the enchanting hazel eyes burst out of his usually genial demeanor. Once, while they were walking on Geary, they came upon a middle-aged man beating his dog with a cane. Maletesta flew into a rage, grabbing the man and shoving him up against a chain link fence. Suddenly, he stopped and turned back to her with an awkward smile. He had no memory of the incident.

Cayenne frowned at the memory and then jumped out of bed to help him with his shirt buttons.

"Cayenne," he said hoarsely, "I do have to go. Put something on quick, before I lose my job."

She made a face at him and reached for a red satin robe on the chair next to the dressing table. She tied it loosely and turned back to him. The petite robe barely covered her jutting breasts and shapely legs.

"There, I'm ready."

Maletesta looked at her, swallowed and took a deep breath.

"Who's at the club tonight?" he blurted. Cayenne, a reserve bartender at the Fillmore's finest night club, the Club Carolina, replied sassily.

"Bobby Bland, and you're gonna miss it."

"Nope. I should be there in time for his first set, but not the warmup acts."

"Only if those smelly old beatniks let you out early. They gonna beat on their bongos?"

"Maybe," he laughed, "but the poetry reading shouldn't last more than an hour. My class put the program together, but I wasn't involved in choosing the featured poet, who does not impress me. Sister Agatha wants more participation from the students in these events, so there it is. Whatever happens, happens."

After Cayenne finished with the buttons of his black dress shirt with the shortened left sleeve, Maletesta ran a comb through his hair. He studied himself in the mirror and smirked at his vigilant eyes and hawky nose. Not bad, but no movie star. He saw Cayenne in the mirror and turned to her.

"Cayenne, I think I'm the luckiest man in the whole world. How did I ever find you?"

"Cuz you dig R&B, Johnny, and R&B led you to me," she replied, snapping on his clip-on tie and lightly running her hand down the front of his shirt. He caught her hand and kissed it.

"You see," she laughed, "it's poetry: R&B led you to me."

"And mysteries," he added, nodding toward the latest Ross McDonald paperback on her dressing table.

The window next to the table looked out on the intersection of Turk Street and Divisadero in the heart of the Fillmore District. Maletesta glanced briefly at the cars in the intersection and sat down on the cushioned chair to pull on his black slacks. Cayenne smiled.

"What?" he asked, buckling the narrow black leather belt.

"You're old Sister Agatha is something else, isn't she? Sometimes I get jealous."

"I owe her a lot," he answered. "She probably saved my life after the war. You'll have to meet her one of these days."

"Well, when?" she shot back.

"Hell, our schedules never seem to work out. Like tonight: I'm at a poetry reading at the school and you're at the club. During the week, when I'm teaching, you're sleeping."

“I’m up by eleven!” she protested, “and I’ve got my own classes to attend at City College, Mister Professor.”

They had moved into her living room. The leather sofa, side chairs and the low Danish modern coffee table were a birthday gift from Maletesta. He stepped into his black loafers and Cayenne helped him with his dark red checkered sport coat at the door. The empty left sleeve was carefully stitched up.

“Now, doesn’t my man look fine?” she smiled as she buttoned the middle button of his coat.

“Not half as fine as his lady,” Maletesta said, kissing her on the forehead. “*Ciao, bella mia*. See you later.”

“You know what John Hardy says, ‘remember your ABC’s: always be cool.’” They both laughed.

Maletesta was through the door and down the stairs in under a minute. Cayenne went back to the window and watched him get into his cherry 1949 Oldsmobile Rocket 88 parked in the bus stop across the street. Maletesta always parked in bus stops and driveways. Parallel parking in tight spaces was out of the question, even with his adept use of the suicide knob on his steering wheel. She watched as the Oldsmobile roared off.

Cayenne pulled down the shade and went into the bathroom to run the tub. As the steam filled the room, she threw in some fancy-named bath salts that Johnny had given her. She closed her eyes and inhaled deeply. Maletesta had given her many things, but she would not let him pay her rent. Even though he seemed to be rich, he didn’t act like a rich man. He didn’t have to teach, but he loved it.

He was thirty seven; she was thirty. Was it the age difference that mattered? No, that was not the problem, and she knew it. Did he love her? She thought so. She took another deep breath. *Johnny, my Johnny, where will our love go? Where can it go, Johnny? Johnny?* She was too afraid it would never work.

Girl, you stop thinking this way! She dropped her satin robe and stepped into the bathtub. She hummed "Fever" as she slid under the soothing bubbles, smiling as they tickled her nose. She had plenty of time. She did not have to be at the club until eight-fifteen, fifteen minutes before the doors opened. She knew it would be packed tonight, so she would leave early. The club was only four blocks from her apartment.

A half hour later, she was applying her lipstick when the phone rang. After two rings, she groaned, put the lipstick down and picked up the phone.

"Yes?" she said.

"Cayenne . . ."

"Yusef."

"Hey, baby sister, you finally got it! How's it goin'?" the voice drawled.

"Look, Mama said it might break her heart because she named you after her favorite brother Alexander, but you got a right to call yourself any fool name you want to. So, what do you want?"

She took a cigarette from the silver box on the table and lit it.

"Alexander's a slave name! Don't you understand that? The people in the Muslim world they know . . ."

"Yusef," she interrupted, "I'll be late for work."

"Work? That juke joint?" he spat through the phone.

She paused. She wouldn't let herself be drawn into the same old argument. She blew a smoke ring into the mirror above the telephone table.

"And just what line of work are you into now," she said finally, "still handing out Ko-rans door to door?"

There was a silence on the other end. Cayenne frowned. Her brother was never at a loss for words. Then he spoke.

"Pepper, baby sister, I'm in a jam. A big one."

"What kind of jam?" She softened. He'd used her kid name.

"Some white dudes been followin' me around. I think I'm on to something. I can't tell you, but I gotta blow town for a while. Do you have any ready money?"

"Sure I do, but what's the matter? Yusef, tell me, what's the matter? What can I do? I mean it." He had never asked her for money before.

"I can't . . . uh, makes no sense. I'll call you tomorrow."

"Yusef, meet me at the Club tonight!"

There was no answer.

"Yusef! Yusef!" Cayenne yelled into the phone.

"OK, I'll be there. Don't worry, baby sister."

"Yusef, please take care. I love you."

Cayenne replaced the phone on its receiver, leaned against the wall and looked at her watch: 8 pm. She would have to run now. She grabbed her coat and left her apartment.

THREE

Burlingame

Saturday, December 12, 1959

"I . . . I . . . I . . ."

The speaker paused in his rhythmic delivery. From the back of the campus auditorium of All Saints College in Burlingame, Sister Agatha estimated that he repeated the first person pronoun about thirty-one times. She sighed quietly but kept her eyes on the figure sitting on the stage.

The speaker was dressed in a black tee shirt, black dungarees and black sneakers with a black Greek fisherman's cap lightly set on his head. Perspiration rolled down his forehead and trickled into his scraggly blond beard. He rose slowly from the sitting position and stretched his arms over his head. The room was dark, the only light being provided by two four-foot candles placed on either side of the speaker. In front of him was a sea of dimly-lit heads, an audience of students intently silent. Somewhere behind him, the bongo drummer began again. This time it was a slow tattoo: tok-tok, tok-tok, tok-tok.

The speaker's eyes were closed. But as he lowered his arms to his side, he abruptly opened them wide. He brought his hands in front of his face and stared at them as he had never seen them before. Then he suddenly clasped himself, pulling his shoulders forward and gripping his biceps with his hands.

"I . . . I . . . I . . ." he continued, his face filling with anguish. "I . . .I . . . I . . ."

The drummer picked up the tempo: tok-tok, tok-tok, tok-tok, incessantly until the rhythm met the pulsing beat of the human heart.

"I . . . I . . . I . . ." matched the furious tempo of the percussion instrument as the speaker spit the words out.

Suddenly there was silence. The drumming stopped. The speaker lowered his hands to his side again. His head dropped slightly; then he turned sharply to his right and took three broad steps to the edge of the stage. With an about face, he stalked to the other edge of the stage and stopped, facing the audience.

"Am," he whispered, "I . . . am."

The audience took a collective breath. The speaker brought his arms up gain.

"AM! AM! AM!" he screamed. "I AM!"

The candles were blown out, leaving the room in total darkness.

For a moment the audience sat dumb, stunned. Then a thunderous applause erupted with scattered cries of "Bravo!" Students were on their feet, clapping wildly. The clamor bounced off the paneled walls of the darkened room. Some of the students hugged each other in joy. This *was* poetry!

John Maletesta leaned against the back wall.

"What bullshit," he muttered.

"John, you shush!" said a lyrical voice in the darkness over to his right.

"Oh, excuse me, Sister, I didn't know you were there," Maletesta apologized toward the

voice.

Sister Agatha chuckled.

"As an English teacher, John, I would think you would be more tolerant to evolving poetic art forms." She adjusted the rimless spectacles on her nose.

"With all due respect, Sister, I'm trying to teach our students Whitman and TS Eliot," he whispered. "I think some of the Beat poetry is really exceptional, but this is very light weight stuff." He pointed toward the stage. "I also have some other ideas about that character . . . not very evolved, I might say."

"Sinclair?"

"I'd say he's got more than free verse on his mind."

"Oh, don't be such a sour puss, John."

Before Maletesta could answer, the house lights came on and they both looked toward the stage. From a door behind the stage, the poets who had read earlier in the program emerged, looking slightly self-conscious, their type-written manuscripts held tightly in their hands, blinking into the lights. The musicians came next: an emaciated man with bongo drums, a smiling man with an alto sax, and a confused-looking woman with a medieval recorder. They all received polite applause from the students as they stepped down from the stage. For a moment, then stage was empty, and then the star of the reading appeared.

Jean-Paul Sinclair, the new darling of the San Francisco poetry scene, strolled across the room, a disarming boyish smile on his face. He was in his early 30's with wavy blondish hair, thick eyebrows and a strong chin covered by a wispy beard like an adolescent's first growth. He wore a long red scarf, the ends of which shimmered as he walked. It gave him the air of a dashing aviator in an old black and white movie.

The female students surrounded him, some holding paperback editions of his collected works. They clamored for his autograph, treating him like their younger sister's favorite rock 'n roll star. Sinclair took it all in stride, with just the right balance of stagey humility and complete confidence. He handled the group comfortably—a clever word here, an autograph there, an attentive frown, an easy laugh.

Bastard should run for office, Maletesta thought as he reached the institutional coffee urn on the long folding table near the main doors of the auditorium. He skipped the little pieces of stale fruitcake on paper plates, but allowed himself a cup of over-brewed coffee, his thoughts as dark as the murky liquid that steamed out of the spigot into the ceramic cup. He had long ago taught himself to hold down the spigot with the index finger of his right hand while holding the cup with the other four fingers. *I am,* he thought, *this is poetry?*

"Eat something, John."

Christ, he thought, turning, *Sister Agatha again.* But as he turned to speak with his boss, the president of the college, his whole demeanor changed. His eyes lit up; his frown became a smile when he looked past Sister Agatha.

Tal. He spotted his daughter among the students.

Tal was in a heated discussion with another student who was holding an open book of poetry in front of them. She gesticulated with her hands as she spoke. Her long black hair flowed over the collar of the Navy pea coat she'd recently bought at Kaplan's surplus on Market Street. She punctuated her literary points with those quick smiles that wrinkled her nose in a most charming manner. Maletesta beamed with pride watching his adopted daughter. Images flashed through his mind: the little Dayak orphan he'd found in the jungle of Borneo thirteen years ago; his determination to bring her back to the States; grammar school, high school, and now a sophomore at the College of All Saints. He swelled inside. She had not seen him yet, and he relished the moment as spectator.

"You know, John, I think you would be impossible without Tal," Sister Agatha quipped as she bit into a piece of fruitcake. She was a short round woman in her late fifties who had hired Maletesta after the war and sent him on the ill-fated archeological expedition that forever linked the three of them together.

Maletesta raised an eyebrow at her good naturedly.

Tal saw them and came over.

"Hi, Dad. Hi, Sister Agatha. Isn't Jean-Paul cool? Isn't he *really cool*!" Her eyes were shining.

"Well," Maletesta began. He was torn between wanting to give her a hug--which he couldn't because it would embarrass her--and tell the truth about what he really felt about Jean-Paul Sinclair. He paused too long.

"Let's face it, Dad. You're just not with it. You never like anything that *I* like!" There was a sliver of anger in her voice, but she turned it off quickly. "How did *you* like him, Sister?"

"Oh, I think he's quite interesting," Sister Agatha replied, diplomatically, "but I'm more comfortable with a few more words in my poems."

That brought a laugh out of the three of them, and Maletesta tried to seize the initiative.

"I'll be leaving in a few minutes, Tal. Would you like a ride back to the City?"

"No thanks, Dad. I'm going back with Terri and Antoinette. See you at home later."

She reached up and kissed him lightly on the cheek and then made her way back into the crowd. Maletesta watched her disappear. She was 19 now. He was trying to allow her as much freedom as she needed to grow, but it was hard to let go. After his wife Annemarie died in the accident eight years ago, there was just the two of them. "Just two peas in a pod," Tal had called them.

But it was different now. He knew it was time to open the pod and let the other pea out, but it was still difficult.

"As bad as it is," Sister Agatha asked, "would you like another cup of coffee?"

"Thanks, but I need to step it up and go. Bobby 'Blue" Bland's at the Club Carolina tonight. I'll see you on Monday, Sister," he answered and began walking toward the double exit doors which led to the parking lot.

"Drive carefully," she called to his back. "By the way, you know we're on Christmas break now."

"Oh yeah," he called back. "Thanks. Guess I won't see you on Monday after all."

As he reached the doors, he glanced back into the room and flinched as he saw Tal talking to Sinclair. She was smiling and nodding at whatever he was saying. He swore under his breath and banged open the exit doors as he left. He was still fuming when he reached his car in the parking lot.

FOUR

Fillmore

Saturday, December 12, 1959

"The problem with Butchertown," a Black horn player once told him, "is that almighty stench from all those animals getting slaughtered. Ooo-weee, sometimes you can hear 'em bawling, man, as they're walking up those wooden ramps to their *doom.*"

The horn player, a friend of Cayenne's whose name was Yancey, shuddered at the memory.

"So don't blame those old cows when they make a run for it and end up in the middle of Third Street. No sir! Run for it, animal, the man's got a hammer! And then there's the damned junk yards with all those wrecks and mud and mangy dogs. And the stink. Sheee-it, man, that's why Fillmore is where it's at."

Maletesta thought about Yancey and the Fillmore as he drove north on 101 from Burlingame and pushed the needle on the speedometer of his Oldsmobile over seventy. On his right the airport appeared and disappeared. The industrial menace of South City loomed in the windshield and then vanished as he passed the exits for Hunter's Point and the ship yards. He was running late to catch Bobby Bland's first show at the Club Carolina.

"Yes, the Fillmore is where it's at," Maletesta murmured as the speedometer climbed.

"Now, look here," Yancey had continued, "we *own* shit in the Fillmore, you know what I mean? My brother-in-law *owns* a barbershop. I mean *he owns* it, man, not some whitey downtown. This is *our* neighborhood, man, you know what I mean? We got Bop City, the Alabam, the Blue Mirror, the Chicken Shack, Melrose Records, we got it."

As he turned onto Geneva Avenue, Maletesta laughed out loud at the memory of Yancey's analysis. He saw Yancey--resplendent in a silver silk shirt and black sports coat-- sitting across the table from him in Bop City, taking a breath before delivering his punch line.

"And we got shoe repair, churches and funeral parlors," Yancey expounded. "Sole your shoes or shoe your souls, brother, we gotcha covered. Amen."

A few national writers referred to the Fillmore as the "Harlem of the West," but Maletesta knew that it was more than that. The Fillmore was dominated by Fillmore Street, a mile-long pulsating artery which was the life blood of the neighborhood. Fillmore Street was a village with other smaller villages attached to it, all with a distinct southern and mid-western character, and the bustle of Fillmore Street could be momentarily halted at any time during the day when the drivers of two cars driving in opposite directions stopped to exchange pleasantries. The village had its own rules of behavior and civility.

As Maletesta stopped at the red light at Ocean and San Jose Avenue, his memory turned sour. A wave of anger overcame him as he remembered his recent discussion with his thesis advisor at Stanford. The discussion hadn't gone well.

"As far as the Black population is concerned," Maletesta had argued during the meeting, "the city of Saint Francis exists in name only. Two months ago, white students at Mission High put a "no niggers allowed" sign in the window of the ice cream shop across from Dolores Park and damned near started a race war!"

His thesis advisor, whose name was John Beck, shook his head incredulously.

Maletesta paused and cleared his throat.

"Unfortunately, the white students at Mission and other schools are only reflecting the attitudes of their parents, the police and City Hall."

Maletesta attempted to light a Fatima. Beck frowned. There was no ashtray on his desk, so Maletesta put the cigarette back in the pack. Beck's assistant, a graduate student whose name was Harris, sat next to him and smiled weakly.

"As you know, Doctor Beck," Maletesta drew a deep breath and continued, "thousands of Black people emigrated here from the South during the war. They came mainly for the jobs in the shipyards . . . and, of course, our government needed them. However, when the war was over, things changed. The old guard of San Francisco assumed that the

Black people would go home . . . back to the Jim Crow South."

"Yes, and . . .?"

"Well, they didn't go back, did they?"

"No?"

"No, they didn't. And now the system we call civil society had a problem, and it responded to the problem of Black people staying here by excluding and separating them from the rest of us, the white people."

"Yes," Harris interrupted, "I read an article in the *Sun Reporter* about how Black people can't get fair mortgage rates to buy a house or even be allowed to buy a house in certain neighborhoods. Isn't that right, Professor Maletesta?"

Maletesta nodded.

"Absurdly enough, they even tried to stop the center fielder of the Giants from buying a home in the white Forest Hill neighborhood."

"Willie Mays," Harris proudly clarified.

"Giants?" Professor Beck queried, a baffled look on his face. "Giants?"

Beck was a plump man nearing seventy. He'd chaired this Department at Stanford since the end of the war and had heard and dismissed many a doctoral thesis from bright young scholars. This one was different because he was older, an English major and a disabled vet. *Good God, and last week young girl proposed a thesis about the history of women's rights!* Beck settled back in his chair and nodded slightly at the English teacher from Burlingame.

"Pray, continue," Beck murmured, glancing at the pocket watch in his vest pocket and scowling at Harris.

Maletesta's mind reeled. *Gianni, this isn't going anywhere. This old bastard will never change. Get the hell out of it.*

Maletesta shook his head like a horse with an annoying fly. He shook it again.

Deploy the men, Gianni! Deploy! Lonnie, cover our back. They're coming! Cover our back!

"No!" Maletesta blurted, "no!"

Beck and Harris startled in their chairs.

"So," Maletesta almost shouted to get himself under control, "the excluded people created their own culture, you see, their own culture, separate and maybe better than the culture that excluded them!"

"Steady now, professor, steady now," Beck admonished him.

Maletesta wiped the sweat off his forehead with his right hand.

"They made a city within a city, a self-sustaining, self-contained Fillmore."

"Hmmm," Beck nodded.

"In a way, the Fillmore is similar to the European ghetto model, but there is an important difference here: music. I'm talking about rhythm and blues!"

Maletesta grew animated, his animated eyes lit up, and his right hand moved like a symphony conductor as he made his points.

"Rhythm and blues is the connective tissue of the Fillmore within itself and with all the other black communities in our country. R&B has its own charts, its own following, and its own radio stations."

"I've heard some of their disc jockeys," Harris added enthusiastically. "They have really neat names like Jumpin' George and Rockin' Lucky."

"Rock-ing Lucky?" Beck was perplexed.

"Yes, Rockin' Lucky," Maletesta corrected. "He's a DJ—that's a disc jockey--who plays new record releases on "take it or break it for Langendorf," the bread company. The show is based on how many listeners call the station, so if enough callers don't like the new record and say "break it," the record is broken on the air. As silly as that might sound, it's actually an exercise in community power that white Top 40 radio does not have."

Beck sighed and managed a meagre smile. *Take it or break it? Good heavens!*

Maletesta read the signs and knew that his thesis was finished, but he soldiered on.

"The record charts and new releases are available in stores like Melrose Records on Fillmore Street," Maletesta continued, leaning forward in his chair. "Essentially, the record store becomes a cultural center."

"A cultural center," Beck noted as he adjusted a manila folder on his desk.

"You see, we think of segregation as just in the South, but actually and especially for musicians, it's all over the country. They can't play the major halls and the hotel ballrooms, so, once again, the excluded culture responds with its own system."

"Yes?" Beck suppressed a yawn.

"Yes. Black musicians play in a unique circuit of clubs which are located in black neighborhoods all over the country. It's called the 'chitlin' circuit.' And then there are the jazz clubs . . ."

Beck stood up and spoke as he walked toward the door of his office. Harris remained in his chair.

"Professor Maletesta, I don't wish to waste any more of your valuable time, but I regret to inform you that your proposed subject really does not fit within the parameters of our Doctoral program. I hope you continue that you continue to write magazine articles."

Maletesta also stood up.

"Excuse me," he said, and Beck turned around at the door.

"Professor Beck, I recommend that you put your parameters where the sun don't shine. Thank you for your time."

“I beg your pardon?’

“You can beg my pardon all day long,” Maletesta said as he burst past Beck through the doorway, “*baciami il culo, stronzo!*”

FIVE

Fillmore

Saturday, December 12, 1959

The Club Carolina was a major stopover on the "chitlin circuit." Owned by James "Sassy" Butler, the Carolina was plush. The carpet was plush; the upholstered booths along the wall on the right were plush. The bar along the opposite wall was mahogany, as were the cocktail tables and chairs set out between the bar and the booths. Small solid brass lamps flickered in the booths and soft overhead lighting cast a warm glow over the room. The dance floor in front of the stage at the far end was large enough to encourage dancing, but not so large as to turn the club into a ballroom venue like the Fillmore Auditorium on Geary. The stage and house lighting was designed and installed by a downtown theatre technician.

Sassy James—they said that his mother gave him that name when he was nine months old—presided over his musical kingdom from an upstairs office which had curtained windows looking down into the club. Sometimes he sat at the bar, but mostly he stayed in the office connected by intercom to the box office, the bar, backstage, and the booth in the parking lot. Trusted and well-paid associates were at the other ends of the intercom.

James possessed two qualities which were rare among club owners and saloonkeepers: he did not deal in dope or girls, and he was a patron of musicians. He actually loved musicians. He treated them like royalty. He fronted money for recording sessions, he paid rents, he went bail for junkies, he got horns out of hock. It was no accident that everybody in the R&B world wanted to play the Club Carolina.

Maletesta gave the keys to his Oldsmobile to the valet in the parking lot, bought a pack of smokes in the cigar store across the street, and jaywalked back to the club. He paid the cover charge at the box office and was greeted in the foyer by the elegant Miss Helene, Sassy James' official greeter. Miss Helene was a tall woman in full evening gown who made club patrons feel like coming into the Club Carolina was the best decision they had made in their lives. However, there was no missing the intent of the two bullet-headed enforcers, stocky men in pall bearer suits, who hovered near her. No tie, no entry. Too drunk, get out. Looking for trouble, you found it.

"Good evening, professor, you're looking exceptional tonight," Miss Helene beamed, her eyes noting his black shirt and Bo Diddley sport coat under his overcoat.

"John, please. Thank you, Miss Helene," Maletesta replied, "and you too, as always. How many hearts have you broken tonight?"

He grinned and allowed one of the bullet-heads help him remove his overcoat which he handed to the hat check whose concession was next to the inside doorway.

"How you do carry on, professor," Miss Helene sighed, as Maletesta slipped through the heavy drapes.

He paused inside while waiting for his eyes to adjust to the low lighting of the room. The room was packed. Cocktail waitresses were scurrying between the crowded tables carrying trays of drinks, some holding trays above their heads. In the dim light they reminded Maletesta of rare birds with glassy plumage that twinkled as they passed under the ceiling lights. There was no room at the bar that he could see, but as he moved closer, he saw Cayenne pouring a tray of drinks for one of the waitresses.

On stage, the house band was cranking through the audience warmup with one of the backup singers doing a fairly close imitation of other popular singers. Maletesta watched as the singer did a pretty good rendition of Ray Charles--sunglasses, awkward movement and all. The twelve musicians in the band were dressed in shiny blue suits which glowed slightly under the stage lights. The horn section was on a one foot riser stage left, and the piano and four backup singers were on a similar riser stage right. The drummer was center rear flanked by the bass player with a red Fender Precision bass and the guitarist with a cherry red Gibson guitar. The whole stage was lit except for the area in front of the rhythm section.

Down of the dance floor, a few couples were dancing and several women stood with all their attention riveted to the center stage, giggling in anticipation. Behind them, their male escorts shuffled their feet, smoking and jostling each other. A haze of smoke hung over the entire room, and the babble of voices was deafening.

Maletesta found an empty stool and squeezed himself in between two older men who nodded an acknowledgement to him. He nodded back, fished a cigarette out of the pack in this shirt pocket and lit it. Most of the Club Carolina personnel knew about his relationship with Cayenne; maybe they didn't approve but were perplexed by the one-armed white man who dug their music. To Sassy James, being Italian counted a little, but not much.

Maletesta laid a fiver on the bar as Cayenne was finishing an order for one of the waitresses. Within two minutes, she set an Old Crow over ice in front of him, winking as she picked up the bill. She was wearing a white silk blouse and maroon slacks with a shimmering gold bracelet on each wrist and a gold choker peeking out through the open collar of her blouse. For a moment, Maletesta drifted away in her beauty and her elegance . . . and those eyes that reached into his soul. He knew the other men at the bar were studying her closely. He didn't like it but was learning to live with it.

Cayenne served several other customers at the bar and another waitress order at the station before she came back with his change. Maletesta gestured to a group of four young white men sitting at a table close to the stage. He was accustomed to being one of the few white men in the club.

"Who are they? They don't even look old enough."

"Helene's got a soft spot for young musicians. Sassy doesn't care as long as their ID's pass and they spend money."

"Nursing one beer a set?"

"Yeah, but they're a great audience. They clap for everything."

At the moment, almost as if on cue, the Ray Charles imitator wrapped it up with a quick showy bow, and the young men applauded wildly. The rest of the crowd was saving their emotions for the main event.

"They love it," Cayenne chirped, "just like you do, soul brother number eight million and twenty six."

The band suddenly broke into a familiar riff, and the house and lights dimmed even lower that they were before. A follow spot suddenly appeared and hovered near the curtain at the rear of the stage. A stage hand whisked a chrome plated microphone stand onto the dark area at the front of the stage. The horns blasted the riff a notch louder as the drummer accelerated a series of rolls between the riffs. The crowd was on its feet, moving as one to the time of the music. From offstage somewhere in the dark came the announcer's voice:

"And NOW . . . ladies and gentlemen! On stage at the Club Carolina! In his ONLY Bay Area appearance! The moment YOU'VE been waiting for . . . here's THE MAN! I mean THE MAN . . . the sensational . . . the incomparable . . . the dynamic . . . BOBBY BLAND . . . BOBBY BLUE BLAND!!!"

The singer bounded out from behind the curtain, and the band immediately jumped into the opening number, "Farther Up the Road." The follow spot brought to center stage. Resplendent in an electric light blue suit with an open white Mister B-collar shirt and shot cuffs, Bobby Bland pulled the microphone off its stand and hit the first verse, "farther up the road, someone's gonna hurt you like you hurt me."

The Carolina went crazy.

The women in the front screamed. The women in the back screamed. The women in the middle screamed. The men whistled, hooted, clapped or nodded their heads in time to the music. The lights went from hot to cool to hot again as Bobby Bland continued his vocal onslaught. By the third number, his jacket was off and the women in the front were calling "yes, yes, yes" and "try me, baby" with tears rolling down their faces.

The joint was a jumpin' Maletesta sang to himself as he beat out a light tattoo on the bar with his glass. His journey from opera to rhythm and blues was accidental but thorough. A year ago, he wrote a magazine piece on the new poetry of the beatniks, and the New York editor--mistaking Maletesta for a pop culture writer--requested something on the West Coast "chitlin' circuit." He had never heard of it but never refused a challenge. He called Ralph Gleason of the *Chronicle,* and Gleason started him off with a list of clubs and radio stations. Four months later, Maletesta had not only completed an authoritative article on Bay Area R&B, he had fallen in love with Cayenne Phillips.

Up in his office on the second floor, Sassy was smiling, looking down through the one way glass at the musical hysteria below him.

"This, gentlemen, is the good life," Sassy opined to the two bullet heads. "We makin' money; people havin' a good time. Bobby's happy. He likes this room, likes our people: no trash, no jive-ass turkeys . . ."

The buzzer on the intercom interrupted him. He pushed a button on the machine on his desk.

"Yeah," he growled.

"Got a hassle down here, Mister Butler. It's Cayenne's brother; he's got no cover but he wants in. Hat check went to get Cayenne, but he's got a wise ass mouth on him…"

Sassy flicked the intercom off. The bullet heads were already out the door and headed down the stairs.

"Throw that son of a bitch out!" he yelled after them.

Maletesta saw the hat check girl come up to the bar and call Cayenne. He saw the look of concern on Cayenne's face as she darted back toward the lobby. He slid off his stool and tried to follow her, but the crowd was too dense. Several "excuse-me's" later, he was only half way to the lobby. Cayenne was coming back through the curtains when Maletesta finally caught up with her. He put his hand on her arm.

"What's the matter? Is everything all right?" He had to shout over the din.

She put her mouth up to his ear.

"There's nothing you can do about it," she said flatly and squeezed her way back to the bar.

When he got back to his stool, she was methodically mixing drinks and setting up trays.

"Two bourbon sevens, a gin 'n tonic and a gin screwdriver," called one of the waitresses at the bar's waitress station.

"You got it," Cayenne answered and began filling the order.

Maletesta marveled at the way she handled glasses, ice cubes, bottles and mixers so quickly and deftly. He knew this was why Sassy had taken a chance with a woman bartender. She made a lot of money for the club, but--unlike many bartenders--none of it went into her pocket. Sassy didn't need to have a watcher watching her as he did for other bartenders. Maletesta wondered if he could keep up with her if he hadn't lost his arm in the war. He finished his highball and decided that—luckily--he didn't need both of his limbs to teach or write occasional articles.

Cayenne was suddenly aware of him and smiled absently. He blew her a kiss as he left. Bobby Bland's first set was just ending, but he had to be up early and Cayenne was working until last call.

The bullet heads watched him as he made his way through the lobby and followed him out to his car in the parking lot. They didn't return to the club until he had driven off. He frowned at them in the rear view mirror and then put it out of his mind.

SIX

North Beach

Sunday, December 13, 1959

It was long past midnight and the night was growing cold, but life looked pretty good to Jean-Paul Sinclair as he staggered down Bannam toward his flat at the end of the alley. He had just left Gino and Carlo's, the bar down the street on Green, where he'd stood for a round of drinks with the locals. Unlike many of the other Beats and their camp followers, money—bread, scratch, jack, dough—was not a problem for him. He had a trust fund no one knew about except the family he left in Dayton, Ohio where he was known by his real name, Paul Seiberling. One day his father had handed him an account number and said, "Paul, I know you can't seem to keep your feet on the ground around here. I have a proposal for you. I want you to see the world—take your time--and when you find out what piece of crap the world is, you can come back and join me in the hardware business. My door is always open."

After two years of bumming around in Mexico, a year in Southern California trying to sell bad scripts to small time movie producers, and a year in Big Sur absorbing nature, he emerged in San Francisco on the crest of a cultural explosion which would become known as the Beat Era. He wrote his father and told him he would not be joining him in the hardware store. His father answered simply, "good luck."

Paul Seiberling, who was now Jean-Paul Sinclair, had developed some talent as a poet. He was not a Ginsburg or a Snyder, but he had a knack for attending the right parties and gallery openings, being in the right place at the right time, and having the hippest repartee when a reporter was looking for quotations. If the press was at a reading, somehow Sinclair was there. If a hungry gallery owner was at a coffee house looking for the coolest performance at the next gallery opening, Sinclair was there. It didn't hurt that he was photogenic, like McClure.

Whatever it was, fate or luck, there was no denying the rising star of Jean-Paul Sinclair. He had a nice pad in the heart of North Beach. He was more or less liked by the beats and the locals. Universities were calling him. Publishers were offering him deals. He even had a real estate deal that would make his father proud of him. Best of all, young women were eager to be in the company of the almost famous poet.

Except tonight, he thought. *She'd run like a deer. Hell, I took her up and down Grant Avenue on my arm, Mike's, the Bagel Shop . . . man, her eyes glowed when she looked at me. I didn't move too fast, did I? Did the idea of champagne on the roof top frighten her? Nah, too young, too green, that must be it.*

Reflecting, he saw the young college student running down the street.

Yeah, too young. Nice though, really nice! Maybe next time.

One of Sinclair's more likeable personal attributes was his personal optimism, which was not always reflected in his poetry. He was actually humming "The Way You Look Tonight" by the time he reached the street door to his flat. Things were too good to be brought down by a skittery chick. Hell, win some, lose some.

Sinclair lived in a third floor flat in a pre-Earthquake building on Bannam, an alley tucked in between Grant and Columbus. He liked it. It was quiet. A half block away there were two bakeries, a restaurant and a bar. *What more could anyone want*, he wondered in an alcoholic daze as he began climbing the stairs to his pad. Hey, he even had access to the roof where he often gave parties and invited prospective girl friends to see the city lights. North Beach had become a neighborhood of wild parties with bongos, booze and maryjane. Sinclair's roof was well adapted for parties. It had a three foot parapet which made it difficult for stoned celebrants to fall over. He also had set up small tables and chairs with collapsible picnic umbrellas. Noise wasn't an issue because he was the neighbor downstairs.

Tonight, Jean-Paul Sinclair didn't feel like going to bed when he entered his flat. As he crossed the living room to the kitchen, the steam radiators were coming on, clanking and hissing with the heat which was rising from the boiler in the basement of the building. He yawned and took a bottle of champagne out of the refrigerator. His original scheme had failed, but he wasn't ready for sleep yet. He sat down at the kitchen table and began thumbing through the galleys of his latest book of poetry, *The Dog Saw Me Naked and Other*

Poems, but he decided he didn't feel like editing work tonight. He picked up his copy of the collected works of Walt Whitman and-- with the book under his arm and the bottle in his hand--went back into the hallway and up the stairs at the end to the roof access door.

The fog was heavy on the roof, so Jean-Paul opened one of the picnic umbrellas at a table, turned over the wet pad on the chair and sat down, setting Whitman on the table. He clicked on a battery-powered lamp and clumsily unwound the wire cap on the bottle of champagne. He tried to ease the cork out, but it came out with a loud pop. He giggled and stood up, ceremoniously holding the bottle out in from of him in a mock salute.

"To you, San Francisco! You made me, and I'm going to make you!" Jean-Paul laughed into the dark around him and the street lights below.

As he swallowed the bubbly liquid, he thought he heard the sound of steps behind him. Walking on tar and gravel roofs was a noisy affair. He turned and saw two men in dark raincoats.

"Hey, what's happenin'? What it is, what it ain't, what it's gonna be? Sorry, I don't have another bottle. Are you the new guys from the first floor? How . . ."

Jean-Paul's sentence was cut off as he staggered back under the force of a blow to his left temple. His feet gave way under him as he took another blow to the head. The champagne bottle fell from his loose grip and rolled across the roof as he slumped onto the wet gravel.

Without a word, the two men in raincoats lifted him up and dropped him over the side of the parapet. Jean-Paul Sinclair, the latest celebrity poet of the North Beach scene, was dead moments after he hit the foggy, silent sidewalk on Bannam.

SEVEN

Sharp Park, San Mateo County

Sunday, December 13, 1959

"A nine, three eights, and two sevens. Hell, I taught you to shoot better'n that."

Howard Fraley, the range master, the wrong side of sixty now, squinted through the spotting scope on the bench next to Maletesta. He was commenting on Maletesta's score on a target twenty five yards away. Maletesta set the Smith and Wesson K32 down on the bench and flicked the cylinder open with his thumb. He knocked the empties out by deftly flipping the barrel up and depressing the ejector rod. He then placed the revolver in a slot cut into his shooting box which held the gun at a 30 degree cant and reloaded it with target wadcutters.

"You old buzzard," Maletesta said affectionately, "it's cold as hell, wet, and I can hardly see my sight picture."

Maletesta knew that wasn't the reason for his sloppy shooting. He had planned to visit his parents today and he'd made the decision to tell them about his relationship with Cayenne. *I need to tell them today. Today! I don't care how they take it; it's my life, not theirs! They've still hanging on to the old country thing: find a nice Italian girl. No! The hell with that, I will tell them about Cayenne and me.*

"Out late, I'd wager," Fraley grumped, "carousin' . . . can't keep a steady hold. Sight picture? Bull pucky!"

Maletesta suppressed a smile, closed the cylinder and took up the Camp Perry shooting stance that Howard had taught him almost eighteen years ago. He no longer needed to anchor his left hand in his trouser pocket because it was no longer there. He cocked the Smith, settled the sights on the bull at six o'clock, took a few shallow breaths and squeezed off a round. The gun bucked slightly. He cocked it again as he brought it up on the target.

"X. That's more like it," Howard proclaimed.

"I wasn't 'carousin'."

"Hmmpf."

Maletesta fired again.

On this cold Sunday morning the two men were a study in contrast as they stood behind the waist high shooting bench at the Sharp Park Municipal Range: the one—dark, skinny, angular, one-armed—now methodically squeezing off six .32 rounds; the other—pudgy, neat, close cropped white hair half covered by a Smokey the Bear hat—squinting through a tripod mounted Bushnell spotting scope and hooting wildly as Maletesta's wadcutters blew out the center of the target.

Many years has passed since a teenaged Maletesta had tried out for the VFW rifle team that Howard Fraley coached. An electrician by trade, Fraley was newly relocated from Butte, Montana. He was enthusiastic about coaching a high school team and, having no children of his own, took an interest in the young baseball player with such a natural instinct with a rifle. Maletesta became their all-around rifle champion, shooting winning scores off hand, sitting, kneeling and prone. Fraley and the young rifleman developed a bond not only of the master teacher and the star pupil but also one with genuine affection for each other.

Then came college and the war, and all of John Maletesta's skills with a baseball and a rifle ended abruptly when he lost his left arm in a forgettable battle in the Philippines.

Fraley presided over the Sharp Park range with the help of his wife, a little woman who was usually found sitting on a high stool at one of the windows of the "club house," a plain cinderblock building which served as range headquarters. Located just inside the gate of the chain link fence which ran around the perimeter of the property, the one room building held a registration desk, lockers along the wall in which ammunition, targets and other supplies were stored, a blackboard where scores were recorded during matches, and a cork board which held thumb-tacked 3X5 cards advertising sales of guns, equipment, and duck club memberships.

Mrs. Fraley, wrapped in her old blue shawl, presided over the range through one of the floor-to-ceiling windows on the north side of the club house. On a small table next to her were a clock, a pack of Chesterfields, an ashtray, three sharpened number 2 soft pencils, a crossword puzzle book, and the microphone for the public address system. Shooting rounds lasted twenty minutes, and she was the timekeeper.

As Maletesta reloaded for the fourth time, Mrs. Fraley's voice boomed metallically over the range.

"Cease firing," she ordered, slowly and methodically trough the crisp wet air. "Open all actions . . . unload all weapons . . . step behind the line."

Maletesta took two of three steps back behind the faded white line painted on the cracked asphalt path along the firing line. He fished a cigarette out of his pocket and watched a red tail hawk gliding purposely over the canyon wall which ringed the north side of the range. Howard looked up and down the line, checking to make sure all the other shooters were following directions. When he was satisfied that they were, he gave a thumbs up to Mrs. Fraley in her window.

"Check targets," crackled the loudspeaker.

Maletesta was through for the day, so he and Howard ambled down the firing line, passing shooting benches and ground pads.

The Sharpe Park range, owned and operated by the City of San Francisco, was nestled in a canyon accessible from Highway 1 by a one lane road which dead-ended a half mile past the range. It was surrounded by clusters of well-developed pine trees that seemed to be always shrouded in fog. Today was no exception, as this was December. Maybe the sun would make an appearance, maybe not.

"Hear about that shootin' in North Beach?" Howard asked.

"No, when?"

"Last night, radio said, guy got shot down right outside a church."

"They give any reason?"

"No. Gangsters, I'd wager. Mafia doin's."

Maletesta chuckled.

"You watch 'The Untouchables' too much, Howard."

Maletesta and Fraley had almost reached the clubhouse when a horrible stink hit them. The stink emanated from a long-barreled rifle that a teenage boy was cleaning with a wooden rod and water soaked patches. The smell was that of rotten eggs.

"How often do you have to do that?" Maletesta asked, dramatically pinching his nose.

"Usually only after you've finished shooting," the boy answered," but we're trying to get a tighter group." He seemed unaware of the odor created by swabbing out the black powder with water.

"Group? I'd think you'd be happy just to reach the target with that thing," Maletesta smiled. Howard sat nothing, watching the conversation develop.

"In the Civil War," the boy answered quickly, "it wasn't unusual for snipers to hit enemy officers at 300-400 yards with these muzzleloaders . . ."

"I reckon I should introduce you two," Howard interjected. "John, this here is our resident historian, Jimmie Stromeyer, and that's his older brother, Jerry and their sidekick, Red Wilson. All of 'em on our smallbore team. Fellas, this here is the gent I've told you about many times, the guy who broke all the records in 1940, John Maletesta."

"Wow," Jimmie beamed, putting his hand out, "your target is still hanging in the office." "Next to the picture of President Roosevelt," Red noted in awe.

Maletesta shook hands all around. The boys were dressed in flannel shirts, blue jeans and sneakers, and Jimmie had a new-looking Union Army kepi perched on his head. With the Civil War centennial approaching, replicas of weapons, uniforms and other paraphernalia were being marketed all around the country.

"I've never fired one of those," Maletesta noted, pointing to the Civil War Springfield. "Looks like a lot of fun."

"Would you like to try it?" Jimmie asked, picking up the muzzleloader and offered it to Maletesta. He suddenly realized that, since Maletesta had only one arm, his rifle shooting days were in the past. The youth blushed bright red.

"Uh, I mean . . ." he stammered.

"Don't worry about it, son," Maletesta said quickly. "I'm still pretty good with a handgun. Let me watch you guys let one off when the next round starts."

A few minutes later, Mrs. Fraley's voice crackled out again "ready on the right . . . ready on the left . . . load . . . commence firing."

Maletesta and Howard watched the three teenagers stood the old rifle on its butt plate, poured a charge of FFg black powder down the barrel, and rammed a patched lead ball on top of it. Red Wilson laid the rifle on some improvised sand bags and cocked the huge hammer. He pushed a percussion cap onto the nipple, sighted down the long silvery barrel and pulled the trigger. There was a sharp "kerbloom," and the three youths disappeared momentarily in a cloud of smoke.

Howard coughed and Maletesta laughed at the disappearing act created by the one hundred year old rifle. The boys quickly set the rifle on end and began the loading procedure again. Maletesta and Howard headed back toward the club house thinking about a cup of coffee.

"Nice kids," Maletesta said.

"Yeah," Howard answered. "Kinda sad about the Stromeyer's dad. He died last summer."

"What happened?"

"Nobody knows for sure. He was down in L.A. on a business trip. The *News-Call* said he "jumped or fell" out of his hotel room. Didn't make sense to me. Damned shame."

"That's too bad."

"Their Uncle Leo brings them down here once a month. Drops 'em off and then goes over to the golf course for a coupla hours--golfer, but a good guy." Fraley frowned at the notion.

One of the boys let out a whoop as he looked through the spotting scope on the bench and waved to Fraley.

"Ha!" Fraley exclaimed. "They musta got on the paper!"

EIGHT

Ingleside, San Francisco

Sunday, December 13, 1959

"Hey Pop, how you doing?"

"Gianni! What a surprise!"

Joe Maletesta walked around his wood lathe and hugged his son. They were standing in the basement of the white stucco house on Borica Street. Maletesta had parked his car at the curb and walked down the long driveway through the open garage door where he found his father working.

"Nice looking piece of wood," Maletesta noted. "What are you making?"

"Yeah. Maple. A stool for your mother," Joe answered, returning his attention to the lathe.

Maletesta stared at this father's hands: big knuckled, thick fingered and heavily veined hands from forty years of work as an iron worker. His forearms were huge. Though he was in his late fifties, he was still a formidable figure, tough and stocky. Now that he was a shop steward now at Bay Street Iron Works, his work load was not as heavy as it used to be.

The lathe was cutting the piece of maple into a finely-turned furniture leg. Like many workers who worked with their hands all week, Joe loved the satisfaction of building something with his hands on the weekend. Mowing the lawn and pruning the shrubbery were chores. Building something? Never a chore. His wife tended the vegetable garden in the back yard.

"So Gianni, what's new? You down the range this morning?" Joe asked as he turned off the lathe. He still spoke with a slight Italian accent.

"Uh-huh," Maletesta answered as he leaned against the work bench nearby and lit a cigarette. He glanced around the tidy basement, taking in the wood screws and nails in mason jars, the tools hung neatly on the wall. Farther back were the wine vats. The sun was streaming in from the windows facing the back yard, but his father still had the lights on. He wondered if the old man might be losing his eyesight.

"Yeah, though it's pretty quiet this time of year, though I must say that my new Smith and Wesson is a real tack driver."

"You and those guns! Six, seven years old, all the time pretending you had one in your hand: bang, bang, bang! Almost drove your mother crazy." He paused, thinking about it, wiping his hands on his pants.

"We got used to the guns, but sometimes we almost went nuts with all the book stuff! You always had your nose in a book and came up with another crazy idea!"

Joe shook his head at the memory of it and stepped back from the lathe.

"Like that time you told your Uncle Carlo that silly thing about Leaf whatshisname discovered America, not Columbus. Pissed him off royally! I enjoyed the hell out of that even though it wasn't true. Anything to piss Carlo off."

"Well . . ."

"The Fraleys still down there?"

"Yeah."

"Nice people."

Joe put another piece of maple in the lathe and flicked the switch.

"You and Ma see Uncle Carlo at all anymore?"

"Nah," Joe spat theatrically into the saw dust on the basement floor. "Good riddance as far as I'm concerned."

"That's too bad."

"He's no good, and your ma knows it too."

For a few minutes, the only sound in the basement was the sound of the lathe.

"How's work, Pop?"

"Ehh, same old, same old, as they say. Lotta work: fire escapes, railings, fancy gates, you name it; we'll make it," he answered. "Funny thing, you know, Pacific Iron sold their business, and they were doin' good. Funny."

"So, what's new in the neighborhood?"

"Nilson's place up the block is for sale. Some coloreds been looking at it. I don't know, Gianni, I like the neighborhood like it is, you know?"

Maletesta said nothing.

Suddenly, the lathe stopped and Joe looked at his son and smiled.

"Tal was by the other day. What a wonderful girl. She still doin' OK in college? Almost finished, huh?"

"Yeah," Maletesta hesitated. "Uh . . . Ma at church?"

"Nah, she's upstairs cooking. She went early today, got lots of sins to atone for," he laughed. Joe had not been to church since the day his son returned from the war with one arm.

"Stay for lunch, Gianni. Your mother's own ravioli . . . used to be your favorite."

Joe turned all of his attention back to the lathe and Maletesta knew that meant the conversation was over.

"Sure, Pop, see you in awhile."

Maletesta climbed the stairs out of the basement which led to the kitchen. He stopped halfway up and turned back to his father.

"Hey, Pop, do you know why the new Italian Navy has glass bottom boats?"

Joe looked up quizzically.

"No," he ventured slowly, "why?"

"So they can see the old Italian Navy."

He left his father chortling, opened the back door at the top of the stairs quietly and tiptoed into the kitchen. His mother was setting the kitchen table for two. Her back was to him. She set a bottle of red wine in the middle of the table and a glass tumbler at each setting. She straightened the knives and forks, moved a bread plate an inch and stepped back to inspect her handiwork. The kitchen atmosphere was thick with the aroma of ravioli, tomato sauce and garlic.

"Need another plate, Ma."

"Gianni! Bambino!"

Guilia Maletesta threw her arms around him and pulled his head down to kiss him on each cheek.

"Mmmpf," she said, making the same kissing noise she had made when he was a baby. It embarrassed him even after he'd grown up, but he tolerated it. Unlike the stereotypical older Italian women, Guilia was thin and boney and had the angular face her son had inherited. Her thick gray hair was pinned up and her dark brown eyes were bright. She beamed proudly at her only child. It had been years since she'd cried for hours after visiting her one-armed son in the hospital and watched him struggle to pull on a coat or cut the meat on his plate. Then the terrible accident that happened to Annemarie eight years ago. *Madonna mia*! *How can a man survive that?* Guilia regularly cursed all the drunk drivers! She almost agreed with her husband that they should be hanged.

"Oh, Gianni, it's always so good to see you! You just added another month to my life! Sit, sit down here. We'll have a glass of your papa's wine!"

"How is it this year?"

"Fine," she answered, raising her eyes to the ceiling. She retrieved another tumbler from the cupboard and filled two glasses at the table.

"*Salute!*" she proclaimed, raising her glass.

"*Salute*, Mama," Maletesta returned, clinking his glass against hers.

They each took a sip and set their glasses down on the table. She put her hands on her knees and winked at him slyly. He caught the gesture.

"What?"

"Tal came by on Thursday on her way home from school. Her friend Antoinette dropped her off. We had a good talk. She said you have a girlfriend, now, huh? That's good, Gianni! What's her name?" She smiled broadly.

"Oh, Ma, it's no big deal . . ."

"No big deal? Gianni, it's time! Is she nice? What's her name? When can you bring her over for dinner?"

"Ma, it's not serious," Maletesta protested and regretted the betrayal the moment he said it. He knew it was serious.

"Ah, c'mon, Gianni! It's time for you to get serious. You're not getting any younger, you know. C'mon, what's her name?"

"Cayenne."

"Like the pepper? That's cute. Hmmm. Is she English? That sounds like what English people would name somebody, no?"

C'mon, Gianni, tell her the truth!

"Ma, I smell the sauce burning."

"Oh!"

She jumped up and ran to the stove to turn the gas burner down. Then she opened the back door and yelled down to the basement.

"Joe! *E tempo di mangiare*!"

The lunch was uneventful for Maletesta. By a deft switching of topics from the 49rs to the Giants to the unusual sale of Pacific Iron Works, he avoided talk about Cayenne and his problems with Tal. Since he was on Christmas vacation, John agreed to meet his father for lunch at the North Star cafe, Joe's favorite place in North Beach and only a few minutes' walk from the iron works on Bay Street.

Suddenly, as Guilia was serving a second helping of ravioli, she dropped the spoon on the platter.

"*Madonna mia*, I almost forgot! *Madonna mia*!" she exclaimed, a look of panic on her face.

Maletesta and his father jumped to their feet. Joe grabbed his wife's hand.

"What is it?"

"Gianni, you must promise me, on your heart, never to go to North Beach at night, no more! No more at night, Gianni, promise me!"

"Why not, Ma, it's just North Beach . . ."

"No," his mother interrupted, "it's dangerous, Gianni! Two people got killed there last night. It's all over the radio. One man was coming out of Saint Peter and Paul."

Guilia touched her forehead.

"*Madonna mia*, outside Saint Peter and Paul!"

"Oh, Ma, you worry . . ."

"No! And they pushed another man off the roof! Gianni, I don't want you down there!"

Joe sat down and resumed eating.

"Guilia, who knows why these things happen? The Beach? The Mission? It could happen anywhere."

"I think Pop's right."

Before Guilia could answer, the phone rang and she ran to pick it up in the hall off the kitchen.

"Hello," she said. "What? Oh, hi Tal. Yes, he's here. Wait a minute, dear."

Wide-eyed, she wiggled a finger at Maletesta and he walked quickly to the phone.

"Tal, it's me. Is something wrong?"

“Dad,” the voice at the other end answered, “the police just called. They want to talk to me.”

NINE

Cow Hollow, San Francisco

Sunday, December 13, 1959

"Tal, just tell me one more time, please."

Maletesta paced around the living room of the lower flat of their Edwardian home on Steiner Street, absently puffing on one cigarette after another and stubbing them out in the standing brass ash tray next to his favorite overstuffed chair with the bright floral pattern. The conversation started over an hour ago.

"Dad, I just told you! Didn't you get it?"

Maletesta dropped into the chair in exasperation. Tal sat opposite him on the sofa, her legs crossed underneath her in a modified lotus position. The flat was five spacious rooms connected by a central hall. Off the kitchen in the rear was a small porch with stairs that led down to the back yard. An elderly woman, Miss Colbert, insisted on keeping the upstairs flat where she had lived since Roosevelt's first election. She was partially deaf, so noise was not a problem. Maletesta and Tal checked in on her regularly and picked up her groceries from the market three blocks away. Miss Colbert was unaware of the fact that Maletesta actually now owned the building. Her rent remained at a rate from the 1930's.

As Tal recited her story again, Maletesta stared out the bay window that faced Steiner. Over the tops of the roofs across the street, he saw a few pigeons waddling on a building cornice, preparing for another flight to the steeples of St Vincent de Paul's church up the hill. The disappearing fog heralded a bustling Sunday afternoon, and the sidewalks would soon be filled with neighbors, shoppers and tourists.

Maletesta enjoyed the Cow Hollow neighborhood for the amenities it offered. Unlike his parents' side of town where movie theatres were closing, the Marina neighborhood had three going strong. The Marina was warmer and many small stores and markets were within walking distance. Municipal transportation was the best in the nation. Buses ran on Union Street, Fillmore, and Lombard. He could reach anywhere in the Bay Area through transfers or another ticket. Years ago he'd taught himself to drive one-handed, but he usually took the bus downtown to the train station where he caught the commuter train to the college in Burlingame.

When he didn't feel like cooking—which was often—even when Tal was living at home, he could walk to a dozen neighborhood restaurants. Their favorite Italian deli, Lucca's, was down on Chestnut. Maletesta was no longer a religious man, but when he felt he needed a place to gather his thoughts, he was more at home in the wooden Episcopal chapel of Saint Mary's across the street than the concrete edifice of Saint Vincent's. If that didn't suffice, he walked. And walked. And walked. Over Union to North Beach. Down Filbert to the Marina. Up Steiner to the Fillmore. Through the Presidio to Fort Point. The sight of the one armed man striding down these streets slightly off kilter was a familiar one to the neighbors.

"Well?"

"Well, what?" Maletesta answered blankly.

"Dad," Tal said angrily, "you weren't even listening! You asked me to tell you the whole thing again, and you just looked out the window! What a joke, this is! A bad joke!"

Tal wore faded blue jeans and an over-sized gray sweatshirt. She jumped off the sofa and stood next to him with her hands on her hips.

"I *was* listening," he said defensively. "I guess I don't understand why you went walking around North Beach with that bum. *You told* me that Antoinette was giving you a ride home."

"She did, but I wanted to look at the books in City Lights, so I took the 41 over to Columbus and ran into Jean-Paul outside the book store. He signed his new book for me . . . and . . . he's not a bum! And I resent you saying that about him! You call all of these people bums because they haven't caved in to the conformism and materialism that runs this society . . . they don't worship at the altar of the almighty dollar!"

Tal stomped back over to the sofa, sat down, and then immediately got up again and started toward the door.

"Tal, wait, please," Maletesta pleaded, jumping out of the overstuffed chair. "Let's put that aside for a moment. Why do you think the police called? Jesus, they're working on Sunday! What do they want?"

"How do I know what they want?" she snapped, slapping her arms to her sides. "Maybe they want to push me around like they push the beats around! Last month I saw them roughing up Bob Kaufman again outside the Bagel Shop."

"OK, OK, but look, honey," Maletesta was exasperated, "it must have something to do with last night. What did he actually say again?"

"Who?"

"The cop who called, for Chrissake!"

"You don't have to swear, Dad! He said, 'I'm Inspector Brennan, and I'd like to talk to you as soon as possible. Tomorrow morning would be fine.' I told him I'd call him as soon as I talked to you."

"Might be Matt Brennan," Maletesta ventured. "Brennan pops up in the columns every once in a while. It's usually about some sensational murder. He's Homicide. Jesus. What do you think he wants to talk to you about, for crying out loud?"

"I don't know. He didn't say." She slumped back down on the sofa. "Why should it be about last night? I was home at 12:30. I didn't see any crimes, unless reading poetry is a crime. Some of the cops think it is."

She tucked her feet underneath her again. Maletesta looked at her and saw the defiance he remembered when she was eight and he had to battle with her over what time she would take her bath. She'd won. He looked at the grand father's clock near the fireplace. It was nearly four thirty.

"I'll call him," he announced. "What's his number?"

"I can call him . . ."

"Tal."

She gave him the phone number the policeman had given her. He dialed it, but there was no answer when he called. After another try and eleven more rings, he put the receiver back in its cradle.

"Didn't think they'd answer on Sunday," he said as he hung up the phone. "I'll call in the morning. You hungry?"

She looked up at him, a cheeky smile lightening her face.

"I feel like a hamburger."

"You don't look like a hamburger," he answered. It was a stale joke that delighted her as a child. She rolled her eyes at him.

"Really lame, Dad, as in l-a-m-e . . . how about Mel's on Geary?"

"To re-visit your high school memories?"

Tal laughed.

"Oh, c'mon, Dad. It's fun. We get to see wild and crazy teenagers and listen to the rent-a-cop yelling 'all right, in the car or off the lot' through his bull horn."

"By definition, *you're* still a teenager."

"Not for long, though," Tal replied, sticking her tongue out at him. "I'm counting the days, you know. "

"OK, let's go," Maletesta said, sticking his tongue out at her as he walked toward the front hall. Tal grabbed her pea coat and darted out the door before him.

"I'll get the car," she called back over her shoulder.

TEN

Richmond, San Francisco

Sunday, December 13, 1959

There wasn't much traffic on Sunday night, so Maletesta and his daughter arrived in the fog at Mel's drive-in on Geary about fifteen minutes after they left their house. No one could see it, but the sun had already set on this short December day and late afternoon had abruptly turned into night. Drivers had their headlights on. The lighted marquee on the Coronet announced in large letters, "Ben Hur Opens Wed. Dec. 23."

The parking lot outside the drive-in was nearly full with teenagers in sedans mainly borrowed from their parents. Some older teens made their scene in rodded up old Fords, Chevys, and Dodges, some of them works in transition covered in flat gray primer. All of the cars were eclipsed by a stunning candy apple red 1958 Impala hardtop parked front row center. The younger brother of a local singing sensation with hits on all the charts preened behind the wheel of the hardtop, enjoying the attention without noticing it. His own singing group was mediocre, but girls waved at him, hoping they might have a chance with the star if they hung out with his little brother. Car hops bounced between the rows of cars, taking orders, giving directions on how to lower the car windows, and delivering trays of hamburgers, shakes and fries.

Maletesta and Tal parked in a side lot and walked into the diner. As they opened the door, the din inside was palpable, a mix of loud cracking teenage voices giggling and shrieking, order pickups called out from the kitchen, and a Rockola juke box blasting out Bobby Freeman's "Betty Lou Got a New Pair of Shoes." Freeman was another local favorite who played high school dances, sock hops and pep rallies.

The red leatherette, formica and chrome booths in the front were full, so Maletesta and Tal navigated their way through the waitresses and table hoppers to a recently abandoned booth in the back.

"What a great idea of yours," Maletesta grumbled, as they dropped into the booth.

"Oh, c'mon, Dad, don't be such an old curmudgeon," Tal answered, picking up a menu. "Hey, maybe you can study them for a paper!"

"Sure, a paper titled 'Urban Madness and the Hamburger Culture.'"

Their waitress, a skinny teenager with a severe case of acne, cleared their table, swiftly gathering up used silverware, plates and glasses, straws, and crumpled napkins.

"I'll be right back to take your orders," she mumbled and dashed toward the kitchen with a trayful of diner debris. The noise did not subside. Bobby Freeman was followed by Little Richard and Ronnie Hawkins.

When the waitress returned with her order pad, Tal was flipping through the selections on the table juke box.

"Any Bobby Blue Bland?" Maletesta asked as he scanned the menu.

"Dad," Tal laughed, "this is a drive-in in the Richmond, not the Fillmore."

"There're no drive-ins in the Fillmore."

"What would you like?" the waitress interrupted, raising a pencil to her pad.

"A grilled cheese sandwich and a cup of coffee, please," Maletesta answered.

"Fries?"

"No thanks."

"And you?" she asked, turning to Tal.

Before Tal could answer, a voice broke out behind them.

"Hey, pimples, how about some more coffee back here?"

The waitress blushed beet red.

Frowning, Maletesta half turned in the booth to the direction of the voice. He saw a young blond man with a white sidewall flat top who had obviously spent a lot of time in the gym, judging from the biceps bulging from his white tee shirt. The man laughed and a dark-haired young woman across the table from him giggled.

Tal broke in quickly.

"I'll have a hamburger with fries and a strawberry shake."

"OK," the waitress murmured as she jotted down the order. "Hamburger with fires and a strawberry shake, grilled cheese and coffee."

"Thanks," Tal replied.

"Hey, pimples, I said how about some more coffee, huh? You got lead in your pants?" More laughter and giggles burst from the booth.

"I'll be right back with it," the waitress blurted and dashed toward the kitchen.

The din continued around Maletesta and his daughter, noisy teenagers unaware of the festering drama in the rear booths. Tal watched her father's jaw grinding and his eyes grow cold.

"Dad," she pleaded, "please don't make a scene. There are a lot of jerks like that in this world." She nervously re-arranged the silverware on the table in front of her as she spoke.

Maletesta said nothing. His mind was churning. *The eagle-owls are calling. The eagle-owls are calling, calling. Deploy the men, Gianni! Goddamn it, the Japanese are coming! Deploy the men. Protect the men, Gianni, for Chrissake, the Japanese are coming! Check their positions; check their positions!*

Maletesta shook his head to dispel the images.

"What?" he asked Tal.

"It's OK, Dad; it's OK," she whispered, placing her hand on his hand which still held the menu.

A few minutes later, the waitress returned, walking toward the blond man's booth with a carafe of coffee.

"Thata girl, pimples. Get the lead out of your ass!" the blond man shouted at the waitress as she made her way toward his table. He laughed again.

Suddenly, Maletesta shook off Tal's hand and stood up in front of the waitress as she passed their table.

"I'll take that," he stated, taking the carafe of coffee out of her hand. The waitress stood there, unsure of what she should to do in the situation. She tried to say something.

"It's OK, miss," Maletesta said. "Don't worry. Thanks."

Maletesta turned away from the waitress and strode to the blond man's table with the carafe of coffee in his hand. Tal gasped.

"Here's your coffee, flat top," Maletesta announced through gritted teeth when he reached the table, "special delivery."

"Thanks," the blond man began to say as Maletesta splashed some of the hot coffee on the cup and saucer on the table and then poured the entire pot of coffee onto the man's chest and lap.

The man screamed in pain and then, soaked in hot coffee, jumped up to confront Maletesta. As he emerged from the booth, Maletesta dropped the carafe on the table and caught the man's right hand with his own right hand. Then he twisted it around to his back, tangling the man between the bench and the table. The man's dark haired companion screeched as Maletesta quickly changed the grip to an arm lock, pulled the man out of the booth and pushed him toward the door.

"God damn . . ." the man shrieked as he was being hurled forward.

"Shut up," Maletesta rasped.

The juke box continued blasting. This time it was Link Wray with the street fight guitar anthem, "Rumble." Most of the customers were unaware of what was happening, but those in the booths near the fracas sat stunned by the action unfolding in front of them. Maletesta hurled the man through the door, smashing his face into the safety glass as the door swung open, almost hitting a car hop who deftly jumped out of the way while keeping her tray intact. Maletesta gave one more push and the man tripped over one of the concrete car tire bumpers and tumbled onto the asphalt parking lot. The dark haired girl followed behind them screeching "oh, my God, Randy, oh my God!" Heads popped out of car windows nearby, startled expressions on their faces.

The man cursed again and tried to get up while reaching into his pocket for something. Maletesta side-kicked him hard in the shoulder and sent him sprawling, dropping a flattened can opener as he rolled on the pavement. A moment later, he scrambled to his feet, his eyes wide with fear. The dark-haired girl helped him up and they stumbled quickly across the lot.

Less than two minutes had passed since Maletesta had dumped the coffee on the man. He stood outside the door, breathing heavily.

"*Apai, apai*!" Tal called, running up to him.

He turned and saw a stranger, and then slowly recognized his daughter.

"What, what? What's the problem?" he asked, a puzzled look on his face. He shook his head a few times.

"Let's go, *apai*," Tal said, taking his arm.

A gray-haired security guard came huffing over to Maletesta, his hand on the butt of an old revolver in a worn holster.

"What's going on here?" he demanded.

"Nothing," Maletesta replied flatly, "just taking out the garbage."

The security guard scanned the parking lot importantly and then returned to his post on the other side of the lot. Maletesta turned to Tal.

"Will you settle up, Tal?" he asked, producing a couple of tens from his pocket.

"Sure, be right back, Dad."

He picked up the flattened can opener on the pavement.

"A church key, for Chrissake," he muttered, tossing it into a nearby dumpster.

When Tal emerged from the restaurant, they walked silently across the parking lot to their car. No one paid any attention to them. The drive-in scene returned to normal.

They said nothing until they got into the car and Tal switched on the ignition.

"Dad," she asked, turning toward him, "are you OK?"

She paused as she backed the Olds out of the parking lot. Maletesta looked through the front window of the car like there was nothing to see. He yawned and then frowned.

"You haven't called me *apai* in a long time, Tal. It's nice to hear Dayak." He shook his head again. "I don't remember what happened, some punk . . . I grabbed him . . ."

Maletesta stopped, shaking his head again. They were silent as Tal drove down Geary.

"Let's get a pizza," Maletesta said suddenly. "That place on Chestnut near Fillmore."

"OK, but I have one condition."

"You have a condition for pizza; you have a condition for pizza?" He turned to her with an incredulous look on his face.

"Yes," Tal announced, smiling, "the condition is that you won't start counting the people who are eating pizza with forks, as you usually do."

"Ha! All right," Maletesta conceded.

ELEVEN

Fillmore

Sunday, December 13, 1959

"Ben, wake up! Wake up!"

"Huh? What you doin', woman? It's the middle of the night."

"I heard something! Down in the yard! Like a gunshot!"

The old woman had stopped shaking her husband to rouse him. He climbed out of bed and pulled on his robe. The floor was cold, and he slid his feet into an old pair of leather slippers. Then he switched on the lamp next to the bed.

"You're always hearin' things," he said, rubbing the back of his neck. He was in his late seventies with a fringe of white hair around his head. "Probably a car backfire. This isn't the fourth of July when those fools up the street fire off their heaters. There's nothin' out there."

The woman was adamant, sitting up in bed in a lemon-colored night dress and night cap with her arms crossed. A dog barked outside.

"Ben Grieve, somebody fired a shot down in our alley. And there's Ralph next door barkin.' Now, get the flashlight and take a look," she directed and then added, "careful now."

"Ralph's always fussin.' Leave you to sleep outside in a shed all night and you'd be fussin' too, woman. How come nobody else is carryin' on about it?"

He stood up wearily.

"They be peekin' out their windows, but they be doin'nothing," she answered. "Now, git."

"Claudine, you'll be the death of me, woman," Ben complained, but he limped out into the hall which led to the back porch, picking a flashlight off the top of a chest of drawers.

The Grieves bought the small Victorian house on Eddy Street twelve years ago with their savings from his job as an elevator operator and hers as a beautician. The house was mortgage free, neat and well kept, and the Grieves tended a sizeable vegetable garden in the back yard as well as blue hydrangeas in the front planters behind the black iron fence.

The back door creaked as Ben fearlessly pursued his mission. He held the three-battery flashlight out away from his body like it was a snake. He knew they'd shoot at the light if they had a mind to. Many years ago, he was in combat and he remembered the cold hell of the Meuse Argonne at night. Their captain told them not to light any cigarettes which would attract the German snipers. He pointed the flashlight and flicked it on. The beam danced on the back stairs before him. He hesitated.

"C'mon, Horatio."

Claudine was now behind him in her robe, a broomstick in her hand.

"Who's that?" he whispered back to her as he descended the stairs.

"You remember, at the bridge?"

"Woman, this ain't no bridge. Now, clam up."

The two of them crept down the stairs to the yard, Ben periodically bouncing the beam of the flashlight off the stairs, the yard and the fence. They could not see anything beyond the fence. The sky was clear, but they could see nothing, other than their winter garden, chicken wire and the stepping stone path leading to the gate in the fence. Ralph barked once more, and they heard a television playing in one of the apartments in the building next door.

"That's what it was," Ben griped, "probably the Late Show, a gangster movie with lotsa shootin.' You get me outta my warm bed for this . . ."

"Ben, out there in the alley . . ."

Claudine was near the gate, peering over the fence.

The beam of the flashlight jumped over the fence and landed on the body of a man sprawled near the garbage cans. It was not moving.

"He must be a drunk. Hey, mister . . ." Ben started.

"That's no drunk, Ben Grieve. Better call the police."

The Grieves beat a hasty retreat back into the house to the telephone. In the darkness, they did not recognize the body of the dead man. His name was Yusef X, but his family in Georgia knew him as Alexander Phillips.

TWELVE

Hall of Justice, San Francisco

Monday, December 19, 1959

The phone rang four times while Inspector Matthew Brennan scowled at it over his newspaper and looked at his watch. It was 8:30, so on the fifth ring, he decided it was not going to stop, put the *Examiner* sports section down on his desk and reached over for the phone.

"Homicide. Brennan," he answered petulantly, taking his feet off the corner of the desk.

"Brennan who hit .336 in '41?" asked the voice on the other end of the line.

"Who wants to know?"

"Cleanup."

"No shit! Maletesta?" Brennan peeled open a pack of Black Jack gum and arced the wrapper toward the steel waste basket he shared with the next desk. He missed. At the next desk, Inspector Bogdanovich gave him a thumbs down and went back to typing a report about a smash and grab jewelry heist in a Union Square shop.

“Yeah, how they hangin’?” Maletesta’s tone was light and friendly.

“Well, I’ll be damned,” Brennan said, chewing. “I heard about your arm. That was a tough break . . . well, I’ll be damned. You know, I wondered if this beatnik Toolah Maletesta was related to you when her name came up regarding this North Beach guy, Sinclair. You don’t run into many Maletestas.”

“Talah. We call her Tal. Yes, she’s my daughter . . . and she’s not a beatnik. She’s a sophomore at All Saints College in Burlingame,” Maletesta responded.

“Hey, good for her. Smart, huh? Well, you know, these days college kids get a lot of funny ideas in their heads. You know, and they start following around these beatniks like Sinclair . . . looking for thrills or whatever, I certainly don’t get it. What a lulu . . .” Brennan drawled, enjoying himself.

“Brennan, you called my daughter. What’s this about?” Maletesta interrupted.

“Well, we need to ask her a few questions, you know, that’s all, just routine.”

“Questions about what?”

“Let’s say we’re trying to establish some kind of a time frame for the other night in North Beach. Being a parent’s a pain in the ass, isn’t it? I’m lucky, so far, my kids are still in grammar school—Star of the Sea---but you just can’t tell, can you, you know? Now, take these kids with their reefers? Butter wouldn’t melt in their mouth, you know, and then, wham, somebody’s dead. Then you got your regular hoods—

the pachucos and the gitanos in the Mission, the Van Dycks and the Black Sheep in the Fillmore, and all those what-do-they-call-em, 'car clubs.' You know, like the Lairds in the Richmond and Sunset: one or two cars and four hoods in each of 'em looking for trouble."

Brennan picked up a new piece of gum from the pack and smiled at the cop at the next desk. Bogdanovich snorted and shook his head. Brennan was at it again, like a cat with a trapped mouse.

Maletesta had had enough of the lecture.

"What do you want?" he demanded.

"We just want to have a little talk with your daughter. Someone ID-ed her in North Beach with Sinclair on Saturday night. Said she was upset . . ."

"Who?" Maletesta interrupted.

"Well, let's see . . ."

Brennan flipped open a spiral notebook and slowly began turning the pages, humming Good King Wenceslaus off tune as he turned them. Maletesta fumed at the other end of the line, working hard to keep his voice and temper under control.

"Ah! Here it is," Brennan finally announced. "Ange-lin-a Ste-fani. Nice-uh Eye-talian lady. Works inna da bakery onna da corner." He could barely contain himself from bursting into laughter. "She says she know your daughter by sight."

"Yeah," Maletesta exhaled slowly, "we go there once in awhile for panetone and cannoli. What else you got?"

"John, that's all I can say until I talk to her. You know, procedure."

"Yeah, like when I pulled those punks from Galileo off your back after that pickup game at Funston?"

"A long time ago, a long time ago. Say, what are you doing now?"

"I teach English at the College of All Saints."

"Hey, not bad. That an all-girls school?"

"Yeah. What time are you coming over?"

"Four o'clock. All girls? I mean, what a great place to teach, huh . . ."

"Four o'clock, Brennan," Maletesta repeated and hung up the phone. He lit a cigarette and stomped over to the den to the dart board on the wall. He pulled three darts out of the cork board, stepped back several paces and let fly. Two of the darts buried themselves in the target; the third went wild and landed in the nearby frame of the "Flower Carrier," a Diego Rivera print he liked.

Brennan sat staring at the lights in the ceiling for a moment. He had enjoyed himself immensely. He had a hunch he was smoking something out, and so far, everything was going just fine. The rest of the room was a hubbub of noise—phones ringing, officers moving about, talking, coming, going, typing, banging file drawers—but Brennan heard none of it.

"Brennan, you know, sometimes you're a real bastard," Bogdanovich said, but Brennan wasn't listening.

THIRTEEN

Cow Hollow

Monday, December 14, 1959

The doorbell rang as the chimes in the grandfather's clock in the living room tolled four. Maletesta looked at the clock and cursed under his breath. He glanced over at Tal on the sofa, working on a term paper that was due after the Christmas break. The morning newspapers, the *Chronicle* and the *Examiner,* lay unopened all day on the coffee table. The radio had been silent all day as father and daughter Maletesta brooded over their new situation.

An open book tottered precariously on Tal's left knee as she made notations on a stack of 3X5 cards on her right. Several more books lay open on the cushions around her. Her long black hair was pulled up into a pony tail and she flicked it subconsciously when the heard the bell. She took a deep breath and shifted her attention to the Christmas tree in the corner of the room. The tree was a noble fir, her favorite. She and her father bought it at the lot on Clement Street last week and decorated it on Thursday. At the top of the tree--a little bit worse for wear—stood a proud tattered angel Tal had made of cloth and cardboard many years ago during her first Christmas in the United States.

Maletesta looked through the peephole in the front door. Yes, it was Brennan. He hadn't changed much in almost twenty years, red headed with a Hollywood kind of good looks that rekindled an old tinge of resentment in Maletesta. He remembered the oohing and ahhing from the girls in the stands when Brennan was at the plate and Maletesta was in the on deck circle. *Still chewing gum like a matinee idol.*

"Matt! Long time no see," Maletesta said heartily as he opened the door. He put out his hand and Brennan took it lightly. His blue Roos Brothers suit was well cut, unlike the off the rack sacks from the Emporium that the other plain clothes cops wore. His hair was slicked back with Brylcream, and he was taller than Maletesta. He stretched himself even taller as he greeted Maletesta, a habit he had developed in an attempt to intimidate suspects and police brass alike.

"Yeah," he said, almost as an afterthought as he walked past Maletesta into the living room. He spotted Tal and flashed his wallet at her. She put aside her papers and stood up when he entered.

"Brennan. Homicide. You must be Toolah."

"Yes. Talah, or Tal. I'm pleased to meet you," she said nervously and dropped back down on the sofa.

"Have a seat, Matt," Maletesta offered when he caught up.

Brennan pulled a reproduction Louis XIV chair over to the sofa. The chair was uncomfortable, and Brennan scowled slightly as he sat down and opened a small spiral notebook. He retrieved a retractable ball point pen from an inside coat pocket and clicked it loudly into action. Maletesta sat in a ladder back chair opposite him.

"This shouldn't take long," Brennan began, shifting his glance from Maletesta to his daughter. Maletesta noted that Brennan now had slightly drooping eye lids. They reminded him of the snake he had shot in Borneo.

"I'm just concerned about your movements Saturday night. Well, first, you know, procedure." He clicked the ball point pen twice. "How old are you?"

"Nineteen."

"Ah . . . hmm . . . how do I say this? You don't look much like your dad here, and I know you weren't around when we were playing baseball."

"My birth parents in Borneo—where I met Dad-- are dead. I met Dad about 13 years ago when he was on an anthropological expedition. He adopted me back here in the States."

"What's the point, Brennan?" Maletesta interrupted.

Brennan clicked the pen again, made some notes in the book and turned to Maletesta.

"Well, cut to the chase, they always say. She was seen all over North Beach Saturday night with a beatnik named Jean-Paul Sinclair. Now he's dead."

If he said it for shock effect, it worked.

"Dead!" Talah shrieked.

"Splattered all over Bannam alley. Somebody pushed him off the roof of his flat early yesterday morning. What a mess. You didn't see the papers today?"

Tal put her hand to her mouth and ran sobbing from the room. They heard the door to her bedroom bang down the hall.

Maletesta rubbed his knee with his right hand, his jaw working. Brennan sat calmly, a look of innocence on his face. He wrote something in his notebook.

Maletesta stood up.

"Get out," he said quietly.

Brennan glanced at Maletesta's resolute eyes and knew not to push the issue. It didn't matter anyway. He had accomplished what he had set out to do. He stood up and faced Maletesta.

"Gosh, John, I didn't mean to upset her," Brennan said in an over-friendly voice, "but she was at the scene of a crime, you know. She was seen with him at The Place and later at Mike's Pool Hall. We'll need to talk more some time soon."

Brennan continued, snapping his chewing gum.

"You know," he said, walking toward the front door, "it just doesn't look good. Say some kid gets rejected by someone they idolize, you know, like Elvis . . . then maybe they blow their top, you know? It happens."

Maletesta opened the door and turned to face Brennan.

"Brennan, don't you ever come back here unless you have a warrant. Get it? Not without a warrant! Now, get the hell out of my house!"

"John, I might just get . . ." he tried to say as Maletesta slammed the door on him.

Brennan walked to his car smiling.

The telephone in the hallway rang as Maletesta headed back toward Tal's room.

"Hello," he blurted, picking it up.

"Gianni, *come va*? You didn't tell me how many for Christmas dinner. You and Tal and how about your new girl friend, huh?"

"Hi, Ma. No, just Tal and I. Sorry I didn't call; I'm kind of in a hurry right now."

"Whaddyuhmean hurry? Hurry's no good for you or anybody. And why not the girl friend? You think she won't like us? She'll think we talk funny or somethin'?"

Maletesta sighed heavily.

"No, no, of course not, Ma. It's just that . . . hell, I don't know! I don't know! I really can't stay on the phone . . ."

"Gianni, never forget where you come from. Even though your father and me didn't go to college like you . . ."

"Oh, Ma. It's got nothing to do with that, for Chrissake! Look, I have to go. I'll call you tomorrow, OK?"

"Gianni . . ."

"I'll call tomorrow, OK?"

"Sure, sure. I'm only your mother . . ."

"*Ciao*, Mama," he said and hung up.

Maletesta knocked on Tal's bedroom door.

"Tal, honey, I want to talk to you," he said and turned the door knob. It was locked.

"No!" the voice said from behind the door. "Leave me alone."

"Tal, we *need* to talk. Please."

"Dad, please leave me alone . . . we'll talk later, I promise."

Maletesta thought of breaking the lock, but the thought of that drastic action was no more serious than the times he had considered removing the door because she slammed it so often. Also, he knew his daughter well enough. They would talk later, and he would respect her time to be alone. He opened the liquor cabinet in the living room and took out a fifth of Old Crow. He set it on the end table next to the overstuffed chair and retrieved a short tumbler from the kitchen. He poured himself two fingers worth and sat down. He slugged back half the glass and stared at the lights on the Christmas tree. Some of them were out. *I'll go down to Woolworths tomorrow and pick up some new bulbs.*

Maletesta knew cops like Brennan. They didn't care whether you were guilty or innocent. All they wanted were arrests; convictions might or might not come later. He also knew enough about the legal system to know that an ambitious prosecutor with some odds and ends of circumstantial evidence, some flukey witnesses, and a cop's testimony could convict anyone. Or just ruin them for life, even without a conviction. The gossip never ended: "weren't you the girl who was involved in . . ."

I can't let this happen to Tal! He reached over and emptied the tumbler. *I'll have to find out what had happened to Sinclair by myself. I know . . . I'll hire a private detective!*

He refilled his glass.

No, I can't hire a private detective. Jesus, those guys are seedy: they chase down wandering husbands and unfaithful wives; they spy on clerks stealing cans of soup out of store rooms. Small time crap.

He stood up abruptly and began pacing the room.

"I can't trust anybody with this; it's a perfect set up for blackmail," he said aloud and carefully sat down.

W*hat the hell can I do? I'm a teacher, for God's sake, not a detective. Shit!*

He stood up again, ran his hand through his hair several times and took a deep breath. Then he took three more deep breaths.

Well, there's one thing in my favor: I know a lot of people in this town. Maybe I can start calling around and find out something.

No! What the hell am I thinking? I'm a teacher! *Call your friends, Gianni, and ask them for information: information about what? Hi, my daughter's accused of murder, do you have any ideas?*

With another expletive, he dropped heavily back down on the chair.

So, you're a teacher, Gianni, so what, huh? This is Borneo all over again. Straighten up and fly right! Get your ass in gear, man! Move it!

His mind reeled with images of Tal and beatnik poets and court rooms and cops and judges frowning at the defendant in the box. *Jesus!* He couldn't fit the pieces together, but he had to do something, start somewhere! Find out who this poet is . . . or was. That's a place to start. *You know a lot of people, Gianni, start calling!*

What was her name at Vesuvio's? Maria. She knows the Beach. So does Uncle Carlo. I can't worry about the family dispute now. Sister Agatha? Hell, she knows everybody in City Hall, seems like she's related to half of them. Is it enough up against someone like Brennan? How the hell do I know?

Maletesta refilled the glass and threw it back. Somewhere in the back of his head he noted there wasn't a coaster on the table and Tal would be mad if she saw him put down a glass without one. The old housekeeper, Mrs. Dawson, had drilled many 19th century conventions into Tal regarding the setting of silver, the placement of napkins and the like. He retrieved a coaster out of the stack in the drawer and placed the glass on it.

"Thank you, Mrs. Dawson," he said to the ceiling. "Now, do you anything about a murder investigation?"

He waited a minute.

"No, I thought not."

Brennan has the whole damned police department and the DA behind him.

"The hell with it," he shouted and reached for the bottle again.

Maletesta sipped the third glass slowly. He stared at the framed photograph of Annemarie on the side table. *God, I need you, baby. I'm afraid, Annemarie. I'm afraid for Tal.* He looked at the shaking glass in his hand and willed it to stop shaking. It did.

The room grew dark as the sun slipped down and the only light in the house came from the twinkling bulbs on the Christmas tree.

FOURTEEN

Cow Hollow

Monday, December 14, 1959

Two outs, runner on second, a few feet off the bag. Not a big lead. Fat chance he's going anywhere with Mick on the mound and Xavier behind the plate. The batter stepped out of the box. Now he's stepping back in. You hot dog, c'mon! Left handed, solid swing. If he gets anything on it, it will be coming my way. Better fade a little toward the line. Not many in the stands today in this lousy weather. Ha, there's Annemarie with two of her friends behind our first base dugout. Ball two. C'mon, Mick, get his guy, c'mon! Ah, here it comes, high but soft. I've got it, easy, easy, get your glove up, nice and easy . . . no . . . where's my arm, oh Christ, where's my arm? I'm falling . . . Annemarie, catch me, please! Annmarie, help me! They're after Tal! I'm falling, baby, help me! Talah! Can you see Brennan down there, see him, he's looking everywhere, but he hasn't seen us. Come here quick, Tal, hide over here with me behind these bushes. The soldiers won't find us, hide back here . . . Annemarie, please catch me . . . The soldiers are after Tal.

Maletesta awoke with a start, cold sweat pouring down his forehead. He had fallen asleep in the overstuffed chair.

Tal stood next to the chair, pulling a throw rug over him.

"It's getting cold, Dad. I didn't mean to wake you up."

With a deep breath, Maletesta shook off the nightmare and gazed up at his daughter. He took her hand and pulled her down on the lumpy arm of the chair. It was how they had read *Winnie the Pooh* many years before. He saw the chubby little girl transfixed by tales of make believe. Then he saw the young adult, home from college for the holidays. And now his daughter, a suspect in a murder case.

"Talah, we have to talk about what happened." Maletesta only used her full name when he was upset. "You're in a very dangerous situation, and we can't take it lightly. I know cops like Brennan. They enjoy playing cat and mouse with people while they're setting you up. They go to the papers. They ruin people's lives."

"But, Dad, I didn't do anything! I don't understand what's happening."

"How often have you been out with Sinclair?"

Tal jumped off the arm of the chair and stood facing him.

"Never!"

Tal paused, twisting her fingers, looking at her father and then around at the room. He waited. She had untied the ponytail and her hair hung loosely over her shoulders. She twisted a few strands to calm herself.

"Well . . ." she stumbled. Even as a child, she could not lie. She might not mention something, but she would never lie. "Once before, I guess. I mean, before last Saturday."

"When?" Maletesta asked.

"Umm, last month. I went up to talk to Jean-Paul after he had finished a reading at the Coffee Gallery. He said a group of them—including Bob Kaufman and Allen Ginsburg--were going to Lupo's for a pizza after the reading and asked me to go with them. Antoinette was with me. We drove back to school after. It . . ."

Tal stopped and bit her lip.

"What?" he prodded gently.

"Dad, I've never felt like this before. It was kind of scary, but it was exciting, too . . . I mean, Jean-Paul Sinclair *asked me* to go along with them to the pizza restaurant. *Me.* Talah-studying-literature-in-college-Maletesta!"

She paused, thinking about the event, her eyes glowing.

"He was also very gallant. He held doors open . . . he looked after everybody else in the group . . . he did all the ordering . . . he's—I mean was—like a Cavalier out of a story book. I think you would have liked him, Dad . . . if you had a chance to know him."

Tal bit her lip to get herself under control. She moved to the Louis XIV chair which was vacated earlier by Brennan. She had said more than she intended and watched her father closely. Maletesta took a deep breath and exhaled.

"What about Saturday?" he asked. "When I last saw you at school, you said that Antoinette would drive you home. Then you said that you took the 41 over to the Beach."

"Yes, I was in City Lights and Jean Paul saw me. He met with his new publishers and was wandering around the stacks when he ran into me. He asked me if I wanted to go over to Tosca with him for a drink."

"You went?"

"We stayed for about twenty minutes . . ."

"They didn't card you?"

"It was too crowded. Jean-Paul played some opera arias on the juke box, and then we went walking up Columbus, dropped in a couple of places on Grant, and, uh . . ."

Maletesta tried very hard not to look peeved. After all, he kept telling himself, the girl *is* only nineteen years old.

"Uh . . . what?" he asked, quietly.

Tal's forehead wrinkled and she fidgeted with her fingers.

"He asked me if I would like to see his pad," she blurted out quickly. "I said yes."

"Jesus H. Christ!" Maletesta exclaimed, standing up. "Did you go to every God damned place in the Beach? And his pad? Where did the damned bakery lady see you?"

"Dad, if you're going to lose your cool like this, I'm going back into my room."

Maletesta lit a cigarette, stomped across the room to the clock and turned back toward her.

"Lose my cool?" he shouted, "lose my cool? Don't you get it? You could end up in San Quentin! There are a lot of people in prison on a lot more flimsier evidence!"

"More flimsier? Gee whiz, Dad, aren't you an English teacher!" She crossed her arms chest and sat looking at him defiantly.

Maletesta returned to the overstuffed chair and violently crushed the cigarette out in the ash tray. What had he done wrong with this girl? He couldn't believe she was playing grammar games in this situation. He was exasperated.

"Look," he said after taking another slow deep breath, "let's keep it simple. When did you last see Sinclair?"

Tal paused, putting her thoughts together. She looked at her father like he was in the slow learner's class. Then she spoke clearly and resolutely.

"About eleven thirty . . . we were walking down Green toward Bannam. He'd told me earlier that's where he lived, in an upstairs flat on Bannam. God, Dad, it was just too much: here I am in North Beach walking with Jean-Paul Sinclair . . . a published poet with a major work coming out . . ."

Tal stopped. Her lips were quivering, and she closed her eyes.

"I felt that . . ."

She abruptly clamped her mouth shut, unable to speak.

"It's OK, Tal," Maletesta murmured. "Let is out."

After a few moments of sobbing, Tal began again. She was now back on the burgundy colored sofa with her legs crossed under her and a box of Kleenex on the cushion next to her.

"When we got to close to his flat, he put his arm around me and said I was the most exotic woman he had ever seen . . ."

Maletesta groaned silently.

"He said he had champagne upstairs and he wanted to show me the fantastic view of North Beach from his roof top patio . . . uh . . . his face was close to mine. Even in the dark I could see the brightness in his eyes."

Tal stopped.

"Tal."

"I panicked, Dad! All of a sudden I was afraid! I broke away and ran!"

Tal sobbed, her shoulders rising and falling rapidly, pulled out tissues and wiped her eyes.

"I heard him laugh behind me. He was laughing! Laughing! God, I felt like such a fool, like a baby. I felt like . . . such a baby!"

Tal rubbed her face with both hands and ran her fingers through her hair several times. She couldn't look at her father, and a silence fell between them.

"Tal," he said after a few minutes, "we need to get through this . . ."

"Dad, you don't know anything!" she blurted. "You don't know anything! Anything! And I don't want to hear anything from you! I don't want to hear something from Ann Landers! You just don't understand!"

Another silence.

"Look, honey," Maletesta said soothingly, "why did it take you so long to get home? Weren't there any taxies around?"

"I wanted to walk. Finally, I did wave down a taxi, but I walked for awhile first."

"Where?"

"I don't know . . . down Columbus, back up Stockton. I finally got a cab somewhere around Union, I don't know . . . somewhere near that place where grandpa eats with his friends?"

"Yes, the North Star," Maletesta clarified.

Tal got up from the chair.

"Dad, I don't want to talk about this anymore tonight. I'd like to go to bed. Is that OK? I'm sorry about what I said before. I'm just tired."

She bent down and kissed him on the forehead.

"OK. Honey, have a good dream . . ."

The telephone rang before he finished. Tal picked it up in the hall. She came running back into the living room.

"Dad," she shrieked, "it's Cayenne and she's crying! Something awful's happened, and the line's gone dead!"

Maletesta jumped out of the chair and bolted over to the closet for his coat. As Tal helped him into his overcoat, he stopped and reached toward the back of the shelf in the closet. He retrieved something from behind a box of electrical fuses: a very small Bernadelli .25 automatic pistol. Even with an extension magazine, his hand almost completely covered it. He racked the slide against the edge of the shelf and pushed on the safety.

"Holy cow, Dad!" Talah exclaimed.

"Don't worry," he said, pulling on his dark fedora, "but put on the double lock." He slipped the automatic into his coat pocket and bolted out the front door.

FIFTEEN

Cow Hollow

Tuesday, December 15, 1959

A dim morning light peeked through the kitchen windows as Maletesta opened the refrigerator and pulled out a bottle of orange juice. He filled the glass he had placed on the kitchen table and put the bottle back. He lit a Fatima on one of the gas elements of the stove, took a deep drag and sat down on the cushioned bench in the nook, setting the cigarette in a glass ashtray. He looked around the kitchen. It wasn't very big, but the nook with its built-in benches and table reminded him of the many comfortable hash houses and off the arm joints he had known over the years. Annemarie had loved them too and for a moment he saw her on the other side of the table, her eyes riveted to a new book of philosophy she had found. He saw the wondrous little crease between her eyebrows when she was concentrating, her grey eyes scanning the pages. She was sipping her coffee. *How many years now since the accident?* He quickly blinked the image of Annemarie away.

Mrs. Dawson, the housekeeper and cook he hired after Annemarie died, left last year to care for her seriously ill sister in Kansas. Though she was close to seventy, Mrs. Dawson had acted as a second mother for Tal: a confidante about dating, an advisor of clothes and hair styles, a teacher of finesse, manners, and diction. Her cultural interpretations were definitely old-fashioned and locked into a Midwest time zone, but she was a vast improvement over what Maletesta could offer a pre-teenage girl, even though she left a girl with Dayak roots in Borneo sounding sometimes sounded like a kid from Kansas City. When Mrs. Dawson left, it felt like someone in the family had died.

Now Maletesta had two real deaths on his plate: a beatnik poet and Cayenne's brother, Yusef. He had spent half the night at Cayenne's apartment. She had cried uncontrollably for a long time and then fell into a blank open-eyed silence. They sat like out of place statues on the leather sofa in her living room, not moving or agreeing when it was time to move. Maletesta had tried to get her to drink or eat something, but to no avail. She held a locket in her hand which contained a picture of Yusef and kept turning it over and over and over.

"Why?" Cayenne moaned. "Why? Yusef never hurt anybody. He just talked things . . . he never hurt anybody. He was gonna go back to school . . . to State next year . . . he never hurt anybody. Why, Johnny, why would anyone want to hurt him?"

Maletesta made her a cup of tea in the kitchen and laced it with honey and brandy. Eventually she drank it.

"How did you find out?" he asked softly.

"Cop called."

"What was his name?"

"Brendan, Bremmer," she waved her hand irritatedly, "whatever. My phone number was on a piece of paper in Yusef's pocket."

Maletesta nodded.

"Promise me, Johnny," Cayenne said suddenly, looking him straight in the eyes, "promise me you'll find out what happened. You're smart; you know how things work. Talk to Sassy, he knows people. Talk to the cops, even though they don't give a damn about a Black man being murdered. Find out, please. Please, Johnny. Promise me, Johnny."

She began to cry again.

"How will I tell Mother? This will break her heart . . . break her heart . . . ohhh."

Maletesta closed his hand over her two small hands in her lap.

"Cayenne," he swore quietly, "I will find out, and whoever did this thing will pay. I promise you."

He persuaded Cayenne to get into bed, and after she dropped off to sleep, he slipped out. He was home at three o'clock.

Maletesta yawned and looked at the clock on the kitchen wall next to the pantry shelves. It was after eight. Tal was still asleep. He had to get moving. He finished the orange juice and walked down the hall to the bathroom. Twenty minutes later he was showered, shaved and dressed and back at the extension phone in the study with a pad and a pen in front of him. He scribbled a page of notes and then made two phone calls: one to Sister Agatha of All Saints College and the other to Sassy James of the Club Carolina. As he gathered his notes, the telephone rang.

"Hello," he snapped.

"Lieutenant?"

Maletesta froze.

"Yes?" he answered tentatively.

"It's Lonnie, you know, Vennemeyer. You remember?"

The man giggled nervously and coughed.

"Yes, of course, Lonnie," Maletesta stuttered, "how are you? We haven't talked in a few years. Uh, are you still in the program? And, remember, Lonnie, it's John now, no more lieutenant."

"OK, lieutenant, er, John. It's good to hear your voice, man. Yeah, yeah, I'm still in the program. Uh, I kinda fall sometimes . . . but, I get up, you know, I get up. That's what they tell me is important. That's the important thing, you know, to get up! Hey, call your buddy if you think you're going down, but I don't always remember that, you know, nah, sometimes, uh . . . well."

"How's your wife, Louise, isn't it?"

"Yeah, no . . . uh, she left me, yeah, after I lost the job at the muffler shop. Can't blame her, you know, putting up all those years with a screwup like me, you know, that's hard for anybody . . . uh."

Maletesta's shoulders sagged, and he sat down on the chair beside the desk. No one spoke for a half a minute. He could hear Lonnie breathing heavily.

"Lonnie," he said, "what can I do? Do you want to fly out here? Are you still in Lexington? I can find you a place here and probably a job . . . I mean it."

"Yeah, well, thanks, lieutenant, you always were a standup guy. It's just that . . . uh . . . I don't think anything'll make much difference now, you know? All these years? Nah."

Lonnie cleared his throat loudly.

"The dreams, you know, lieutenant. They're back."

"Yeah, Lonnie, I know. Why don't you come out here?"

Another pause.

"I can't close my eyes, lieutenant. God damn it, I can't close my eyes! I can still see it! God damn it, I can't close my eyes . . . can't even close my God damned eyes!"

"Lonnie, please, give me your phone number. I don't want to lose you."

"Thanks, lieutenant, but, you know, er, John, I'm already lost, you know? Thanks, though, I'll call you again."

"Lonnie, Lonnie, give me your number! Lonnie!"

SIXTEEN

Leyte, the Philippines

December, 1944

"Baker Two, Baker Two! This is Baker One! Japs everywhere! We are being overrun!

Hold your position! Hold your position! Do you read me?"

The walkie talkie crackled and was silent. Lieutenant John Maletesta looked at Corporal James "Lonnie" Vennemeyer. They could hear the small arms fire increasing on their right flank about a mile away. Maletesta pushed the walkie talkie button down.

"Baker One, this in Baker Two. Do you read? Come in, Baker One. Over."

There was no answer.

"Baker One, come in. Come in, Baker One," Maletesta repeated.

"Looks like Captain Calloway's in for it," Vennemeyer said. Vennemeyer had a long-jawed face with unnaturally

doleful eyes. He peered out into the encroaching darkness as if he could see Calloway's unit.

"And nothing we can do about it, damn!" Maletesta replied. He took a deep breath and slowly exhaled.

"Lonnie, pull the scouts in and gather up the rest. We'll dig in here on the high ground."

"Yes sir."

Vennemeyer disappeared silently into the trees. Maletesta scanned his "high ground": a slight rise in the forest floor dotted with small boulders and clumps of brush. From here, Maletesta's platoon could form a 360 degree perimeter to defend themselves. The scene from Hemingway's "Fight on the Hilltop" flitted through his mind as he reviewed the position, but he brushed it away quickly.

I'm not El Sordo, and there's no air force to worry about here.

Maletesta removed his helmet and scratched his head, contemplating the position around him. He put the helmet back on and strode around the site with an athlete's grace, calculating fields of fire.

A few minutes later, the platoon emerged from the trees and gathered quietly around him. Counting the two Filipino scouts, there were only fourteen of them left. They slept in the rain the night before and kept moving all day. They were hot and tired and shifted on their feet as they stood in formation. In the six weeks since landing on the gulf, they had been in at least one firefight with the enemy every other day. Maletesta pointed out a position to each of the men as he circled the hill with them. They pulled out their shovels and began digging in as the small arms fire from afar diminished and the sky grew dark. They ate cold rations and waited. They were too tired to worry and there was little talking between them. Fortunately, there was a full moon, so there would be no surprise attack.

At eight o'clock by Maletesta's Waltham watch, the firing from Baker One's position ceased. The night was quiet with the exception of a pair of eagle-owls calling to each other and a slight high breeze rustling the leaves of the trees.

"Captain Calloway?" whispered Vennemeyer, who came up on Maletesta's left.

"Maybe some of them made it back to the river. Anyway, be ready. Pazienza, huh?" Maletesta replied.

"Yeah, yeah, I know—patience. Between you and Barreras, lieutenant, by the time this war is over, I'll know three languages."

Chortling, Vennemeyer returned to his position.

Maletesta whistled low in imitation of a night bird. One by one, each man in the platoon answered. They were in place and ready. Maletesta checked the chamber of his M2 carbine. Satisfied there was a cartridge in it, he pushed the safety off and peered down the slope.

Nothing.

He settled his legs farther into the shallow depression he had dug behind the rocks. As he brushed some dirt off the walnut stock of the carbine, his thoughts went inexplicitly to his mother's walnut dining room table. He could smell the red oil he used to polish the table on the holidays. He thought about Annemarie and their Christmas date and smiled.

Maybe they're not coming this way.

Maletesta set the carbine down of its butt, reached into his back pack and pulled out a battered baseball: his good luck charm, the home run ball he hit during his tryout at Seals Stadium. Minor league, one step from the majors. He squeezed the ball and tossed it in the air, catching it lightly.

I'll be back.

He squeezed the ball hard.

I'll be back.

Abruptly, he shoved the ball back down into his back pack and picked up the carbine.

Have I forgotten anything?

He had placed the .30 machine gun facing the densest part of the woods below them. The rest were in a rough circle about sixty feet in diameter with the two grease guns on opposite sides. Lonnie with his BAR was in the center, I reserve, ready to back up any weak spot.

Wait a minute! Something moved! That bush wasn't there before!

Maletesta squeezed off a shot into a bush about fifty yards down the slope. The bush jumped and yelled and he fired two more rounds into it.

"Banzai! Banzai! Banzai!"

All hell broke loose on all sides. The bottom of the slope around the perimeter was alive with crawling, running and dodging Japanese soldiers. Maletesta emptied his carbine, shoved another banana clip in and emptied that one too. He was aware of the intense gunfire around him, the furious bursts from the full automatics and the steady blasts of the M1s. Bullets from enemy fire buzzed around him, smacking into trees and rocks.

He looked back quickly at Lonnie and over at Jimmie Higgins on his right. Higgin's M1 had jammed, and he was trying desperately to clear it.

"Lonnie, cover Jimmie!" Maletesta yelled.

Vennemeyer slid in behind Higgins, firing as he moved.

"Jesus, I'm hit! I'm hit. Oh Jesus, I'm hit!"

It was Daly, about twenty feet to the left of Maletesta. He had dropped his rifle and rolled out from behind his tree, clutching his side. Maletesta saw three Japanese soldiers moving quickly up the slope toward Daly. He stood up and ran toward Daly, letting off a full automatic barrage from the hip at the three shapes coming up the slope. One of them fell; the other two fired back at Maletesta and retreated back down the slope. He pulled Daly back behind the tree, just as a Japanese non-com suddenly appeared out of nowhere, a Nambu pistol in one hand and a samurai sword in the other. As he saw Maletesta, they both fired simultaneously. The non-com's shot went wild. Maletesta's hit it mark and the non-com sank to the ground.

As suddenly as the engagement began, it was over. The firing stopped. The air was heavy with the smell of gunpowder and the groans of the wounded and dying. Maletesta's platoon could hear the Japanese crashing back through the woods in full flight. They reloaded their weapons and watched the forest warily.

Maletesta tore Daly's shirt open and looked at the nasty oozing hole below his rib cage. Daly's face was pale and wet with perspiration. He writhed in pain.

"You'll be all right, Mike, you're going home," Maletesta said and motion to Higgins, who carried the medical, to bring the morphine. "You'll be back with Millie before you know it, Mike. You're a lucky guy. Hurry up, Jimmie. That's it."

Felipe Barreras, one of the scouts, scooted over to where Maletesta sat taking stock of the situation.

A miracle, only one wounded.

"I see if they're really gone?" Barreras whispered.

"OK, kaibigan. Careful though. So far, so good," Maletesta smiled and punched Barreras on the shoulder. Barreras gave a thumb's up back to Maletesta.

Barreras slipped down the slope and Maletesta watched him disappear into the forest. Then he stood up cautiously and stepped out from behind the tree. The non-com lay sprawled over its roots. There was no movement or sound in the woods.

They're gone, thank God.

He leaned the carbine against the tree and lit a cigarette. He exhaled loudly and shook his head in disbelief at Vennemeyer, who stood at a nearby tree, scanning the forest.

Only one wounded. Vennemeyer held the BAR loosely by his side.

"Luck o' the Irish, Lonn . . ."

Suddenly, the Japanese non-com was on his feet swinging his sword. Instinctively, Maletesta raised his left arm in defense and tried to back step. In a blur he saw the flash of the blade slicing through his arms and the blood spurting out. He screamed. He saw the non-com hammered back by a burst from Lonnie's BAR. He saw his arm on the ground. He screamed again.

SEVENTEEN

College of All Saints, Burlingame

Tuesday, December 15, 1959

"I do not believe that any sane person would suspect Tal of murder. I've known that girl for over twelve years, John. Murder? That's the silliest thing I've ever heard!"

Sister Agatha stood by the multi-paned window near her desk gazing absentmindedly at the "new" Science Building across the quad. It was completed ten years ago with the precious gems Maletesta had brought back from the otherwise failed anthropological mission to Borneo. She walked over to the magnificent world globe in the corner of her office. It was three feet in diameter and situated on a stand made of Honduras mahogany. It had been given to her years ago by her old radical uncle, Con Buckley. She spun it and, for perhaps the millionth time, watched it glisten in the early morning light as nations, countries, and oceans became one. The oneness of the spinning globe pleased her immensely. Upon returning to her desk, she carefully lowered herself into the chair, wincing at the grinding of joints no longer young. Despite the school's extensive funding, her office remained as spartan as it was thirteen years ago when she had recklessly authorized the expedition to Borneo. No carpet, no soft chairs, no frills, only the faint aroma of lemon oil furniture polish.

She sighed and turned to Maletesta who was sitting in the hardwood chair on the other side of her desk. Maletesta had taken the train to Burlingame earlier that morning. All Saints kept an on-call shuttle service at the train station manned by an ex-con named Ducker who maintained a pristine four-door 1938 La Salle for the transport of various souls to the college. The con delivered him to the school's front gate.

"If this were an old novel, I'd say 'harrumph,'" Sister Agatha added.

"I've known that girl forever," Sister Agatha continued. "She would not harm a fly! Why, once when she was here shortly after you both came back from Borneo, we went for a walk around the campus. I remember it quite clearly to this day. There was a beetle crossing the path as we approached the dormitories. Most children would have stepped on it! Talah carefully stepped over it. What kind of idiot says she was involved in Sinclair's murder?"

"A cop named Brennan," Maletesta replied, pulling out a Fatima cigarette from the inside pocket of his navy blue sports coat.

Sister Agatha pushed a ceramic ashtray of Alcatraz across the desk to him as Maletesta lit his cigarette with his Zippo.

"I cannot imagine that habit is beneficial for your health, Professor Maletesta, no matter what the advertisements on television proclaim."

"You mean like 'the thinking man's cigarette?" he answered a he snapped the lighter shut.

"Harrumph again is all I can say." Sister Agatha said as she settled in her chair and pursed her lips. "I rather like that word; it's very useful for different occasions."

Maletesta shrugged with a smile. Sister Agatha moved slightly to take weight off her arthritic hip.

"That's better. Did you say the policeman's name is Brennan?"

"Yes," Maletesta replied, "we played baseball in college. As you know, Sister, we actually made the playoffs. Baseball was looking good."

"Yes, I know, John."

"Unfortunately, that kind of thing doesn't matter to guys like Brennan. For him, the 'old school tie' is a noose."

"Hmmm."

Sister Agatha leaned forward over the desk in a gesture of confidentiality.

"I do not tell many people about this, John, but my father—God rest his soul--had a blind pig," she almost whispered.

"Excuse me?"

"He had a blind pig."

Maletesta looked perplexed. "You mean, like a lame dog or something?"

Sister Agatha straightened her rimless spectacles.

"No," she clarified, "a blind pig. It's a slang term for an illegal saloon during Prohibition, also called a speakeasy. My da ran one down on 18th and Capp. I was already in the Order, but none of my younger brothers and sisters were allowed to go there, nor ever talk about it."

"He was a bootlegger?"

Sister Agatha blushed.

"In a manner of speaking, yes. That's how he bought his house in Glenn Park in the early days of the Depression. He would never have been able to afford it on his salary from the public works department"

"Well," Maletesta commented, "good for him, I suppose, but I just can't imagine one of your relatives being like Al Capone."

"Oh no," Sister Agatha agreed, "My father was not a violent man, and he got out of the business when Repeal came. He kept his job with the City, and his life of crime was over."

Maletesta chuckled.

"The point is, John, that to operate his blind pig, my da had to pay dues to the local 'club owner's benevolent association.' Do you know who the president of the association was?"

"No, but I know you'll tell me.'

"Lieutenant Patrick Brennan, Mission Station."

Maletesta let out a low whistle.

"And," Sister Agatha continued, "Da always said that's how Brennan bought his very posh house in Laurel Village."

Sister Agatha leaned back and folded her hands on the desk.

"They're both gone now, but San Francisco is small town, John. The information may be useful to you somewhere during your investigation. I would not have brought it up, but I do not like the direction that policeman has taken. Perhaps he has some questionable issues of his own."

"Thanks," Maletesta answered, stubbing out his cigarette on Alcatraz. "It's interesting, but I don't think it will help me find whoever killed Sinclair."

"Now, Sinclair—poor soul," Sister Agatha mused, "who in the world would want to kill him? He was another harmless person, in my opinion."

"Doesn't make any sense, does it? Unless it was someone who appreciated real poetry," Maletesta chortled.

Sister Agatha raised her eyebrows in distaste.

"For shame, John, the man was murdered."

"OK, OK," he put up the palm of his right hand. "Actually, I have a friend who works at Vesuvio's who knows a lot of people in North Beach. I'll be talking to her tonight . . . ."

"Good."

"Then there's my uncle Carlo," Maletesta said tentatively.

"Oh dear, do you mean the uncle who you told me is some kind of a gangster?"

"Well, there's always been bad blood between my pop and him. Pop says he's in the mafia. My mother, who is his sister, prays about it and says he just owns a juke box franchise. We've haven't seen him for years. Anyway, he's at the bottom of the list. I can't imagine Carlo would know anything about the murder of a beatnik poet," Maletesta shrugged, "but I'll do whatever I need to do to get Tal clear of this."

Maletesta stared at the floor for a moment and then looked up.

"I'm just not sure I'm up to this, sister: I'm a teacher, not a detective."

He tapped his left foot unconsciously. Somewhere outside a bell rung for classes that were not being held. Finally, Sister Agatha levered herself out of her chair, walked around the desk and looked down at her one-armed English professor.

"John Maletesta, thirteen years ago, you sat in this same chair and gave in to defeat and-- quite frankly--self pity . . ."

Maletesta winced, but Sister Agatha held up a precautionary finger and continued.

"Yes, it *was* self pity. Your dream of a career in baseball had ended, and you weren't able to find another life. I asked you to accompany our small expedition to Borneo. Ultimately, you agreed, and when you came back, you were a different man. You left your self pity in that jungle and came back a strong man and a new father . . ."

Maletesta started to speak.

"You survived your wife's accident, and you raised that wonderful little child to become a brilliant and compassionate young woman. The gems you brought back from Borneo set you up for life but, most importantly, helped us change All Saints from a finishing school for girls into a genuine college for young women. At the same time, you've been the bedrock of our English Department . . ."

"All right, enough already," Maletesta protested, raising himself out of the chair.

Sister Agatha placed her hands on her hips and laughed.

"You have work to do, professor Maletesta. By the way, you once convinced me that Dashielle Hammet should be included in the great American writers of the 20th Century, so why don't you study the methods of his 'Continental Op'? It can't be that difficult to develop a plan to exonerate your daughter."

She shooed him out of her office as if she were sweeping the floor.

"One more thing," Sister Agatha said to Maletesta's back as he walked toward the door, "the House Un-American Activities Committee is coming to town."

Maletesta turned and smiled.

"You better watch out, you better not cry, you better not pout . . ."

Sister Agatha held up a hand to cut off his song.

"That's very seasonal and very witty, John, but not funny. They've subpoenaed Uncle Con."

"What?" Maletesta asked. "Subpoenaed him for what?"

"As you know, he was in the Abraham Lincoln Battalion in Spain," Sister Agatha answered quietly.

"Oh for Chrissake," Maletesta exclaimed, "what is it with these witch hunters? That was over twenty years ago! Investigate him? That's crazy!"

"Nonetheless, it's true," Sister Agatha replied, "and there's no need to bring Jesus Christ into it."

"Excuse me, Sister, but a lot of those guys had a pretty rough time after the war."

"Yes, they were blacklisted. Uncle Con was lucky in that way; he kept his job on the waterfront. I have not always approved of Mister Harry Bridges' tactics, but he takes care of his people, even if it means antagonizing the government and putting himself into jeopardy."

"And now this for Uncle Con after all he's been through. Not very fair, is it?"

Sister Agatha walked over to Maletesta and waggled her right index finger again at him.

"Please. You already know that life is not *fair*, Professor Maletesta," she said, "and that's why we need to work to make it *just*! Now scoot!"

EIGHTEEN

North Beach

Tuesday, December 20, 1959

Vesuvio's was one of the favorite watering holes of the poets and artists of the Beat Generation. Located down the street from City Lights Books and across the street from the Tosca Café and XII Adler Place, Vesuvio's was an eccentric bar owned by an eccentric owner who welcomed eccentric people.

The owner collected ancient postcards and projected them on one of the walls with a slide projector during the evening. Certain chairs were reserved for certain people. If you were sitting in a certain painter's wicker chair, you'd better be out of it when that painter came in. The window table was usually occupied by beat poets who want to be seen. When tourists recognized the poets at the window table, they'd fall all over themselves and rush in to buy drinks for the poets in return for a little chit chat to take home to Aunt Martha and Uncle John the insurance salesman in Hicksville. Shocking inside news about what San Francisco was *really* like.

The Beats were on to this scene. Sometimes, a beat will tell a tourist, "I've already had enough to drink, just give me the money."

Maletesta took the 41 bus down Union Street to Columbus and walked the rest of the way to Vesuvio's. He wanted to think. The lead waitress at Vesuvio's was Maria de las Casas, whose parents were from Galicia in Spain. He met her during one of the International Brigade reunions that Sister Agatha's Uncle Con Buckley had invited him to attend. Like Buckley, Maria's family had fought against the fascist troops of Franco and Mussolini and Hitler's Luftwaffe in an ill-fated defense of a democratic Spain. They'd lost, but the fire in the bellies of the anti-fascists never went out. The reunions, which were usually held in one of the local Basque restaurants, were full of high energy and idealism forged in the fire of battle. Maletesta smiled as he thought of those reunions with the middle aged radicals pumping their fists and screaming across the table over the issues of the day. They had strongly held opinions about everything.

In one of his conversations with Maria at a reunion, Maletesta learned that she knew North Beach better than anyone he knew, including his father. Unlike his father, she knew the Beat side as well as the Italians, the working class, and the jumble of ethnicities and occupations that constituted this unique neighborhood.

Maletesta sat at a corner table. There were very few customers in the place at this hour. Maria spotted him almost immediately and came over to his table. She had a dancer's slim body and devastating green eyes. She wore tight blue jeans and most men watched her as she moved between the tables. Her smile flashed in the dim lighting of the club.

"John, doll baby, what'll it be?" "Doll baby" was a title reserved for her close friends in North Beach.

"Any kind of draft, Maria," he answered, shaking out a cigarette, "and I have a problem that I hope you can help me with."

"Name it, you know that. I'll be right back."

When she returned with the beer, she stood by the table expectantly.

"Did you know Jean-Paul Sinclair?" Maletesta asked.

"Sure. Good-looking guy!" Maria answered, smiling. "A real skirt chaser, you know, but it's too bad what happened."

"Like his poetry?"

"Well, no," she hesitated, "I mean, he wasn't a Bob Kaufman. He felt a little like somebody putting on an act; a very good act, but still an act. I often wondered . . ."

"What?"

"He behaved like one of those guys who have money from somewhere. You know, you think maybe some time they'll go back home and open a car dealership."

They both laughed. Maletesta took a sip of his beer, and Maria went to serve another table. She was back in about ten minutes.

"Why are you interested in a dead poet, doll baby?" she asked.

"The cops are trying to hang it on Tal."

"No! That's crazy! The sonofabitchin' bastards!"

"I know," Maletesta stubbed out his cigarette and shook out a second, "but I've

got to prove her innocent. Who would know about Sinclair, where he hung out, what he did, who owed him money, you know, that sort of thing?"

She thought a moment, her fingers on her lips.

"Well, Shig-Shig at City Lights would know, but he's out of town right now . . . let me see, who else?"

Maria snapped her fingers.

"El Pilar."

"Who?"

"El Pilar."

"Spanish?"

"No, no, no," she laughed. "Last year he was The Fez and wore one of those Arabian hats without a brim. When he blew into town four years ago, he was the Duke of Donkeyshire."

"Whaaat?" Maletesta burst out laughing. "Are you kidding me?"

"The truth: cross my heart, five fingers to heaven, and a cellar full of rats," she swore and then added sheepishly, "he's kind of goofy."

Maria took off again to a group of tourists who had alighted on the window table. After she shooed them off the designated table, she took their orders. Eventually, she returned to Maletesta's table.

"Where do I find this El Pilar?' he asked.

"Just walk along Columbus," she replied, "on some corner you'll find a guy dressed in a monk's outfit-- at least, this week—you know, like Saint Francis? He's got the shaved tonsure and everything. When you see him, ask him if you can buy a poem."

"Buy a poem?"

"Oh, it's just his thing, a way to open a conversation. He's one of those nosey types, you know? Seems to know a lot about other people's business? No one else will know much about Sinclair. I bet he covered his tracks pretty well."

"Thanks," Maletesta said, placing a ten dollar bill on the table and getting up from his chair.

"Hey, doll baby, what do you think of the trade?" Maria was one of the thousands of San Franciscans who had become avid baseball fans when the Giants moved into town a year and a half ago.

"For Blasingame?"

"Of course."

"I think his best years are behind him."

"I mean, do they really need another hitter?" Maria asked. "They got Mays, Cepeda and now this rookie, McCovey?"

"*That* guy is really something," Maletesta agreed. "I saw his first game: he went four for four. Holy moley, what a swing! He'll be here for a long time."

Maletesta paused and looked down into those green eyes.

"You know, Maria," he confessed, "I still haven't decided what I feel about the Giants. I still have a soft spot for the Dodgers: jeez – Jackie Robinson, Pee Wee Reese, Big Don Newcombe, hell, you know, the Bums!"

"All those guys are gone, doll baby, and the team's not in Brooklyn anymore," Maria clarified. "They're in Lost Angels."

"OK, OK," Maletesta conceded. "How are the kids?"

"They'd better be doing their homework."

As Maletesta turned to leave, Maria touched his arm.

"Hey, wait a minute, I have something to show you. Sit down a minute."

He sat down as Maria darted quickly into the back room and came back with a small thin package wrapped in butcher paper. She placed it on the table and carefully unwrapped it. Before him lay one of the most beautiful water color paintings Maletesta had ever seen. He took a deep breath as he turned it toward the light with his hand. A Monterey Cypress stood in isolation as a fog moved into it.

"My God," he exhaled, "Who painted this?"

"My neighbor, Victor Wong," Maria replied proudly. "Our kids are almost the same age, so we babysit each other's kids."

"Incredible. Does he do oil too?"

"No. Victor says oil is too easy; you can paint over your mistakes. In water color, you can't make a mistake."

A small group of tourists came through the door.

"I better run," Maria said, re-wrapping the painting.

"Thanks for the showing."

Maletesta sauntered up Columbus back toward Union. Had he passed "El Pilar" on his way to Vesuvio's? He didn't remember seeing anyone dressed like a Franciscan monk. As he crossed Stockton to Green, he saw someone in a robe coming toward him from the 622. The 622 Green was a family style restaurant that often gave away free meals. As the figure approached him, Maletesta recognized the man's tonsure as he passed under the street light. He saw a chubby man, maybe in his late 40's, with a short medieval beard.

"El Pilar?"

NINETEEN

North Beach

Tuesday, December 20, 1959

Walter Throckmorton was a bright but nosey little boy. He peeked through the bedroom door of his parents' bedroom when they were in bed. He eavesdropped on the teachers' meetings at school, hiding in the bushes outside the half open window of the staff room. He spied on other little boys who set off cherry bombs in the toilets of the school restrooms. He wasn't a snitch. He never told on anyone. He just *knew* things, and that made him happy. And strong in his own way.

He never changed as he grew older. When he was in high school, Walter would slip out of his parents' house at night and sneak around the neighborhood looking into windows. He was almost caught one time when a couple took a break in their connubial activity to raise the shade higher so that they could see the moon and instead saw someone in their garden. Terrified at the possibility of discovery, Walter ran like hell down to the cemetery where he hid behind an outsized monument while a barefoot man in trousers stomped around the street.

By then, his parents had come to the conclusion that they had raised a strange child. He told them that he did not want to go to college when he graduated from high school; he wanted to travel. It was in the beginning of the Depression, so his parents, who were barely scraping by, welcomed his decision. On the day after graduation, Walter cashed in some bonds his grandmother had given him and announced to his parents that he was leaving. In an awkward moment, his parents handed him a pack of penny post cards so that he could keep in touch.

Walter tossed the post cards into a garbage can outside the Greyhound Bus Depot in Newark, New Jersey. He was on his way out to the Southwest in the hope of spying on secret Indian rituals he'd read about in National Geographic magazines. Sitting in the seat behind the driver, he imagined the discoveries that awaited him and the knowledge he would accumulate. He dreamed of the power of knowing secrets that very few other people knew. He dreamed of a time when he would return to Newark and everyone would recognize him for what he knew.

Years passed and Walter Throckmorton of Newark, New Jersey simply disappeared. He had taken many different jobs throughout New Mexico and Arizona, using a different name for each job: hotel clerk, insurance salesman, night shift janitor, grocery clerk. The names came and went with the jobs. By the late 1940's, Walter Throckmorton had no idea what his birth name was.

No one knows just who he may have spied on or what secrets he may have learned, but at some point he discovered the hallucinogenic properties of peyote and, after several years of spiritual experimentation and two failed marriages, he came to a fuzzy conclusion that the Southwest was no longer the place for him. On the day he turned forty-three, he packed a small suitcase and walked out of his trailer home in Phoenix, leaving his sleeping third wife behind.

He arrived in San Francisco not long after the publication of *Howl.* Allen Ginsburg became his idol, and in his various personages, Walter began making regular rounds of the places to see and be seen, sometimes near his idol. At night he could be seen at the Bagel Shop, the Place, City Lights, Mike's Pool Hall, Vesuvio's, Trieste, the Bagel Shop, the Spaghetti Factory, the Basque restaurants, and the like. By day he showed up in the laundromats, the library, the art galleries, and Washington Square. To the beats, he was just another crank who made the scene, and the cops never rousted him because they considered him a harmless tourist attraction. Soon, the man from Newark with an ever-changing name melted into the social foliage of North Beach.

"At your service, your excellency," the man in the monk's outfit replied to Maletesta with a flourishing bow. "El Pilar, that is, at your service."

"Maria de las Casas says you know things."

"Maria, yes, lovely spirit. Yes, she is correct. El Pilar does know things. He also sells poems, small works of art, they are." He pulled a string from over his shoulder and a small basket appeared at the end of it. He jiggled it in front of Maletesta. Maletesta dropped two quarters in the basket.

El Pilar straightened his back, elevated his eyes toward the street light and emoted in basso profundo tones:

"Whistle while you work,

Hitler was a jerk.

Mussolini pulled his weenie;

Now it doesn't work."

Maletesta snorted.

"That's a small work of art?" he queried.

El Pilar stepped back abruptly.

"For fifty cents, you expected William Blake?"

"OK, OK," Maletesta agreed and dropped a buck into the basket.

"Ah, now El Pilar will update the old poem into a new and improved poem," he said, stage whispering toward Maletesta. "Are you a fan of the local team named after the 49rs of the Gold Rush? How about the Mayor?"

"Yes and no."

Once again El Pilar straightened his back, gazed at the street light and recited,

"Whistle while you work,

Christopher's a jerk.

Nomellini pulled his weenie;

Now it doesn't work."

Before Maletesta could object, El Pilar added, "What other information do you seek?"

"I want to know everything about a beatnik poet named Jean-Paul Sinclair: his friends, his enemies, how he lived . . ."

"He died," El Pilar interrupted, rolling his eyes heavenward. "All very tragic. His no doubt soon-to-be-illustrious career was just beginning."

Maletesta dropped a twenty dollar bill in the basket, along with a card with his address and phone number. The monk nodded solemnly and theatrically.

"El Pilar will find the information you seek. El Pilar is a solid cat, man, a no jive guy. On this corner, two nights from this night, the straight skinny will be presented to you."

El Pilar bowed deeply, took a deep breath as he rose and expounded:

"But first, a bonus for your generous donation."

"Bonus?" Maletesta asked.

"Yes," replied El Pilar seriously. "Your inside track bonus is to impart the knowledge that the Pilgrims put popcorn in a bowl and poured milk on it to eat it as a cereal. Not quite corn flakes, but let us admit: the pilgrims were strange and weird cats."

He exhaled.

"So, there you have it: a morsel of knowledge most people do not have."

In the dark, El Pilar could probably not see the perplexed look on Maletesta's face.

"Uh, thanks," Maletesta muttered.

"El Pilar wishes *salaam aleikum* and happy trails to you until we meet again."

With that, he slipped the twenty dollar bill inside his robe, flung the basket over his shoulder and crossed Columbus Avenue without further word.

Maletesta smiled at the retreating figure and wondered if he had just blown twenty one dollars and fifty cents.

TWENTY

Paradise Billiards

Wednesday, December 16, 1959

"Too bad you missed Eddie Vienna, bub," the cook said as he set a chili dog and a cup of coffee on the counter in front of Maletesta.

"The Georgia Shooter?"

"The same."

"Here in the Paradise?" Maletesta asked as he picked up his fork.

"Yeah, last night."

Maletesta sat at the near-empty grill counter on the back wall of Paradise Billiards on Market Street where Sassy James had told him he would meet with a black private detective named Osceola King between one and two o'clock. King had not arrived.

He put the fork down, pulled a small silver-plated folding knife out of his jacket pocket and pushed a button on the knife. A curved three inch blade sprang out of the handle. He then cut the hot dog into bite-size pieces by rocking the blade through it.

The cook, who was round shouldered and wearing a white shirt and an apron that hadn't been washed in recent times, watched in amazement. Maletesta wiped the knife on the napkin of the counter, closed it and put it back into his pocket.

"What do you call that, bub?"

"A rocker knife," Maletesta replied as he picked up a fork. "They began making them after the Civil War."

"That legal?"

"I don't know, maybe you should call the police department and ask them."

"Ok, Ok, I get it. No offense, bub. So, how do you like the dog?"

"So far, so good."

"That's an all-beef dog you got there, bub. We get 'em from over in Butchertown. No pork or chicken in that one."

The Paradise was about half full in the early afternoon, which meant half the tables were empty and the hooded lights over them were turned off. Men in shirt sleeves and suspenders played quietly at the other tables. It was a one floor walkup from Market Street and first time visitors learned to respect the church-like solemnity of the pool hall. The sign at the top of the stairs said "No Spitting and No Swearing."

It wasn't much different than when he used to come here before the war, Maletesta mused after scanning the room for the third time. *I was pretty good in my three sports: baseball, rifle shooting and pool.* He put down his fork and wiped his mouth with the paper napkin on the counter. *I had two arms then. You need two arms to play baseball, two arms to shoot a rifle and two arms to shoot pool.* He tried unsuccessfully to push the thought out of his mind. *It's not the same, Gianni. It's not the same. You can't go home again, the man wrote. No, Gianni, you can't go home again.*

The cook wiped off the counter in front of Maletesta with a dirty rag and leaned into him. "You look like a savvy guy, bub. Got a story."

"Yeah?"

"Kid comes in last night with his paycheck," the cook confided. "Upholstery cutter. I know him. Gets paid on Tuesdays, comes in a coupla times a month. Pretty good player, not as good as he thinks he is. Gets in a game with a guy who brings his own cue stick in a fancy leather case. Watch out, I'd think if it was me."

Maletesta swallowed and placed his fork on the plate.

"You know how it goes. Hustler lets him win for a while; kid gets cocky, ups the ante and then gets his ass kicked."

"Kid should have known better."

"No, no, that's not the end!" the cook exclaimed. "The kid's sitting over there on that bench," he nodded toward the wall, "hanging his head. He's blown the rent money; how does he explain it to his wife?"

Maletesta looked up and waited.

"Guess who comes over to talk to him?" the cook asks, his hands on his hips.

"Tell me."

"Eddie Vienna! He goes over and listens to the kid's story. Then he goes to shoot with the hustler."

The cook grinned.

"The punk don't know who he's playing with! Well, it's no lie that Eddie looks like kind of a shlump, you know."

"Yeah, I've seen him: horn-rimmed glasses, huge cardigan, shiny slacks."

"Exactly. So, long story short, Eddie gets all the kid's money back, gives it to him and says, 'get the hell out of here and don't ever come back.'"

"Good story, thanks," Maletesta said.

There was no sound other than the clicking of the balls, the scraping of blue chalk on cue sticks, oaths uttered under breath at a missed shot, and a short thump of a cue stick on the floor in appreciation of a good shot. The thumps were not loud; they were given to compliment the shooter, not to entertain the audience. At one table, some college students spilled talcum powder all over the floor in their efforts to slick up their cues. A player at a nearby table looked over, scowled at them, and then went back to his solo game of one pocket. A haze of cigar and cigarette haze hung over the whole place.

There were bleacher-like stands along a side wall where older men sat on wooden benches. Some of them peered out into the room to watch the games, others read the Racing Form or the sports sections of the local newspapers, and there were always a few who were sound asleep. The wall opposite the stands was adorned with huge 19th century oil paintings in gilded frames depicting horsemen in red and white uniforms riding with hounds and scantily clad young women in elaborate bedrooms looking expectant. There were also a few exotic palaces of unknown origin. Each painting had a little brass mounted fixture with a bulb aimed down at it, but the illumination was defeated by the veneer of tobacco smoke and dust which coated the paintings. The grill and the counter where Maletesta sat were situated at the back of the room.

Maletesta finished the chili dog, pushed the plate away and checked the grease encrusted clock on the wall behind the grill. A quarter to two. He glanced around the room again. *I can't waste any more time on this crap. God knows what the cops have by now. I'll call Sassy later and tell him it was a washout.* He placed a five dollar bill on the counter and pushed himself off the stool.

"You Maletesto?"

TWENTY ONE

Paradise Billiards

Wednesday, December 16, 1959

Maletesta turned and saw a heavyset middle aged Black man in a pearl grey suit and matching fedora approaching him. The man's tie held a vivid display of hand painted mallards flying toward the counter. The tie was held in place with a gold guitar tie clip. The man looked pointedly at Maletesta's empty left sleeve.

"You Maletesto?" the man repeated.

"Maletes-TAH. Who wants to know?"

"Man named Mister James said there would be a man named Maletes-TOH at the Paradise who wanted to do business."

"It's still Maletes-TAH."

The man laughed, revealing a gold canine with a miniature white star in it.

"Ah, all those foreign names sound alike to me," he said, sitting down on a stool, leaving one stool between Maletesta and himself. "My name is Osceola King: CB King to my friends, *Mister* King to you."

Maletesta sat down again and pointed at the tie clip.

"Well, *Mister* CB King, are you any relation to BB?"

"He's my second cousin."

King shot his cuffs revealing small gold cuff links in the shape of quarter notes, and then spoke again.

"Of course, all Black people named King say the same thing. You can believe me or not. I don't really care." He looked at the polished fingernails of his left hand and smiled.

"So, then, mister King, do you also play guitar?" Maletesta asked, gesturing to the tie clip.

King laughed heartily.

"I play piano," he answered. "Bach, Beethoven and a little Monk . . . you dig? As if it's any of your business, Mister Italian name."

Maletesta began to slowly drum the fingers of his right hand on the counter.

King smiled again.

"Do you know that there are actually some Black people who don't know anything about *the Blues* in the popular 'chitlin circuit' form?"

Maletesta shifted on his stool.

"I'm sorry, but it doesn't look like this is working out . . ."

King nodded his head twice in acceptance of the apology.

"All right, Mister Italian name, let's start again . . ."

"My name is Maletesta, first name John."

"OK, first name John, Mister James told me to help you, and Mister James and I go way back to Marshall, Texas. So, what do you want?"

"I want to know about a man named Yusef X, also known as Alexander Phillips."

"What about him?"

"He was murdered last Sunday in the Fillmore. Somebody shot him in an alley off Buchanan. I want to know why. Sassy James told me that you know everything that goes on in the Fillmore. I want to know what Yusef was doing and why someone would want to kill him."

"Why?" King asked, "Are you some kind of head beater?"

"No, Mister King, I'm not a cop. I'm just a teacher trying to help a friend."

Maletesta paused to see how the private detective would accept that. The clicking of balls on the pool tables continued in the silence that followed. King slowly arose from his stool and moved closer. As he turned toward Maletesta, his suit jacket opened slightly and Maletesta recognized the nickel plated butt of a Luger pistol in a shoulder holster.

"So," King asked deliberately, "then you're some kind of do-gooder? Is that what you are, mister Maletesta, first name John? You plan to help 'Negroes in need?'"

Maletesta's patience ran out. He stood up and faced Osceola King, his eyes blazing.

"*Mister* King," he answered. "I'll make it simple. I need your information to help a friend of mine. I was told that you might be able to find it. I want to know what it will cost and when you will deliver it. If you can't answer those questions or if you don't want to do the job, then don't waste my time!"

The two men glared at each other for several seconds. A few of the pool shooters at nearby tables sensed the situation and stopped to watch the scene. Neither Maletesta nor King spoke or moved. There was a loud crack at one of the tables as a player broke a rack of balls, but neither man noticed. There was a slight scraping noise as another player chalked his cue.

"You want any more coffee, bub?"

Maletesta glanced to his right. The cook stood behind the counter, coffee pot in hand. In Maletesta's vision, he was a blur. The entire room was becoming a blur and there was a roaring in his ears.

"Coffee?" the cook asked again, raising the pot like he was presenting a championship belt in a ring after a knockout.

"Coffee?"

Suddenly, Maletesta recognized the cook.

"No. No, thanks," Maletesta pushed his hand through his hair and smiled slowly.

Osceola King broke into laughter. He buttoned his jacket.

"He doesn't want any more coffee," King said to the cook between bursts of more laughter.

"No more coffee," Maletesta repeated to the cook, laughing.

"You guys are weird," the cook muttered and went back to his grill.

"All right, Mister *Maletesta*," King said when the laughter subsided, "let's talk business. Who's this guy again?"

The two men sat back down on the stools.

"His mother baptized him Alexander Phillips, but recently he's been going by the name Yusef X."

"Was he one of those black Mohamedans?""

Maletesta spun slowly on the stool, looking at the floor.

"I don't know what he was, but somebody thought he was important enough to kill him. It wasn't a robbery; his wallet, which only had a couple of bucks in it, was not taken. I want to know why someone shot him down in a back alley. By the way, can we drop the formalities?'"

"Sure. My associates call me Cool Breeze."

"Cool Breeze?"

"It's a long story," King answered. "So, who am I working for? You or someone else?"

"My name is John and you're working for me. Is that a problem for you?"

"Not as long as the bill is paid, John."

"It depends on how much you charge and what you deliver."

King lit a Kool cigarette and blew a smoke ring at the ceiling.

"One hundred dollar retainer, eleven dollars an hour, minimal expenses included."

"How minimal is minimal?"

"You reimburse if I have to fly somewhere or rent hotel rooms, small stuff is mine."

"Done."

Maletesta pulled a sizeable wad of bills from his overcoat pocket and placed them on the counter. He picked out five twenties and handed them to King, who eyed the remaining bills on the counter.

"I wouldn't mind having their brothers along for the ride, John."

"Deliver something worthwhile and you will."

Maletesta paused, took a deep breath and exhaled. He did not want to end the meeting like this.

"Look, Mister King, this is really important to me," he said, lowering his voice. "Really important. How soon will you have something?"

King looked at his watch and at the calendar hanging on the wall by the grill.

"Meet me on Saturday afternoon, one o'clock."

"Where?"

"Club Carolina parking lot."

"Deal."

Osceola King walked back between the pool tables out of the room. Maletesta stared at the floor for a few minutes while the cook watched him.

Maletesta dropped a fiver on the counter.

"For running interference," he said to the cook who had a puzzled look on his face.

"Huh?"

Maletesta laughed and walked across the room. No pool shooters noticed.

TWENTY TWO

Hall of Justice

Wednesday, December 16, 1959

"Homicide, Brennan."

Brennan picked up the telephone on the ninth ring. Everyone had gone home and the office was empty, but Brennan was still at his desk, leafing through a three ring binder of photographs of felons recently released from California prisons. He closed the binder when he picked up the phone.

"Maletesta. You got a minute?"

"John! Sure. For you, absolutely, although, I've got nothing new on the Sinclair murder. We're working on it, but so far, nothing. Those guys in North Beach, they really clam up when we come around. They don't like us. Maybe it's because we wash and shave every day, huh? Hey, how's Toollah? Feeling better?"

"Talah. Yes. But I have a question about another matter."

"Shoot, buddy. You know that. You and me, we were two thirds of the three dollar outfield!"

Brennan laughed too heartily and picked out a stick of gum out of a pack of Blackjack on his desk.

"Yeah," Maletesta said evenly, "the three dollar outfield."

Maletesta waited a few seconds before asking the question. He could hear Brennan snapping his gum on the other end of the line.

"What do you know about the murder of a man named Yusef X on Sunday night?"

"You mean the one out in the Fillmore?"

"Yes."

Brennan swung his feet up onto the desk and leaned back in the swivel chair.

"Not much. Somebody shot him a couple of times in an alley out there."

"Any suspects? Any leads?"

"C'mon, John, are you kidding me? Those people are always shooting and cutting each other. Who knows why? He's squeezed somebody else's tomato? He welshed on a bet with Stagger Lee? You know that one by Lloyd Price? 'Stagger Lee threw seven; Billie swore that he threw eight.' You know what I mean, John? Life's cheap out there."

Maletesta inhaled.

"So who's investigating the murder?" he asked.

"Who's asking?"

"I am."

"Why?" Brennan shot back warily.

"Let's say I'm trying to solve a puzzle, but I don't have all the pieces. You know, as part of the old three dollar outfield?" Maletesta chuckled.

"Yeah?" Brennan sounded confused. "Well, we don't know anything."

"Who's on it?"

"Couple of patrolmen asked questions around the neighborhood, as usual, got zilch. That's it, John. That's the pick of the litter for the three dollar outfield."

"I've got one more question, Brennan, and, quite frankly, you haven't given me anything."

"Hold on there, professor. I thought you were working on the problem of the poet who was pushed off the roof."

"I am, and this other matter."

"Busy guy, ain't you? Don't you have no homework to correct?"

"I have another question about Yusef's murder."

"You know, professor," Brennan replied, "I'm looking for a piece of paper here that says I'm supposed to tell a professor from a fancy girls' college in Burlingame all about the workings of the SFPD. Get it?"

"What kind of gun?"

"What kind of gun? Hmmm. Dunno, professor. Nine millimeter bullet was on the report. Probably a Luger or a P 38; they've been floating around all over the place since the war. Fifteen -twenty bucks on the street."

Luger, Maletesta thought, and wrote *Osceola King, Luger* on a pad in front of him.

"Did your guys find any casings on the ground?"

"No, don't think so: none were mentioned in the report. You know how that goes; they had to run to a four car pile-up on Geary shortly after they got there, or was it three cars?"

"Or one car."

"Yeah, maybe. That's how it is, amigo. Life goes on."

"Thanks," Maletesta intoned as he hung up the phone.

"Any time. Stay in touch," Brennan answered, placing the receiver back in its cradle. He frowned at the telephone sitting on his desk, and then went back to the binder of photographs.

TWENTY THREE

Land's End

Wednesday, December 16, 1959

For the third or fourth time that night, the man wished that he owned a dog. It was less suspicious to walk a dog up and down a deserted street than to walk by yourself. If someone asks you what you're doing, you can always say that the dog needs his exercise or has a problem with his bladder. People will nod and smile. They understand all the problems you can have with a dog.

In his Burberry and his trilby, the man was the picture of an upper class English gentleman even though he was neither. His image was created downtown at the Brooks Brothers men's clothing store, not too far from the small corner shop where he bought his expensive Cuban cigars, the kind he sniffed ostentatiously in front of his business associates before he clipped the ends with a stainless steel clipper and lit them. Actually, he preferred Pall Mall cigarettes, but the exotic cigars impressed his associates.

The man passed the darkened hulk of the closed Sutro Baths for the third time. The place gave him the creeps. He didn't like it when he was a child. The midget representations of Tom Thumb and his wife in their glassed exhibits spooked him as he walked down the long hallway to the swimming pools: hot, cold and medium with a big pool the length of the other three. He was afraid of the hump-backed man who passed out the towels on his way to the lockers. An older boy once told him that *pachucos* from San Jose had put razor blades in the slide for the big pool, so he stayed in the small medium temperature pool until it was time to go home. He didn't know the story was a fabrication used by big kids to keep younger kids off the slide.

The man shivered at the memory or maybe the thickening fog swirling around him as he walked back up hill toward the telephone booth. He was a methodical man, and they were late. How in the world had he gotten in this deep? He was just trying to make money out of a unique opportunity. What was wrong with that? Wasn't that a standard business procedure? Wasn't that how Sutro and Spreckles and Stanford and Crocker made their fortunes? Everyone admired them, the financial heroes of San Francisco. Anyway, there was no turning back now. It was too late for that.

He shivered again and pulled his coat tighter as he passed the lighted telephone booth not far from Inspiration Point. Before the fog had rolled in, he had seen a few cars parked out there with their windows steamed up from young couples inside them. He parked his own car farther up the hill so he wouldn't look like some kind of peeping tom or pervert. His movement was athletic, as befitted a man who played handball twice a week at his club. He could still beat the younger, newer members of the club and strutted in recognition of that fact.

Suddenly the telephone in the booth rang.

The man almost leaped into the booth and picked up the receiver.

"Hello," he said tentatively.

"Queen," said the voice at the other end.

"African," the man answered, slightly embarrassed at the childish code he had agreed to use.

"We're finished," the voice announced, "is the money where it's supposed to be?"

"Yes, but . . ."

"Small bills?"

"Yes, but . . ."

"But, but, but. Is this Porky Pig I'm talking to? But, but, but. What the hell's the matter?"

"There are some complications," the man answered.

No answer came from the other end of the line.

"Are you still there?" the man asked after a half minute of silence.

"Yeah?" the other voice sighed. "What complications?"

"You need to complete two more projects."

"You gotta be kiddin' me! Me and my side kick here are on our way out of town tonight. Like the guy on the radio says, 'see yuh in the funny papers.'"

"No!" the man demanded. "These projects need to be completed, and you will be paid! That's the deal we made!"

"Two more?' the voice asked. "Who do you think we are, Frank and Jesse James?" He laughed, singing off key, "Now Jesse had a wife to mourn for his . . ."

"Have you been drinking?" the man in the Burberry demanded.

"Yes, mother, maybe, so what? We did our work, remember? Tonight we hit the road for L.A. Highway 101. We're finished, you know: f-i-n-i-ss-hh-e-dd. Got it?"

"Five thousand," the man said flatly.

"What?"

"You heard me, five thousand. Same deal. Small bills in the locker at the Greyhound bus depot."

"You said *two* projects: six thousand, or we're on our way south. Tonight, buddy."

"All right," the man answered, "but the projects must be completed by Sunday. No complications, nothing traceable."

The voice laughed.

"That's a good one, buddy. 'Nothing traceable.' You been watching them cop shows on the tee vee? The Line Up? Dragnet? He started singing the Dragnet theme, "Dun duh dun, dun duh dun duh dun . . ."

"Yes or no, I don't have all night!"

"Whoa, there, hoss! Does that mean yes for six grand?"

The man in the phone booth stared at the street outside.

"Still there, buddy?" the voice asked

"Fifty five hundred. I'm not a rich man."

"Ok, ok, keep your shirt on. Yes. Looks like we are the James gang, after all," the voice chuckled. "Hi yo, Silver? No, that's the Lone Ranger."

There was a pause and then the voice spoke again.

"Who are these projects, where do they live and what do they look like?"

The man in the Burberry described the situation quickly and efficiently, hung up the telephone and disappeared into the fog.

TWENTY FOUR

Aquatic Park

Thursday, December 17, 1959

"*Come va,* Gianni!"

Carlo Manzone embraced his nephew in a bear hug that almost squeezed the air out of Maletesta's lungs. Then he stepped back and sized up Maletesta.

"You look good, Gianni. You look good, good."

"*Grazie, zio* Carlo," Maletesta replied, smiling, "you too."

He hadn't seen his mother's brother in almost nine years, after that awful Christmas dinner when that fight broke out between his father and Carlo and his father had ordered Carlo out of the house. As usual, the arguments were fueled by too much *grappa* imbibed by the parties involved, but the resulting split was permanent, and the families remained separate.

Carlo Manzone was in his late fifties. Steaks of gray streamed through in his pomaded hair, but he worked hard to maintain a youthful and healthy appearance. His tan came from many hours under the sun lamp at the Elks' Club on Post Street where he also swam and played handball. He watched his diet. He dressed in the latest styles. He moved quickly and precisely. Today he wore a tight polo shirt with short sleeves, tan colored slacks and saddle oxfords. He looked at his nephew through gold rimmed Ray-Ban sun glasses.

The bocce court at Aquatic Park was almost empty on this Thursday morning. Manzone was there only to provide encouragement and mediate arguments between two older friends who were in the heat of a game. Bocce is an ancient Italian sport played with eight large balls and a smaller target ball called the *palino*. From the outside, it looked like a casual game for old men. From the inside, it was an intense cutthroat exercise of skills that carried thousands of years of confrontation.

"How is *zia* Paola?" Maletesta asked.

"She's fine. She's over on the wharf, walking those dust mops of hers and looking for some decent crab."

He grinned and checked the time on his wrist watch. He motioned Maletesta over toward the wooden benches and sat down.

"I have to pick her up in a half hour . . ."

"Dust mops?"

"You know, those yappy little dogs that make all that noise? Pain in the ass? French, I think."

Maletesta remained standing, running his right hand through his hair.

Manzone erupted.

"Gianni, what the hell do you want? How did you know I was here?"

"The cleaning lady who answered your door told me," Maletesta blurted.

"I don't see you or anyone else in your family for eight years," Manzone continued, a pained look on his face, "and now all of a sudden you show up here with 'hello *zio* Carlo; how is *zia* Paola?' What the hell's going on?"

Manzone dramatically straightened his back and folded his arms, reading his nephew's restless eyes. Maletesta sat down on the bench beside his uncle and pulled a pack of cigarettes out of his shirt pocket. He shook one out for himself and offered the pack to his uncle, who declined with a palm up gesture. Maletesta lit his cigarette with the Zippo, coughed and broke the silence.

"Tal's in trouble. Big trouble."

"Come on! Tal's a kid, a nice kid," Manzone said warily. "What is she now, eighteen, nineteen? Nice kid. Don't give me any crap, Gianni."

Maletesta leaned in.

"It's true," he affirmed, exhaling smoke. "The police think she's involved with a murder in North Beach . . ."

"Which one?"

"I don't know how many murders you know about, *zio*, but I'm talking about a poet named Sinclair last Sunday."

"You mean," Manzone interjected, "the guy who thought he could fly?"

Maletesta nodded and added, "Somebody pushed him off the roof."

Manzone, still chortling over his joke, said, "No harm done, some people might say. Those guys are always pissing in the alleys; maybe he was pissing off the roof. Who says he didn't jump? Taking a leak, lost his balance?"

"Homicide says so. The cops say they found signs of a struggle, and they say that a neighbor heard someone yelling. It wasn't a suicide, and there's nothing funny about it."

Maletesta dropped his cigarette on the ground and stepped on it. He turned to watch a gaggle of sea gulls bickering over a half empty bag of potato chips someone had dropped on the walk way near the bocce courts. They darted in and out around the bag, pecking as much at each other as at the chips in the bag. More sea gulls arrived, seemingly out of nowhere, to join in the fray. The air filled with their raucous cries as they battled each other over the bag. A few local pigeons flew in but were outclassed by the larger gulls and never got close. Then one of the sea gulls picked up the bag and flew off with it toward the concrete seating area of the promenade. The rest of the gulls charged furiously after him.

Maletesta turned back to face his uncle.

"Somebody murdered Sinclair, and Tal might have been one of the last people to see him."

"Yeah?" Manzone started to say something, but Maletesta held his hand up to stop him.

"*Zio* Carlo, I know there's bad blood between us, but you know as well as anybody, that I can't take sides against my father. *Capische, zio?* I'm sorry, but you can either help me, or not. I need to find the people who killed Sinclair to get Tal out of it."

Maletesta took a deep breath.

"And I will do whatever it fucking takes to prove her innocence, whether you help me or not!"

Manzone twisted his mouth to the left and then to the right and then stood up. He took off his Ray Bans and ceremoniously polished them with a monogrammed handkerchief he extracted from his back pocket. He cleared his throat several times. Before he put the Ray Bans back on, he wiped his eyes with the handkerchief.

"God damn it, Gianni," he said softly. "God damn it."

Maletesta was startled.

"You know I would put my hand in the fire for you, don't you, Gianni?" Manzone whispered as he turned toward the promenade, his shoulders rising and falling. "After what happened to you in the war? Then in Borneo? Annemarie's accident? Raising that kid all by yourself? God damn it, Gianni."

Manzone turned back to Maletesta.

"I was so God damned proud of you, Gianni."

"*Zio* Carlo," Maletesta murmured, standing up and gripping his shoulder.

The two old Italians on the court began arguing loudly, cursing and gesturing. Like many old people, they looked remarkably alike. Cloth caps, long sleeve shirts buttoned at the neck with no ties, old suit trousers shiny and baggy from years of wear. One of them picked up the *palino* and threw it angrily toward the other end of the court, and it zipped by Manzone and Maletesta. The second man reached into his trouser pocket.

"Hey, *basta*! *Basta*, *stupidi*!" Manzone yelled at them.

The old men stopped suddenly. The man with his hand in his pocket backed up a step, and the other one who threw the *palino* went to pick it up. He smiled sheepishly as he approached the uncle and his nephew. Manzone cuffed his cap lightly as he passed.

"*Tranquillo*, eh? *Tranquillo*," Manzone announced.

He turned back toward Maletesta.

"*Tranquillo,* Gianni, eh, *tranquillo*."

"*Si, zio* Carlo, *tranquillo*," Maletesta agreed, not quite knowing what to expect.

Manzone suddenly embraced his nephew and kissed him on his right cheek. He released him and stood back.

"I will make some calls, Gianni, and ask some questions. I promise you, if it's something I can find, I will find it. You have the same phone number?"

"Yes. *Grazie*, *zio*," Maletesta said and embraced his uncle. Realizing the meeting was over, he turned to walk away.

"Strange, though," Manzone interrupted.

"What?" Maletesta stopped and turned around.

"I was just thinking. Another guy from the Beach took a dive. Last summer."

"Yes?"

"His name was Stromeyer. I knew him a little, you know, we played some handball at the Elks' Club, him and his brother-in-law. Matter of fact, got a game with the brother-in-law this afternoon."

Carlo frowned and wiped his hand across his mouth.

"Still doesn't seem right," he looked at the sky.

"What, *zio*?" Maletesta asked slowly. "What doesn't seem right?"

"Papers said 'suicide,' but he wasn't no suicide kinda guy. I know. I can tell suicide kinda guys. Don't ask me how I know. This guy talked about his family all the time. And," Carlo poked his right index finger at Maletesta, "he was doin' real good in his business, smart guy. Didn't seem like a suicide, but I don't what the hell it was . . . maybe he was drinking. I heard from one of the other members that sometimes he hit the bottle pretty good."

Maletesta said nothing.

"Hey, wait a minute!" Manzone shouted and reached into a pocket. He pulled out two tickets and handed them to Maletesta.

"Gorgeous George! Winterland. Saturday night. Ringside. You can take Talah, compliments of her Uncle Carlo. It will cheer her up. Here, take 'em."

"Thank you, *zio*. How much . . ."

"No, no, no, no," Manzone said, holding both palms up. "Enjoy the show! I got a piece of it, so they give me some pretty good tickets, but Paola and I are going up to Tahoe for the weekend."

"Ok, thanks."

"*Di niente*," Manzone shrugged and turned back to the game.

When Maletesta was about thirty feet away, Manzone called out again to him.

"Hey, Gianni!"

Maletesta turned.

"Merry Christmas!" Manzone yelled. "*Buon Natale*!"

Maletesta waved a thanks and walked back to his car.

TWENTY FIVE

Fillmore

Thursday, December 17

The alley off Buchanan Street was impeccably clean and Maletesta saw the reason for its condition as he walked toward the blind end. An elderly man in a flannel shirt and faded overalls was pushing a broom along the north side of the alley. He had obviously finished the south side where the garbage cans stood with their lids intact perfectly aligned with the buildings behind them. There was no debris on the ground.

Brennan told Maletesta that Yusef's body was found in a nameless alley off Buchanan between Ellis and Eddy. Maletesta took the 22 Fillmore to Eddy and walked the rest of the way. He'd passed some grade school girls playing hop scotch on the Buchanan side walk when he entered the alley. They waved at him and went back to their game.

"Hello," Maletesta said to the elderly man as he neared him.

The man jumped slightly.

"I'm sorry," Maletesta apologized, "I didn't mean to startle you."

"No harm done," the man answered, leaning on his broom. "I was thinking about somethin', that's all. Don't expect visitors here, just the kids."

"I heard that a man was killed here the other night."

"That's right, the wife and I found the body about 15 feet from where you're standin'."

"You found the body?"

"Yes sir. I thought the shots came from somebody's TV, but the old woman says, nope, them's gunshots." The man let out a flemmy laugh from his chest. "*I* was the one in the first war with the 370th and we had a lot of shootin', but *she's* the one who recognized the shots. Funny thing, huh?"

"Did you see anybody?" Maletesta asked.

"Naw. Whoever done it was movin' quick. Say, are you plainclothes? Those other cops didn't even want to listen to me. Just took my name and address." The old man pushed at some crumpled newspapers with his broom "Sad, he was a young man."

"Who, the cop?"

"No, the dead man. Seen a lot of 'em in the war. Not good, that."

"To answer your question, no, I'm not a cop," Maletesta clarified. "I'm just trying to help a friend." Maletesta held out his right hand. "My name is John Maletesta."

The old man took his hand and shook it ceremoniously.

"Name's Grieve, Ben Grieve, and it's a pleasure to meet you, sir."

"And you too, Mister Grieve," Maletesta answered. "Can you think of anything that might help me find who murdered Alexander Phillips?"

"Who?"

"That was the murdered man's name, Alexander Phillips. Sometimes he called himself, Yusef X."

"X?" Grieve asked.

"Yes, I believe he was involved with that group they call the Muslims."

Grieve backed up a step.

"Wait a minute," he said, rubbing his head and squinting at the top of a building across the street. "Wait a minute," he repeated, "I remember that fella. He rang our bell last week: a proud-dressed young man in a suit and a tie. Suit wasn't new, but pressed, you know? Very polite fella, he wanted to tell me 'bout the Ko-ran, but I told him we was AME and not interested in the Ko-ran. Kinda hurt his feelin's, I think."

Grieve paused and shifted his weight on the broom handle, remembering the conversation with Yusef X. Maletesta waited.

"You know," Grieve said finally, "he was a nice young man and real sincere. I had to respec' what he was doin', talkin' 'bout people workin' together and such. So I gave him a dollar and he left . . . and now he's dead. Ain't that a real shame. Just like the war."

Maletesta bid his thanks to Ben Grieve and walked back to the mouth of the alley while Grieve went back to his cleanup work. As he approached the street, Maletesta smiled and paused to watch the girls playing hopscotch on the sidewalk. His memory reached back to Talah as a ten year old outside their house, chalking the pattern on the sidewalk. Somehow, the rules of the game always escaped him. A girl would throw some kind of a marker or key to a square and then jump in that direction. There was always a lot of excitement in the throwing and the jumping.

He watched a girl with pink clips on her braids throw a shiny yellow marker onto a square.

Jesus, it's a cartridge case!

"Hey," Maletesta blurted out, walking toward the girl, "where did you get that?"

The girl turned away quickly and her friends ran behind her.

"What?" she asked defiantly.

"That shell you just threw. It's from a gun."

"I found it."

"You did?" Maletesta said. "Can you tell me where?"

"Sure," the girl replied, pointing down the alley, "right down there by Mister Grieve's gate."

Maletesta looked down the alley and then back at the girl. Then he squatted down beside her.

"I'd like it for my collection," he said, "What can I give you for it? How about a shiny brand new quarter?"

The girl hesitated.

"Well, mister," the girl replied, "whatever it is, they're hard to find. I've never seen one before, so I think it must be real valuable."

"Hey, c'mon," one of the other girls said, "let's play. I gotta be home to take care of my baby brother in an hour!"

"OK, OK," the girl with the pink clips said and turned back to the game.

"Wait," Maletesta said, "how much?"

"One dollar," The girl squeezed her eyes closed and put her hand out.

"Holy moley, sweetheart, you drive a hard bargain!" Maletesta said as he pulled a dollar bill out of his pocket and laid it on her open palm. The girl gave him the cartridge case and ran away giggling with her friends.

Squinting, Maletesta turned it over in his hand. It was rimless--which meant it was from a semi-automatic pistol--but it was not familiar to him. There was no doubt in his mind that it was from the pistol that killed Cayenne's brother. He studied the head stamp on the bottom of the case. There was a "G" at about 10 o'clock with some odd writing after that and then at about 2 o'clock there was an "E." On the bottom half of the case were the numbers "1937," obviously a date but from where?

Maletesta sighed, put the shell into his pocket and walked briskly back to Fillmore Street to catch the 22 bus. About half way down the block, he was approached by a sharp dressed man in sunglasses.

"Hey, man," the man whispered, "have you heard about Big Mary's house? You can have a lotta fun up there. It's only a few minutes away; I can take you there. Lotta fun."

"No thanks, not today," Maletesta answered and continued walking.

"They're dancin' around without any clothes on," the man called after him.

TWENTY SIX

Fillmore

Thursday, December 17, 1959

"Who?" Cayenne asked.

"His name is King, Osceola, Cool Breeze, whatever," Maletesta answered.

"Lotta gold flash, sharp dresser?"

"Yeah, gold guitar tie pin."

"I've seen him," Cayenne said, nodding. "He comes in the club sometimes. Nobody messes with him. The word is he killed a man in Texas. That's why he left in a hurry. I was told he's a friend of Mister James, so he can run a tab that never gets paid. He doesn't drink much, though. He's a two-Manhattan kinda cat."

Maletesta and Cayenne were sitting in the leather chairs opposite the sofa in her living room. Usually they sat together on the sofa.

"Well," Maletesta said, "I hope he can find something out about Yusef. Anything. Sassy said he knows the Fillmore like nobody else knows. "

"Expensive?" Cayenne asked.

"Not too bad, particularly if he delivers."

Cayenne was wearing a black sweater and black toreador pants when she answered the door. She had moved back to let him in but stepped away when he reached out to pull her in close. She directed him to the chairs.

Silence hung in the room.

"Cayenne . . ."

"Yes?"

"I promise you again that I will find whoever killed Yusef."

"You can call him Alexander now. It doesn't matter anymore. I told my mother that I'm bringing Alexander home to Georgia."

"When?"

"We're leaving on Saturday. That's as soon as the coroner will release his body."

Maletesta lit a cigarette, blew a smoke ring and set his cigarette on a crystal ash tray on the coffee table in front of the sofa.

"How long will you be gone?" he whispered.

"I don't know. I've left the Club. I told Sassy I needed some time."

"What about Christmas?" he asked. "We weren't together during the holidays last year, but I thought this year we could spend Christmas together."

"At your folks' house?" Cayenne slowly crossed her legs.

"Uh, I don't know," Maletesta answered, shifting in the chair. "I was thinking about dinner; just you and me. You know, in a restaurant downtown."

"What about your folks? When are they eating?"

"I think earlier, like in the afternoon . . ."

"Are you and Tal going over there?"

"Well, yeah."

"Well, Johnny, why don't I just go with you guys to your folks' house?"

"Uh, they're kind of old fashioned . . ."

Cayenne stood up.

"John, I think you have to make up your mind. I'd like you to leave, please."

"What do you mean?"

Cayenne strode over to the door and opened it.

"This way, professor," she said, pointing to the street.

"Cayenne," he protested as he stood up, "listen to me, baby . . ."

"Not right now, John, I'd like you to leave."

"Call me later?"

Cayenne shrugged.

When Maletesta passed through the front door and started down the stairs, he heard the dead bolt applied behind him. When he got to his car, he looked back. The shades were drawn, and the front room lights were turned off.

Cayenne walked slowly back to the kitchen and sat down at her kitchen table. The walls around her were covered with colorful fliers and autographed photographs of the artists who played at the Club Carolina. Sugar Pie DeSanto and Jackie Wilson, tacked to the door that covered the ironing board enclosure, smiled at her out of the photos.

"They only allow you in the chitlin' club," she said to the photos. "You'll never be welcome in the Fairmont, the Top of the Mark, or the Masonic, or Bimbo's. You understand that? Never."

Her voice cracked.

Cayenne did not drink alcohol, so she turned on the gas under the tea kettle and set up a cup with a tea bag and a lump of sugar in it. She retrieved some leftover meat loaf from the fridge, put a slice on a plate, smothered it in catsup and sat down with it at the table. The kitchen was a mess, and it bothered her. The sink was full of dirty cups and plates, and the sideboards held an assortment of empty cans and food containers from the deli. She hadn't cleaned anything since Yusef died.

I'll clean up everything tomorrow after I pack.

Earlier in the day, she rummaged through the small trunk she carried from Georgia and found the photograph she'd been looking for. She propped it up against the salt and pepper shakers and studied it while she picked at the meatloaf with her fork. Her mother was sitting in a rocker on the porch and laughing joyously at something Yusef--then Alexander--had said. Cayenne had her arm around Alexander who was half bent over in laughter. She didn't remember the joke, but she remembered that the photograph was taken shortly before she and her brother left for California, the "promised land."

"I'll be rich, mama, you'll see, I'm gonna do commercials on television! Easy money in San Francisco!"

"I never see any Black people on TV except Beulah," their mother answered.

"That's right, mama! I'll be the first, and you can come out and we'll buy a houseboat!"

"A houseboat! My, my, Alexander, that would be fine."

Promised land, yeah, and Yusef is a janitor and I'm a bartender. No, Yusef was a janitor. Now he's nothing . . . he's dead . . . and I'm?

The tea kettle began whistling. Cayenne picked up the photograph and pressed it against her chest with both hands.

I'm sorry, mama. I don't think you'll ever know how sorry I am. I'm bringing Alexander home to you in a box. We never should have left. We didn't know anything about the Promised Land, mama. It's not better out here in California; it's just different.

She put the photograph back on the table, walked over the garbage bin and scraped the meatloaf into it. She turned off the gas under the kettle began taking the photos off the walls, carefully stacking them on the table.

I'm still just another Black woman who can't rent an apartment in a white neighborhood. Alexander was right: they'll never let us in . . . never!

She picked up the photograph of her mother and her brother and turned it over and over in her hands, her fingers touching the images of her family. She held it against her chest and then put it back down on the table. She looked at the spaces on the wall.

Johnny? No, Johnny, for all your cool, you won't let me in either.

TWENTY SEVEN

Cow Hollow

Thursday, December 17, 1959

"Tickets to what?"

"The wrestling match at Winterland. Saturday night," Maletesta announced as he entered the room carrying a bag of groceries from the corner market.

"Wrestling?" Tal repeated. "Wrestling? Tell me you're kidding."

Tal continued typing on the Underwood on the big table in the dining room. The table was littered with paperback and hardbound books, some open and some closed with multicolored book marks sticking out of them. There were also several spiral notebooks scattered on the table and a splash of 3X5 cards near the typewriter. She was not a skilled typist and didn't want to be. She typed with two fingers, with stops and pauses and the regular use of an ineffective eraser which made the corrections barely readable.

Maletesta had just come in the door with a bag of groceries from the market on Union Street.

"It's a sellout," he declared, setting the bag on the table.

Tal stopped typing and looked at him.

"Dad, this is a joke, right?"

"Gorgeous George and Lord Blears! Ringside seats. What more can a person want?" Maletesta improvised a smile for her.

"I can see it now," Tal scoffed, picking at the Underwood. "Next it'll be 'how about a night of Roller Derby over at Kezar?' Seriously, Dad, did you say *ringside*? You mean where the guys who fall through the ropes can land on us? Where in the world did you get those tickets?"

"Uncle Carlo told me he wanted to cheer you up. He has a piece of the action."

"What?" Tal stood up. "You saw Uncle Carlo?

"Yes."

"Where?"

"At the bocce court at Aquatic Park. This afternoon."

"Dad," Tal frowned, "I thought you and nona and grandpa weren't talking to him. I mean, it's been years since any of them talked to each other, hasn't it?"

Maletesta thumbed through one of the spiral note books on the table, avoiding her stare.

"Tal," he mumbled, "there's family and there's family . . ."

"Oh, no," she groaned, "a tautology."

Maletesta tried to swat her on the head with the notebook, but she ducked.

"You were never much good at that," Tal laughed.

"No," he admitted, "that's why you're a spoiled child who throws words like 'tautology' at her father."

"Did Uncle Carlo know anything about Jean-Paul's murder?"

Maletesta shook his head.

"How's the paper coming," he asked, "and when is it due?"

"Slowly as in s-l-o-w-l-y and it needs to be in Professor Milton's box by 5pm on January second."

"Five sharp," Maletesta qualified. "Robert Milton's a stickler for promptness. He won't accept it if you're late, even a few minutes."

"I know."

Tal resumed pecking at the keys on the typewriter.

"You'd better get cracking," Maletesta said and picked up one of the 3X5 cards.

"*Tammany Hall,*" he read and put the card down. "As I recall, Tammany became the metaphor for political corruption. I remember seeing a cartoon of Boss Tweed in a history book; he looked like a vulture. What's your perspective?"

"Yes, I know that Tammany is the accepted historical example of political graft," Tal explained, "but my thesis is that, first--along with the corruption—the politicians of Tammany Hall took care of people who needed help and were ignored by the wealthy establishment. Secondly, if they didn't serve the needs of the people who elected them, they wouldn't have been elected over and over, would they?"

"OK," Maletesta said, "that sounds like an excellent choice for a theme. Make sure your references are accurate."

As he was carrying the groceries into the kitchen, Tal spoke again.

"Did you ever hear of William Plunkitt, Dad?"

"No," Maletesta stepped back into the living room, "who's he?"

"He was a Tammany politician who got rich," Tal answered, picking up one of the 3X5 cards. "He has this terrific quote, 'I seen my opportunity and I took it.'"

"What opportunity?"

"Well, he calls it 'honest graft.' For example, if he heard that the City was going to build a street car line through some neighborhood, he'd go out there and buy property. Then the City would have to buy his property to put the line in. Get it? Perfectly honest."

"Seems kind of dodgy to me. Anyway, I'll put together some dinner."

"Cool. I'm hungry."

"Oh, by the way," Maletesta remembered, "I'm going out tonight to meet a strange beatnik character in North Beach who supposedly knows all kinds of inside information about people in the neighborhood."

"Who?"

"Someone called El Pilar."

"El Pilar?" she giggled. "You mean the guy with the basket on a string?"

Maletesta put the grocery bag on the wicker chair near the kitchen door and turned back to her.

"Do you know him?"

"Not really. He hung around Jean-Paul for a while. Everyone thought he was a little crazy, but he carried a little note book and was always writing something in it. Well, almost everybody in that group was always writing something down: a new word, part of a poem, you know, they're very creative."

Maletesta raised an eyebrow.

"So, you don't know anything about him?"

"No. Sorry."

Maletesta put away the groceries in the kitchen cupboards as Tal continued working on her paper. He threw some lettuce, tomatoes, peppers and olives into a salad bowl and began frying two ribeye steaks in a pan on the front burner of the stove. He opened the door to the back landing to clear the air and placed a fresh loaf of Larraburu French bread on the table along with two plates.

"Smells great, Dad," Tal called out from the other room.

Maletesta set the knives and forks on the table and suddenly remembered something. He went over to the doorway.

"Hey, Tal, I almost forgot, do you know what's playing at the Marina?"

"Let me guess: Dumbo."

"No, you ninny, The Blue Angel! I saw it on the marquee when I was coming home from the grocery store."

"The Blue Angel? You've been talking about that movie for years. That's the one with Marlene Dietrich, right?"

"Yes. Was it covered in your film history class?"

"Just briefly. We never saw the film, but Doctor Coffey talked mainly about some odd camera angles that the director used. I can't remember his name. Isn't it also a kind of attack on middle class hypocrisy?"

"Yes . . ."

Maletesta went back to the stove and flipped the steaks.

"I think you'll like it," he called back to the other room. "It's about how a society with artificial standards can be very destructive. Tal, I need a hand here."

Tal carried the frying pan over to the table where she forked out a steak on each plate. Then she mixed the salad with oil and vinegar, tossed out equal portions and sliced up chunks of the French bread.

Maletesta used his large rocker knife with its curved blade to cut his steak. He paused while carving and smiled at the knife fondly. It was a gift from Mrs. Dawson, the former housekeeper. Her father had served under General Grant during the Civil War and, like many veterans of that slaughterhouse, came home an amputee. Rocker knives became popular after the war.

"Mmmmm, really good," Tal murmured as she swallowed her first bite.

"I agree. They're from Iacopi's. Oh, I should also mention that Bruno said to tell you hi and that's he's not happy with all the people moving into the Beach now."

"Surprise, surprise."

They ate in silence for a few minutes.

"Getting back to that movie, it was based on a book by Heinrich Mann, Thomas Mann's older brother," Maletesta continued as he kept eating. "Actually, when I think about it, it would fit right into the Beat culture today. How about tomorrow night?"

"Dad, I'm too old to go to movies with you. The last one we watched together was Cinderella."

"No, no, no," Maletesta objected. "I'm busy tomorrow night. I meant that you should call a friend. Get your mind on something else for awhile."

"All right. I'll call Ray. He's home from UCLA for the holidays, and I haven't seen him in over a year, so that'll be fun. Thanks for thinking about that."

"Ray? A poet?"

Tal's eyes welled up

"No, no, Dad, not a poet . . . just a friend."

TWENTY EIGHT

North Beach

Thursday, December 17, 1959

Maletesta was irritated. In the past hour and a half, he had walked up and down Columbus Avenue from Broadway to Union, smoking four cigarettes and stopping only once for a cup of coffee in the U.S. Restaurant. While inside the pie-shaped restaurant, he never took his eyes off the street from his table at the window. Before leaving, he stepped out the back door on Stockton to look up toward Green for El Pilar. He stalked to Green and waited again under the street light. An ambulance with its siren blaring raced by him as he shivered in the cold.

For a Thursday night, the Beach was busy. *Must be the holidays*, he thought as he stamped his feet and pulled his overcoat tighter. He noted the tourists awkwardly wandering around. Words played in his impatient mind. *Awkward gawkiness or gawky awkwardness? Sounds like Jabberwocky.* Bundled up locals, carrying packages and shopping bags, bustled along the sidewalk pursuing various domestic missions. The Beats slowly emerged onto the scene, some engrossed in their own thoughts and others aware of and dramatically posing for the out-of-towners.

Maletesta went back to Vesuvio's twice and glanced in from the doorway. Maria de las Casas shook her head negatively when she caught his eye across the crowded room.

Walking blindly down Columbus, he found himself across the street from the Telegraph Hill Neighborhood Center. Gloria Unti's modern dance class just ended and black clad dancers streamed out onto the sidewalk. He didn't recognize anyone he knew. A few of his friends took classes from Gloria, including Maria de las Casas. He lit another cigarette and walked back to Green. On his way back, he ran into an obese man in an overcoat buttoned up to the collar and an old fashioned homburg perched on his head. A narrow flash of a bright yellow shirt peeked out of the overcoat collar. The man was walking a terrier with three legs. The dog stopped to sniff and urinate on a fire hydrant in the sidewalk. Maletesta smiled at the man and the dog.

"He's a brave little guy," Maletesta said.

"I don't think so," the man replied in what Maletesta identified was a Balkan accent. "He doesn't know how many legs he's supposed to have, so he just follows his disposition with what he has."

Maletesta nodded.

"Wise man," he said.

"No, wise dog," the man stiffly clarified and walked off with his terrier.

Maletesta shrugged and continued walking. The strange beatnik who called himself El Pilar had not shown up at the appointed hour.

At ten o'clock, Maletesta returned to Vesuvio's for the third time and spoke to Maria.

"God," he exclaimed. "Maria, I feel like a burglar casing all the places on Columbus from here to Union! I even walked into a couple of places and asked the guy behind the counter if he knew El Pilar. All I got was a hostile look; one guy reached for his telephone."

She laughed.

"It's not funny," he objected, "I swear, a couple of store keepers began writing things down on a pad after I passed three or four times. Plus, and I mean plus, I also met a philosophical dog and his companion."

"Whaat?"

"It's not worth retelling. What do you think happened to your friend, El Pilar?"

Maletesta glanced around the crowded and loud room.

"Maria, do you ever count Greek fisherman's caps?" he mused.

"Don't be a smartass, John; it doesn't suit you."

"You got three in here tonight. And not one of them is Pete Seeger."

"Nor a Greek fisherman, doll baby," Maria answered, "but--getting back to El Pilar--I can tell you, for all of his odd getup and awful poetry, he's very regular in his own way. If he told you he would be there tonight, he'd be there tonight."

She frowned and began wiping off the table next to her.

"Something happened. Maybe he got sick; maybe he'll drop in here later. I'll let you know if he does."

Maria hurried over to a new table of customers, and Maletesta walked out of Vesuvio's and down Columbus. All the walking had made him hungry, so he went back into the U.S. Restaurant and ordered a plate of tortellini and a tumbler of the house red He continued to watch the action in the street outside the window as he ate, more hurriedly than usual.

Where the hell is this guy? Maletesta thought as he scarfed down the tortellini. *Maria says he's reliable, so what the hell happened? I need some decent information, and I need it soon or Brennan will be back at our front door with a warrant! Goddamit!*

His legs ached slightly from all of his walking, so when he finished his meal and said good night to the staff, he took the bus back to Union, thinking about Brennan's next move.

TWENTY NINE

The Forbidden City

Friday, December 18, 1959

At 12:40 am, the SFPD patrol car rolled into the red curb zone on Sutter Street and stopped. The young cop at the wheel yawned as he surveyed the scene on the sidewalk through his windshield. The cop--whose name was Powell--would not open his door until he figured out what was going on. Dispatch wasn't clear about the problem. Dispatch was usually muddled these days, particularly after they hired the Boozer, a shirttail relative of the chief's wife. Playing accordion in an Irish bar band shouldn't qualify you for dispatch, Powell thought, but, then again, maybe it did. All you had to do was pick up the phone and relay the situation to whoever was on duty.

Powell learned the hard way not to jump into things. Two years ago, he'd jumped out of his car and right into a drunken family brawl in the Excelsior. He lost a tooth in that one. A few minutes ago, the Boozer told him that a brawl was developing outside the Forbidden City in Chinatown.

He saw two young white men arguing with a middle-aged Chinese man in a tuxedo. Judging from their unsteadiness of the young men on their feet, it looked like they had too much to drink. The cop sighed and shifted his duty belt. More drunks to deal with, and this wasn't even his shift. If Dressler hadn't called in sick, he'd be home in bed now.

Powell recognized the man in the tuxedo. His name was Charlie Low, and he was the owner of the Forbidden City, the most famous night club in Chinatown, even though technically it was located outside the Chinatown gate. He noted a few other customers, mostly white, hanging back, watching the argument.

Powell had been to the Forbidden City before. Last May, he and his wife went there for dinner and a show on his birthday. As he sat in the patrol car deciding when he should intervene in the argument, the images of the floor show that night in May flickered through his mind like a newsreel. First, there was a comedian who he didn't think was very funny. Then there was a singer, who called himself the "Chinese Frank Sinatra." Powell didn't think he sounded like Sinatra, but he was a terrific singer. The last part of the show blew his socks off, a chorus line of scantily-clad dancers. Powell was overwhelmed by the visual onslaught of legs, but he told his wife he didn't think they were very good.

Powell got out of the car and strode over to the antagonists on the sidewalk, slipping his baton into its holder. He scowled at the two men and then turned to Charlie Low.

"All right," he announced in the most authoritive voice he could summon, "what's going on here? You first, Mister Low."

"Officer, these two customers were bothering my dancers," Charlie responded in a very angry voice, "calling them names. Politely, I asked them to leave, but they made a big fuss about it. We finally got them out on the sidewalk, but now they want to come back in . . ."

"Hey, can't take a joke, huh?" one of the men interrupted. "What the hell's matter with you? We were just having fun, you know?"

The man was in his early thirties and was rocking back and forth on his feet like a prize fighter. He wore a skinny dark suit with a dark turtle neck sweater and an olive green Tyrolean hat with a brush sticking out of the band was cocked back on his head.

"You'll talk when I ask you to talk," Powell growled, facing the man with his hand on his baton.

"Yeah, yeah?" Tyrolean hat answered, continuing to shift on his feet, left to right. "I talk when I want to talk, man! I got a right, you know, I got a right to talk when I want to talk, man, you know? It's in the, the Constitution, right, general? Right?"

The other man intervened as Powell was pulling out his baton.

"Hey, hold on there, officer. He's just had one too many Old Fashioneds, ha ha, can't hold his liquor. C'mon, Bobby, it's time for us to hit the road." The man put a hand on Bobby's shoulder. Bobby turned on his heel, shaking the hand off.

"Lay off me, Al! Don't touch me, man, understand?" He pointed at Charlie Low. "This kinda guy don't push Bobby K around, jus' cuz he's got a tuxedo don't change who he is . . ."

Bobby K? Powell thought as he sized up the punk and pulled his baton out of its holder. *Bobby K? What kind of crap is this? Who does this punk think he is?*

As Charlie Low backed into a fighting stance, Powell stepped in front of him and lightly jabbed Bobby in the solar plexus. He stumbled forward, caught his balance and gagged.

"Bastard," he rasped.

"Tell you what, wise guy," Powell snarled, "if you're not on your way out of here right now, I'll run you in for public drunkenness! And maybe I'll throw in attempted assault on a police officer, just for the hell of it. You want that, wise guy?"

"OK, OK, take it easy! We're gone," Al said and pushed Bobby toward their car which was parked in front of the patrol car. He shoved him into the passenger seat and slammed the door. He almost sprinted around to the other side of the car, got in and drove off.

"Thank you, Officer Powell," Charlie Low as they watched the green Buick drive down Sutter Street. The cop looked pensive for a moment and—remembering something he learned at the academy—pulled out a little notebook and pencil from an inside pocket. He wrote down a brief description of the two men and their Buick, including the license number.

THIRTY

Cow Hollow

Friday, December 18, 1959

They arose later than usual on Friday. Maletesta slept fitfully, dreaming of odd looking beatniks running to the sound of sirens. Tal hammered away at her paper long into the night. It was almost 9 o'clock when they stumbled into the kitchen and started the coffee.

"So, he didn't show?" Tal asked.

"No. I walked up and down Columbus looking for him, even hung out on the corners like a lost tourist. Dropped into Vesuvio's a couple of times. The last time, Maria told me it wasn't like him to miss appointments. Finally, I gave up, had something to eat at the US and came home."

Tal frowned and put two slices of rye bread into the toaster.

"Let's catch the end of Sherwood's show," Maletesta said, turning on the radio perched on the shelf above the booth. It was an old Philco Annemarie found in a schlock shop on McAllister.

“Oh, no,” Tal giggled, “not another chapter of Parkey Sharkey’s ‘I Seen California Destroyed by Progress.’”

“I hope not.”

Don Sherwood, known locally as the “World’s Greatest Disc Jockey,” hated baseball and was in the middle of his own sarcastic version of a baseball announcer’s live broadcast of a game.

“Ball one.” Sherwood intoned.

A silence of five or six seconds followed.

“Ball two.”

Another prolonged radio silence.

Maletesta cracked up laughing, but Tal shook her head in exasperation.

“Strike one.”

Maletesta could hardly control himself and almost spit out his coffee.

Talah suddenly reached up and switched the radio off.

“Dad, I don’t like what’s going on. Why didn’t El Pilar meet you last night? Did something happen to him? This whole thing doesn’t feel right. It feels a lot like the time I followed you through the jungle back home. Remember?”

“Yes, I remember,” her father said, putting his cup down.

"I can't help it. Do you remember when I was a kid there, the elders in the village trained me to have a kind of a sixth sense?"

"Yes."

"This is scary, Dad, and Don Sherwood's jokes won't change it!"

Tal ran her fingers through her hair.

"First Jean Paul, then Yusef, Cayenne's brother. Who's next? Why didn't El Pilar show up at your meeting? Did something happen to him too, Dad? Is that cop coming back here to arrest me? You've talked to Maria and Uncle Carlo, and a private detective named King, and it doesn't look like you gotten anywhere! Does it?"

The two slices of bread noisily popped up in the toaster and startled them.

"None for me," Maletesta said.

Tal ignored the toast.

"Well, do you have anything to say? Anything . . . I mean like anything at all, Dad?"

Maletesta stubbed out his cigarette in an ashtray and coughed.

"Talah, somewhere there's an answer to this, and I promise you, I will find it."

Tal didn't answer. She picked up a section of the morning newspaper and held it up in front of her face. As was their usual procedure, Maletesta got the front section first. It was propped up on a newspaper rack. Tal looked at the comics, but was not laughing as she usually did.

"You know, Dad," she suddenly blurted, dropping the paper on the table, "next week is Christmas! *This is so weird!*"

Maletesta sighed deeply.

"Unfortunately, it's just gotten worse, Tal," he said slowly and began reading aloud a short news item on page three.

"*Hit and Run Fatality in North Beach,*" he intoned.

Tal gulped.

"*Last night,*" Maletesta read, *"an unidentified man crossing Greenwich Street near Columbus was struck by an automobile and fatally injured. Witnesses said that the automobile, which did not stop, was a dark green Buick. However, no one saw the license plate number."*

Maletesta looked up at her, took a deep breath and began reading again.

"*The man, who was dressed in monastic style clothing, died several hours later in San Francisco General Hospital,"* he continued. *"Police said next of kin will be notified when the victim's identity is determined."*

"Oh my God," Tal shrieked, "is that El Pilar, who you were supposed to meet? Oh my God, Dad! What's going on? What *is* going on!"

She stood up and spoke rapidly.

"We're in San Francisco, right? This isn't the jungle where I followed you for days when you were looking for that base. This is supposed to be civilization, right? No head hunters here, right? But I can feel it, Dad. We're still in the God damned jungle!"

Maletesta closed his eyes.

"Do you remember, Dad? They said I had a gift. I knew when the river was flooding upstream. So they trained me to feel things that other people could not feel, to sense things that were going to happen. Over the years it's been going away, and I thought I left it behind with my people in Borneo . . . it got too painful: I pushed it away."

"Yes, I know, honey."

"But, I can feel it again. I can feel it again, Dad! I'm afraid, Dad!"

"Tal, please sit down over here, next to me."

She sat down on the bench and clasped her hands together on the table. He covered them with his hand.

"The Beats are right, aren't they?" she whispered. This thing we call 'civilization' and 'society' is just a hollow shell, isn't it? Underneath it all is the same old greed and violence."

She looked directly at him.

"Isn't that right? Is there a killer waiting for us outside?"

Tal stood up and faced him.

"Can we go outside, Dad? Is it safe for us; is it safe for us to go outside!"

Maletesta stood up quickly and pulled her to himself, holding her in a one armed bear hug. She burst into uncontrolled sobbing.

"Tal! Listen to me," he murmured, "*listen* to me. You know I will always tell you the truth."

He held her tighter.

"It doesn't look good, and I don't quite understand it, but we will handle it. *Capeesh,* Talah? We *will* handle it. We *have* to handle it! Together! Just like we've handled all the other stuff that was thrown at us. Do you remember? Do you remember that brave little girl in the jungle?"

"Yes," she answered almost silently.

"I remember her too, Talah. I remember that brave little girl. We handled it, didn't we? And we're still on our feet. And we will do it again. Right, honey? Just like in the jungle."

The doorbell rang.

"What the hell?" Maletesta said and released his daughter. He walked stiffly to the door.

"Careful, Dad."

Maletesta looked though the peephole and saw an unknown man in a post office uniform. He slowly opened the door.

"Good morning. A bit early, aren't you?"

"'Morning, I'm new. Got a special delivery for you. You need to sign for it."

"OK," Maletesta said, signing the form on a clip board. The mail man handed him a small package wrapped in brown paper.

Maletesta carried the package into the dining room and set it on the table. Tal stood next to him, looking wide-eyed at the package as if it were something from outer space.

"Well," Maletesta, picking up the package and tearing the brown wrapping paper with his hand.

Tal flinched.

"Wait, Dad!"

"What?"

Maletesta stopped, and as he turned, Tal grabbed the package and ran down the hall to the bathroom.

"Tal!" he yelled and ran after her.

When he reached the bathroom, the package was in the tub and Tal had turned both taps wide open.

"Turn those off!" he yelled, grabbing the package and holding it close.

"No! Gimme that!" Tal shouted, trying to pull the dripping package away from him.

"Stop it, Tal, stop it! Please, honey, that's enough."

Tal turned the taps off and angrily marched back to the living room.

She was sitting in his chair staring at something he could not see when he returned with the package. He stopped next to the chair and looked down at her. She continued her unblinking stare.

"Tal, honey," he said softly, "we can't let ourselves get crazy over this. We need to keep some kind of normality to get through this mess. If we panic about things that *might* happen, we'll drive ourselves nuts."

She said nothing, but her eyes followed him as he put the package on the table and clumsily tore through the heavy brown wrapping with one hand. It was a thin book, slightly damp.

"*Overland to the Islands*, by Denise Levertov," Maletesta read the cover.

A half sheet of paper fell out of the book as he leafed through it: *"Merry Christmas, Professor Maletesta, from Sister Agatha."*

Tal put her head back and laughed out loud

"A book of poetry from Sister Agatha! Oh my God, Dad, this is better than Sherwood! Crazy!"

Tal stood up and hugged her father, who was also laughing, holding a little book of poetry in his hand.

After a few minutes, Tal announced, "I don't know what you're doing today, Dad, but I'm going Christmas shopping!"

As she ran from the room, Maletesta called, “and I’m going to make another pot of coffee and delve into Denise Levertov’s little tome.”

“No one would guess that you teach English Lit, Dad,” Tal called back from the doorway.

THIRTY ONE

Cow Hollow

Friday, December 18, 1959

Maletesta leaned back in the office chair and studied the desk in front of him. It was a genuine Rucker Fuller "secretary desk" with drawers and knee openings on both sides of the desk. He'd bought it in a Mission Street thrift shop five years ago. The thrift shop guy told him it came from the old girls' school on 362 Capp Street which was now a community center. Maletesta was intrigued by the idea that the drawers on one side of the desk were fake: they did not open. So, presumably, a student could sit down and work there opposite another student but could not open a single drawer on her side of the desk. The concept intrigued him, so he bought it.

The desk was solid oak and rather wide. The multiple coats of varnish probably applied by the school's maintenance workers did little to disguise the ancient scratches and deep gouges in the surface. He felt that the desk was like him, varnished but damaged. His missing right arm could not be varnished over, and the gouges of his nightmares remained hidden. A few years ago, his doctor told him about a prosthetic arm, but after thirteen years with one arm, he was not ready for that.

Maletesta swiveled left and right in his chair and stopped, facing the desk.

He glanced at the yellow pad in the center of the desk and the Parker Jotter pen on it. A fat telephone book sat to the left of the pad and the telephone was on the right. A glass ashtray with several butts in it sat next to the telephone. Behind the pad, there was a pile of term papers in their folders: work to be reviewed and corrected before the end of the year. *Still have two weeks, thank God.* A brass goose neck lamp crowded its way into the desk set, illuminating the scribbles on the yellow pad. Maletesta frowned at the ashtray and opened the top right drawer where he found a single loose cigarette. He lit it and then walked out into the living room to turn on the stereo.

I need to get away from this for a while. The next thing Tal will be drowning all the Christmas presents in the bath tub! Merde! I can't let this ruin our lives.

The turntable was stacked 45's by James Brown, Nina Simone, Jackie Wilson and Lowell Fulson. Tal was still shopping, so Maletesta turned up the volume and bopped around the room in time to the different rhythms of the songs, nodding his head, humming . . . he would never behave like this when his daughter was home. A half hour later, the telephone rang.

"Hell!"

He picked it up in the office and closed the door.

"Gianni, this is your mother."

"Yes, mama," he sighed, "how are you?"

"Gianni, you shouldn't play games with your mother. It's not nice."

"I don't know what you mean, Mama. I'm not playing any games."

"This girl friend of yours, you know what I mean?"

"No," he answered carefully, not knowing where this conversation with his mother was going.

"I mean," his mother persisted, "is she coming for Christmas dinner or not?"

"Uh . . ."

"Gianni, are you trying to hide something from your mother? You know, sometimes someone might think, well, she's not so pretty, so maybe someone might not like her, but, you know, Gianni, you know, beauty is only skin deep . . ."

"Ma," Maletesta interrupted, "it's not about beauty, I mean, you don't understand . . ."

"Gianni, you don't have to worry. Papa and I will welcome whoever you like; she don't even have to be Italian, you know, she can be maybe Irish or German, Gianni, that's OK . . ."

"OK. OK, Ma, but I have to go. I have to do some Christmas shopping, you know? I'm way behind."

"Gianni, listen to your mother! Are you gonna bring your girl to our house for Christmas dinner?"

"No."

"Why not?"

"She's out of town."

"Whaddya mean, she's out of town? Did you have a breakup or something?"

"No, ma, she . . . uh . . . she had to visit her mother. She's sick."

There was a pause at the other end of the line.

"Well," Guilia Maletesta pronounced, "that's very nice; she cares about her mother, not like a certain someone. When will she be back?"

"I don't know, ma."

"So, you did have a breakup! Mothers know these things, Gianni. It's OK. We all got problems. You gotta talk to her. You know me and your father . . ."

"Ma, there's someone at the door. I have to go. *Ciao*. I'll call you later."

The telephone rang again and Maletesta hesitated. He picked it up gingerly, expecting his mother.

"Hello, this is Sergeant Monroe of the Lexington, Kentucky police department. I'd like to speak to a Lieutenant John Maletesta."

"Uh, this is John Maletesta, but I haven't been a lieutenant since the end of the war. What is this about?"

"Well, I'm sorry to report, sir, that a note was left at our station by one of our residents, a James Vennemeyer. The note said to contact you and listed your phone number."

Maletesta breathed deeply.

"Lonnie? Contact me about what?"

"Um, Mister Maletesta, when we got the note, we went immediately to Mister Vennemeyer's apartment and, uh, found him deceased on the floor of the living room. I'm sorry to report that it appears that Mister Vennemeyer took his own life with a service pistol."

"Oh my God . . . what did the note say?" Maletesta asked, his voice crumbling.

"Just five words, sir: 'tell Lieutenant Maletesta I'm sorry.'"

Maletesta squeezed the telephone until his hand hurt.

"Thank you, Sergeant," he said. "Has his family been contacted?"

"We haven't found any next of kin. He's in the city morgue."

Maletesta clipped the phone on his shoulder and picked up a pencil.

"Can you give me the number of a respectful mortuary there?"

"Sure, hold on. I think Hanlon and Harrison are about the best. I'll get their number for you."

Maletesta wrote the number down on a pad, hung up the phone and slumped to the floor. Tears rolled down his cheeks as he cried and cursed loudly, damning everything and everyone who crossed his mind. He was grateful that Tal was still shopping.

THIRTY TWO

Cow Hollow

Friday, December 18, 1959

The "Top of the Hour" story on the 10 o'clock news opened with the recent murder of the bootlegger, Roger Touhy, in Chicago.

"Twenty-two days ago, Roger Touhy was released from prison after serving 25 years for a crime he didn't commit," the broadcaster intoned as grainy black and white photographs flicked across the screen.

"Touhy was shot to death outside his home by two hit men allegedly working for the Chicago Syndicate. Touhy's real crime was that, during Prohibition, he fought with the syndicate over control of the distribution of illegal liquor. They wanted all of it; he wanted part of it. And, ultimately, Roger Touhy paid for it with his life."

On that sentence, the broadcaster took off his glasses looked directly into the camera.

"Apparently, those guys never forget."

"Speaking of murder," the broadcaster continued, as a photo of a smiling Jean Paul Sinclair popped up on the screen, "we've had four violent deaths in the City in the last six days. The police say they are investigating all leads in these murders and have identified several 'persons of interest.' However, there seems to be a bit of desperation here: they are asking any witnesses to these crimes to please come forward." Sinclair was replaced by a clip of Brennan walking quickly by a knot of gesticulating reporters outside the Hall of Justice.

Maletesta turned off the television. *Touhy: is that how Carlo will end up?* He couldn't bring himself to believe that Uncle Carlo was that important in the local world of crime. An attitude, a winter sun tan, fancy clothes, hints of hidden power. Surely, it was a kind of charade, a posturing which infuriated his father and drove his mother to light extra candles for her brother.

And yet there was no doubt about the personal crime wave swirling around him like a rising tide. Sinclair with Tal involved; Yusef with Cayenne; El Pilar with . . . who, him? *Jesus, in less than a week? And who is this fourth murder? This is like an English mystery, or, better yet, Red Harvest.* He smiled. He liked Dashielle Hammet, but *Red Harvest* always seemed a little too absurd to him with bodies dropping all over the place. *God, I hope not!*

Back at his desk, Maletesta flipped furiously through his notes on the pads, reliving the events of the past week. Brennan, snapping his gum and clicking that God dammed ball point pen, waiting to pounce on his daughter. He wasn't looking for the truth: all he wanted was another arrest, a headline in the newspapers. *Yusef. Hell, I don't even know what the poor bastard looked like, but nobody gives a damn about him being shot down in some no name alley in the*

Fillmore. Sinclair is a celebrity, so the press and the TV are demanding arrests for his murder.

He lit a Fatima and stood up, studying the Diego Rivera print on the wall. It always puzzled him. Rivera called it the "Flower Carrier," but there were two people in the painting: a poor peasant almost prone from carrying an unbearable burden and a woman behind him helping him to lift it. *Who is she? Is she his wife, or a woman in the village? Or maybe some good Samaritan passing by? My God, the poor guy can barely get up!*

He tried to remember the lines from Edwin Markham's poem. The whole class had to memorize it in high school. He brightened and straightened up to attention. He was back in his sophomore class, standing by his desk, answering his teacher.

"Uh, yes, I've got some of it, sir:

'Through this dread shape the suffering ages look;

Time's tragedy is in that aching stoop;

Through this dread shape humanity betrayed,

Plundered, profaned and disinherited . . . uh . . . "

"Sit down, Mister Maletesta," the black clad Jesuit had commanded.

Maletesta stubbed out the cigarette in the ash tray.

It doesn't matter who she is, Gianni. The point is that someone is helping someone else. Maybe that's what Rivera is saying.

He sat down and jerked out the center drawer of the desk. The sparkling brass cartridge case he's bought from the hopscotch player rolled to the front of the drawer. He flicked it up with his thumb and caught it.

Earlier that day, he researched the case in his cartridge reloading manual but couldn't find anything resembling it. It looked like some kind of 9mm, so he'd called Bob Chow's gunsmith shop in the Mission Street. A very weak voice answered and told him they all had the flu and they were closing for the weekend.

He squinted at the damned case again. The writing on the rim made no sense to him. *1937 means what? A date? Maybe. So what?* He tossed it back into the drawer and closed it.

Maybe Osceola King will have something for me about Yusef tomorrow when we meet in the parking lot of the Club Carolina. I need something! Anything! I've failed Cayenne. Cayenne, I am absolutely nowhere in finding out what happened to your brother!

Cayenne hadn't called him and when he called her apartment in the afternoon there was no answer.

And then there's that strange character, El Pilar. What did he know? He must have found something about the Sinclair murder or he wouldn't have been killed. Who would kill a harmless old coot like that? The bottom line, Gianni, is that these guys--whoever the hell they are—they're serious, and they're playing for keeps!

So, I have two problems: one, find out who murdered killed Sinclair so I can get Tal clear of this mess, and two, find some kind of justice for Yusef. Who killed him? Why? Is it someone in the neighborhood? Did he cheat somebody? He was doing the Mohamedan thing. Did he piss off some bible bangers? No, they wouldn't shoot a guy in an alley. What the hell? Merde!

Maletesta stood up abruptly and marched over to the hallway to flick on the outside porch light for Tal.

You've screwed up, Gianni; you don't know what you're doing! A week's gone by and you've got absolutely nothing! You've done nothing to get Tal out of this mess. That God damned Brennan will come calling again--this time with a warrant--and you've got zilch! Again, why would anyone kill a poet? Why would anyone run over a kooky beatnik who was checking out the poet? Why Yusef? The whole damned thing makes no sense at all, Gianni, no sense at all.

He went into the kitchen to find something to drink. Tal would be home soon. The movies were over at eleven. He opened the refrigerator and scowled at its contents. No beer, no soda, some orange juice. He closed the door and spotted this morning's coffee pot still on the stove, unwashed. There was at least a cup and a half of coffee in it.

Ah.

He took a tall glass out of the cabinet, set it on the counter next to the stove and poured the old coffee into it. Then he grabbed a few ice cubes out of the freezer and tossed them in the glass. Lastly, he stirred two fingers of Old Crow into the coffee and sipped it.

Ah, Iced Coffee Royale ala Maletesta!

Wait a minute.

Maletesta stopped in the middle of the kitchen.

Why did I just throw all three murders together? Accidental? Coincidental? Am I missing something? Is there some possible connection in the killings? They're not random? No, that's crazy. Well, it's worth considering. I need to think it through all over again. No, how could they be connected? Certainly not Yusef.

It was a warm night and the back door to the outside landing was still open, so he switched off the kitchen light and took his coffee out to the back porch. He sat down in the spindly wooden chair next to the small table with the ash tray. There was a stack of brand new small clay pots from his father next to the table, a reminder that starting plants from seeds in pots was a noble human effort. It was too dark to see the yard below, but he knew very well what it looked like: a jungle of untended weeds. Much to his father's disappointment, Maletesta had no interest in growing anything, be it flower or vegetable. His father often gave him fancy clippers and trellises and potting tools on his birthday, but John just put them in the shed at the bottom of the stairs where they remained unused. A couple of times a year he paid a neighbor's son to clear out the weeds and haul them down to the dumps in Daly City.

Maletesta set his coffee on the table and lit another cigarette. The bars weren't closed yet, so there wasn't much traffic hum from Union Street. He leaned back in the fragile chair and listened to the crickets. They weren't common in the City, but in this drought year, they were out in force.

The cadence of the crickets was methodical and comforting, like the roll of the breakers on the beach: "brrrit, brrrit, brrrit, brrrit." He wondered absentmindedly if they could be considered musicians; they were as steady as a metronome.

"Brrrit, brrrit, brrrit, brrrit."

Suddenly, they stopped. He heard a kind of scraping noise for a few seconds by the back fence, then it was quiet again.

No one knew where the crickets came from, but they were not native to the City. Some people said they escaped from Chinatown where they were treasured as pets. Whatever the reason, they were in the Marina during that warm winter.

The crickets started up again.

"Brrrit, brrrit, brrrit, brrrit."

Maletesta stubbed out his cigarette in the ash tray and was thinking about "The Blue Angel." *Are we a society like Germany in the 1920's with its false prosperity and shallow values? We do seem to punish anyone who criticizes, anyone who objects to the status quo. For God sakes, they've subpoenaed Uncle Con. There's one thing to be said about the Beats: they point fingers at those sanctimonious phonies . . .*

The crickets stopped again, and Maletesta straightened up in his chair. *Something is disturbing them. Someone's in the yard.*

He stood up and slowly backed into the kitchen. He reached up to a small shelf behind the door, retrieved a flashlight, and tiptoed back to the landing. The crickets were still silent, but he could not hear anything else. He aimed the flashlight at the yard and flicked the switch. *Nothing.*

"God damn it, the batteries are dead!" he muttered to himself.

Infuriated, Maletesta threw the flashlight at a side fence where it landed with a resounding bang. Then he picked one of the clay pots off the table and hurled it at the back fence. As it crashed, he flung another one toward the rear fence but it landed on the walkway.

"Come out and show yourself, you bastard!" he screamed toward the yard. His response was the sound of a deep thump from the neighbor's yard as someone landed A slight rustle and then nothing. Maletesta stood on the landing, breathing hard, peering into the darkness.

A few minutes later, the crickets started again.

"Brrrit, brrrit, brrrit, brrrit."

Back inside the house, the telephone rang. He locked the back door and picked up the phone in the hall.

"Hello?" he shouted.

"Mister Maletesta, this is Elizabeth Halliday next door. I heard some odd noises in your yard. Is everything OK?"

"Everything's fine, thanks, Mrs. Halliday. I think a raccoon was in the yard, but it's gone now."

"Oh my."

"Goodnight."

Maletesta retrieved the Bernadelli .25 automatic from the shelf in the closet, shoved it into his pocket and walked out the front door to meet Tal and her friend at the Marina Theatre when the movie got out.

THIRTY THREE

Cow Hollow

Saturday, December 19, 1959

Maletesta was out in the backyard early. He threaded his way carefully through the weeds and dried up plants, looking at the ground. Periodically, he'd stop and crouch down for a closer inspection. He had already noted the scratches and scuff marks on the back fence made by last night's intruder. The day promised to be oddly warm for December.

"Did you lose something, Dad?" Tal called down from their back porch.

"No, just checking out some places to plant in the Spring."

Tal laughed.

"Planting?" she scoffed. "What are *you* going to plant?"

"I think it is time for us to get back into nature," Maletesta answered as he walked toward the back stairs. "You know, plant some things that we can harvest and eat, just like grandma and grandpa do in their back yard."

"You're kidding, aren't you?"

“No, Tal, I think it’s a good idea.”

Tal walked down a few stairs, glancing over the yard.

“What are all those broken pieces of clay pots doing all over the place? How did that happen? Weren’t those pots on the back porch?”

“Yeahhhh . . .”

“Dad, what happened? Did you throw them out there to break them?”

“It’s a long story,” Maletesta replied as he came up the stairs.

“Try me,” she answered.

Miss Colbert emerged from her back door on the top landing and stepped spryly down the stairs as Maletesta was ascending from the yard. She reached his back porch the same time he did. Miss Colbert was a small ancient woman with a shock of white hair and a pinched face who created her eyebrows with a pencil. She drew them about one inch above her eyes, and the unfortunate result was that she looked continually surprised. Miss Colbert was over fifteen years retired from a clerk’s job in the police department but had long ago assumed a police inspector’s demeanor.

“I heard quite a racket out here last night, Professor Maletesta!” Miss Colbert announced, adjusting the crisply ironed apron around her waist. “What was the heck was happening?”

“I saw a black cat, Miss Colbert,” Maletesta smiled. “You know what it is about black cats, of course.”

"Professor, I am not superstitious, and I am extremely disappointed that a college professor in this year of 1959 would possess such a primitive perspective. Surely, you are not serious!" Miss Wilson stared down her short nose at Maletesta.

"Well, you've got me there, Miss Colbert," he replied sheepishly, "I think it was actually a raccoon, but I didn't want to frighten you. They can be very ornery."

"Oh, pshaw, Professor, when I was a young girl in Coos Bay, my sister and I ran them off with our slingshots! I did tell you about my sister, Eleanor, didn't I? She was the first female auxiliary deputy sheriff in Lassen County. Of course, that was after we moved to California. A crack shot, she was."

"Yes, you did tell me about her, Miss Colbert."

"Well, so there," Miss Colbert concluded and went back up the stairs.

Maletesta and his Tal walked back into the kitchen, closing the door behind them. Tal snapped the dead bolt on as Maletesta poured himself a glass of orange juice and sat down at the table. She walked over and sat down on the bench opposite him. He took a sip and set the glass down on the table.

"So?" Tal asked.

"Yes?"

"Dad, even that dotty old lady upstairs knows it wasn't a raccoon. What happened?"

Maletesta said nothing, but took another sip from the glass.

"Dad!"

"All right. Someone was in the backyard last night."

"How do you know?"

"I heard them. You were at the movie. It's a long story."

"Is that why you were standing out on the sidewalk when Ray and I came out? You made me feel like I was in middle school, Dad."

"I'm sorry; I was worried."

Tal looked at the back door and then back at her father.

"So, who was here?"

"I don't know, but it might have something to do with me looking into Sinclair's death, or El Pilar's death or Yusef's death—or the God damned man in the moon!"

Maletesta pounded his fist on the table.

Tal said nothing, clasping her hands together.

Her father sighed deeply.

"You know, honey, this is not over. I've grabbed the tail of a snake, but I don't know how long it is or how poisonous it is. I'm afraid I've put us both in danger. I'm sorry."

Maletesta walked over to the back door and stared down at the yard.

Tal joined him and hugged him, following his vision to the battered back yard with the shards of broken clay pots scattered from one fence to the other.

"I'd better call Grandpa for a new supply of flower pots," Tal giggled

Maletesta looked at her and smiled.

"Hey," he suddenly blurted, "what about 'The Blue Angel?' Did you enjoy it?"

"It wasn't exactly 'The Blue Angel' you described."

Tal began washing the breakfast dishes in the sink, carefully placing them in the rack on the sideboard.

"What do you mean?"

"No Marlene Dietrich, no odd camera angles and a happy ending in color. Ray and I were laughing out loud near the end. It was like Ozzie and Harriet."

"No!"

"Yes!" Tal countered, laughing. "The professor got his job back at the end! He didn't die in all that German angst and middle class hypocrisy you were telling me about. I thought we'd see Ozzie walking across the lawn in his cardigan to straighten everybody out."

"What the hell!" Maletesta responded in disgust. "Who made it, Walt Disney? Did you catch the director's name?"

"Edward Dmytryk, do you know anything about him?"

Maletesta hesitated.

"No, but the name's familiar. I think he was one of the Hollywood Ten. They were blacklisted for refusing to testify before the House Un-American Activities Committee."

"When was that?"

"Nine-ten years ago. A lot of people lost their jobs because their political beliefs were out of sync with the witch hunters. It was not a proud time in our history."

"Really? Did Dmytryk lose his job?

"I don't know, but now those creeps are after Sister Agatha's uncle. You know, Uncle Con."

Maletesta picked up the coffee pot and poured the cold coffee down the drain in the sink.

"OK, I've got to get back to work, and so do you. You're on top of your paper, right?"

"Yes, Dad."

"And no more worrying?"

"Dad, the feelings are not about 'worrying.' They're signs about what might happen, you know?"

"Nothing will happen, all right?"

"All right."

"And just to prove it, I'm going over to the Tip Top and get a haircut."

"Why don't you get them all cut," Tal quipped.

"Oh no, "Maletesta groaned. He stopped at the doorway.

'Look, honey, just to be on the safe side: don't answer the door unless it's someone you recognize, OK? And don't answer the phone."

"Yeah, all right, cool."

"Oh, I almost forgot, I'm meeting Osceola King, that private detective from the Fillmore at noon."

"Where?"

"The parking lot of the Club Carolina."

"Dad, watch yourself, OK?"

"Don't worry; I don't think anyone would be so stupid to try something in broad daylight."

He didn't tell her that earlier that morning when she was asleep, he had slipped his Colt Three-Fifty-Seven with the six inch barrel inside yesterday's newspaper and laid it on the front seat of the Oldsmobile.

THIRTY FOUR

Cow Hollow

Saturday, December 19, 1959

"Tony, you're a dumb ass, you know? How can you be such a dumb ass? I mean, really."

All the customers in the Tip Top barbershop burst out laughing. Tony was just the latest target of Alfredo Pezzi, the owner and proprietor.

"Fredo, you can cut me and stab me, but I'm right and you know it. We're becoming a murder capitol, and we need more cops in this town."

It was another typical Saturday morning at the Tip Top Barber Shop on Union Street near Van Ness when Maletesta entered the shop. The shop was full, but he grabbed the last empty waiting chair near the door. He picked up a copy of the *Saturday Evening Post* on the seat and sat down. He looked around the shop with the *Post* on his knees and nodded to a few familiar faces. Others glanced at his empty left sleeve and quickly looked away. Years ago, his mother brought him to this same shop for his first real haircut. She had treated him to a banana split at the ice cream store down the street after the ordeal. The ice cream store was now a real estate office.

Long and narrow, the Tip Top was the weekly crossroads of information, accurate and inaccurate. An aroma of hair oil, talcum powder, after shave lotion and cigarette smoke permeated the place, and the faint sounds of classical music struggled out of a portable radio perched on a shelf on the rear wall. For many years, the musical background in the shop was provided by a record player which played stacked singles by Benny Goodman and Beniamino Gigli, but eventually the old 78 s broke and nobody missed them. The radio was tuned to an obscure local station that didn't have much of a signal. It didn't matter because none of the Tip Top customers were listening anyway. Most of them only listened to themselves.

There were four chairs in the Tip Top, and the first one inside the door was manned by Alfredo "Fredo" Pezzi, self-appointed moderator of this conversational market place. Sometimes he was quiet; most of the time, he was not. This was one of those times. He was scowling at the angry-looking man in the second chair.

"Where you gonna put those cops," Fredo demanded, "on the roof tops at night? To stop somebody getting pushed off? One cop on every roof? How about a squad car on every street to catch a hit and run? How much do you think that will cost? Outside every Church? It's a dumb ass idea, Tony."

"Well, there's a lotta killing going on . . ."

"Who gives a damn," the man in the third chair piped in, "got ridda two of 'em. They're no damned good, lazy, dirty, practice free love . . ."

"Hey," Fredo interrupted, "free love: maybe they're on to something there."

A ripple of laughter erupted in the shop.

"It's not funny, Fredo," Tony retorted, "and you know it. North Beach used to be a good neighborhood and those bums have ruined it!"

Fredo finished trimming the eyebrows of the man in his chair as the grumbling swept through the chairs. He held his right hand up in his recognized gesture for silence, meaning he was about to make a pronouncement.

"Hey, say what you want about those beatniks, at least they're not trying to move in next to you like some other certain people in this town."

"That's the first sensible thing you said, Fredo,"' Tony answered, "and that's why we need more cops."

"Christ, you and your cops! People been killin' each other since Cain and Abel!" somebody in the back called out.

"It's all about your property," Fredo exclaimed loudly, ignoring the interruption. "Now you take Elliot here," he said, placing his hand on the shoulder of the man in his chair, "he knows all about that kind of thing, right, Elliot? How's the real estate game these days, eh?"

"It's not bad, Fredo," Elliot declared importantly, straightening the sheet covering him in the chair. "Things are starting to move again. You know, the big money is in projecting into the future . . ."

Elliot paused dramatically.

". . . and making smart investments."

"The future? That's a laugh!" Tony guffawed. "In a city full of beatniks? Not much of an investment opportunity, I'd say!"

Elliot glared at Tony.

"We needn't worry about that crowd. The police department is doing an admirable job of keeping them on the run and enforcing the law in all those dumps they hang out in."

"What about the coloreds in the Fillmore? They're not going anywhere, Elliot. How does that work for your investment in the future?"

Maletesta looked up from his magazine which was balanced on his knees as he turned the pages with his right hand.

"Ah, that's the wrinkle," Elliot answered suavely. "There could be big money in the Fillmore, which we real estate people are now calling the 'Western Addition.' We're counting on help from our friends in the government; it's called Redevelopment."

"You're kidding, of course," Tony objected, "all the government does is raise taxes. They can't even get us more cops. Am I wrong, or am I right, huh?" He waved a hand out to the men waiting in the chairs along the wall.

The response was a rumble mostly of agreement with a few dissenters.

"Yes, that's true," Elliot agreed, "but it does a lot more than raise taxes to feed the bureaucrats. It can also set policies that work for us. For instance, this idea they call Redevelopment which takes over the property . . ."

"I heard about that," Fredo interrupted, "and that's a lot of baloney, Elliot. It'll never happen. You know as well as I do that the government can't take over houses in neighborhoods: it's, uh, un-American!"

"That's right, Fredo," one of the waiting chairs agreed, and there was a chorus of agreement from the other customers.

"Look here," another chair piped in, "those guys at city hall can't even find a new ball park for the Giants!"

"Yeah, and what the hell's wrong with 16th and Bryant, I'm asking?" another added.

"Nah, the fix is in for out there at Candlestick, out in Hunter's Point, what the hell!"

A few groans rippled through the shop.

"George Christopher and Charlie Harney," Tony announced, "you know how that goes: Harney's got the land; Christopher's got the deal. As my mother used to say . . ."

"You had a mother?" another asked to laughter.

Tony was undaunted by the sniggers.

"As my mother used to say," he continued, "one hand washes the other. One hand washes the other. They're a couple of crooks and you guys know it."

"Well, maybe you're right," Elliot said in full retreat, "I have heard about some planning projects . . . I was just thinking that it might help the real estate market . . ."

"That's your problem, Elliot," Fredo concluded, "too much thinking."

"City Hall, are you kidding me?" a man in white painters' coveralls chortled. "You guys remember Jimmie the Jet, the fullback at Galileo?"

A few heads nodded.

"I cut his hair a few times," Fredo said, "back when he could still fit in the chair!"

"My point exactly," white coveralls said, "six, seven years ago he got himself a cush job drivin' the mayor around. His mother knew somebody who knew somebody; you know how that goes. But then Jimmie the Jet got so fat . . ."

"He never met a donut he didn't like," Fredo added to a round of laughter which included Maletesta.

"That he couldn't fit in the driver's seat of the damned limo no more," white coveralls concluded. "A limo, I tell you. So, did they kick his fat ass out of there? No, of course not! Go down there to City Hall. Take the stairs down to the basement on Grove Street. At the bottom of the stairs you'll find Jimmie the Fat, sitting in an oversize chair and directing traffic."

"Directing traffic?"

"For the employees who can't remember where they're supposed to go!"

“Nice job,” Tony said, “maybe I can apply.”

“City Hall,” Fredo grumbled, “those chiselers can’t get nothing right. Right?”

Elliot the real estate man did not answer. Maletesta thought about the conversation for a minute and then went back to the *Post*. The conversation moved on to golf, which did not interest him.

THIRTY FIVE

Parking Lot of the Club Carolina

Saturday, December 19, 1959

Maletesta drove wildly through busy holiday streets, impatient to get to his meeting with Osceola King in the parking lot of the Club Carolina. People were going to Christmas parties, buying trees, and shopping for presents and groceries for the coming week. He passed a few almost-empty Christmas tree lots and congratulated himself for buying their tree at the Guardsmen lot last weekend. As he stopped at a signal on Geary, he reminded himself once more that his driving days were soon coming to an end. The suicide knob on the steering wheel that he relied on to navigate was legally questionable, and it was only a matter of time until he got pulled over for something: broken brake light, five miles over the speed limit, whatever. His drivers' license itself was dubious. The last time he went to the Department of Motor Vehicles to take the driving test, lady luck intervened. The test drive instructor was none other than Johnny Esola from his old unit in the Philippines. That wouldn't happen again.

The parking lot of the Carolina was empty. He stopped inside the entrance and glanced at his watch. He was ten minutes early, so he drove to the middle of the lot, turned off the engine and rolled down his window. A blast of gospel choir practice from a nearby Baptist Church shook the car. Maletesta smiled and began tapping his foot and nodding his head to the music. *I wonder if Saint Mary's will ever get it? No, not in a few life times.* He laughed aloud.

"You're one mighty strange white man, Mister Maletesta."

Startled, Maletesta slid his hand inside the newspaper and jerked his head toward the window, almost all in one motion.

Osceola King stood outside the Oldsmobile three feet away, resplendent in a light blue seersucker suit and Panama hat. A brand new black Impala was parked a few feet behind him. There was a quizzical look on King's broad face.

"Jesus Christ!" Maletesta exclaimed. "Why did you sneak up on me like that?"

"I didn't take you for a religious man. And now, here you are, lookin' like you were in one of those Holy Roller trances, like my sister Beatrice."

Maletesta relaxed, opened the door and stepped out. He pulled out a pack of Fatimas, offered it to King who declined, and shook one far enough out of the pack to stick it between his lips. He put the pack back in his shirt pocket and retrieved the old Zippo from his trousers, lighting the cigarette. He ceremoniously snapped the lighter shut and turned to King.

"Well, have you got anything about Yusef?" he asked, turning his head to blow the smoke toward the hood of the Olds.

“I’m sorry to say, not much,” King replied. “Your man hasn’t left much of a trail. Not many people seem to know who he is, or was. And then there’s some who just won’t say. Can’t quite figure that one out.”

Maletesta waited.

“His sister works at the Club Carolina,” King continued. “Ownership likes *her*, but definitely not *him*. There’s a standing order to 86 him whenever he shows up. You gotta work hard for that kind of action. I talked to the old couple who found him in the alley. They had nothing. Stories about the first world war, changes in the Fillmore, that kind of thing.”

“Old news,” Maletesta snorted and flipped his cigarette butt toward the street. “You got anything worthwhile?”

“This Yusef had a real talent for pissing people off.”

“Yes?”

“He was always trying to push this Koran stuff, to Baptists, of all people.” King gestured toward the source of the gospel music. “They didn’t like it, and they didn’t like him . . .”

“You think they would have killed him?” Maletesta asked quietly.

“No, no, no, no. The religious thing’s a dead end, but something else kept coming up about Yusef as I continued my investigation.”

“What?”

"Like he'd go into a shop like Melrose Records and ask to see the owner or the manager. When that individual came out, Yusef would ask him if he owned the place or had a lease. The manager would usually tell him 'none of your business' and then they'd throw him out."

"How many times did this happen?"

"I don't know how many, but here's what I think is strange: in four places, as Yusef was being kicked off the premise, he'd yell out something like "is somebody tryin' to buy you out? Is somebody tryin' to buy you out?"

King shook his head and continued.

"It doesn't make any sense to me," he said. "What *was* that fool doing?"

Maletesta ran his fingers through his hair.

"Damned if I know. You got anything else?"

"No, that's the crop, other than a few mighty pissed off former girlfriends, but none of them would have offed him."

"The other day in the Paradise, I noticed that you carried a Luger, Mister King," Maletesta said carefully.

"That might be true, depending on who is asking and why."

"Yusef was shot with a 9mm pistol. Luger's a 9mm."

"Mister Maletesta, you either trust me or you don't; any other questions?"

"All right, no more questions."

Maletesta took a wad of bills out of the inside pocket of his tan suede sports jacket with the leather buttons and handed them to King.

"Thank you," Maletesta said, "there must be some sense in it somewhere. What in the hell was Yusef after, talking about things like leases?"

King counted the bills as he put them in his wallet.

"I wish I knew. Some people said he was just a crazy guy."

Maletesta put out his right hand out and they shook hands.

"Thanks, Cool Breeze, I really appreciate it. Maybe there's something in that lease thing. I can't imagine what, but I need to find out who killed him."

Osceola King handed him an embossed business card.

"My time is your time, John. The number on this card is a 24 hour service operator."

"See you."

Cool Breeze started walking back to his Impala.

"Wait a minute," Maletesta said suddenly.

"Yeah?"

"Find out if anyone actually *was* trying to buy them out and why. Maybe there *is* something there after all. Call me if you find anything."

"As they say across the street: amen, brother. And--it's nobody's business but yours—but, for the record, mine's a .30 Luger."

Maletesta waved a dismissal at him.

THIRTY SIX

Winterland, San Francisco

Saturday, December 19, 1959

The fans wanted to believe that it was real. They wanted to believe that it wasn't rigged. They wanted to laugh and cheer their heroes and boo the villains. They wanted to believe that good triumphs over evil; if not that night, then for sure by the end of the season. They were the fans of professional wrestling.

Professional wrestling, with its staged outcomes, was not the biggest "sport" in San Francisco. That mantle belonged to the newcomer Giants, but the locals had their own favorites who were here before the New York invasion. San Francisco no longer had their minor league Seals where all three DiMaggio brothers played and their stadium at 16th and Bryant was taken over by the Giants, but the Giants were still not the only game in town.

The other team favorite was the 49rs, a National Football League team who played their home games at Kezar Stadium in Golden Gate Park. Kezar was accessible by numerous bus routes, and if you were driving, there were neighbors who sold parking places in their driveways on game days for a couple of bucks. Almost everyone knew someone who was on the team. Frankie Albert, Joe Perry and Leo Nomellini were hometown heroes and some of the 49rs owned neighborhood liquor stores or sold cars in the off season. There were so many post-game hangouts all over town that sometimes it was impossible to get a dinner reservation after a 49r game.

There were also three race tracks close to the City, and the immortal Sea Biscuit's popular successor was Silky Sullivan who was ridden by Willie Shoemaker, another favorite of the fans. The annual Bay Meadows Handicap race in nearby San Mateo often drew 20,000 people, very few of whom were inveterate gamblers. Then there was boxing which was ingrained in San Francisco for over 100 years, from the Gold Rush bare knuckle punch-outs down through Gentleman Jim Corbett, Abe Attell and Joe Benjamin to Fred Apostoli and Bobo Olson, the middle weight champion who stunned the City when the newspapers discovered that he had two families, neither of which knew the other existed.

Coming up in popularity was roller derby, an exercise in organized mayhem by people on roller skates which was born during the great depression and thus not very far removed from the physical devastation of the dance marathons of that era. The Bay Bombers were San Francisco's team, and the star of the contests at Kezar Pavilion was Ann Calvello, who actually grew up in the City. With her wild makeup and dyed hair, she resembled a Hollywood wrestler, but the truth was she sustained more broken bones than any professional wrestler who bounced around on a trampoline. Roller Derby was considered hokey by the City's high brows, but its physical brutality was real.

Maletesta and Tal easily found their ring side seats at Winterland, two on the aisle. They had stopped at one of the concession stands for a beer, a soda and a bag of popcorn and carried them down to their seats. They nodded to a heavyset couple in the seats next to them, and the couple smiled back between handfuls of popcorn. Maletesta glanced over at the ringside row of the wrestling officials and noted two nattily dressed middle-aged men preening with attitude. *Carlo's associates*, he thought and took a sip of his beer.

Tal surveyed the crowd as she sat down and whispered into his ear, "I can't believe we're here, Dad. This is really too much. I mean, really, too much. Do we have to stay?"

Before Maletesta could answer, a buzz of anticipation ran through the crowd who had filled the place to see "Gorgeous George," the reigning celebrity of the wrestling world. The fans were anxious and noisy, waiting for the man they loved to hate to appear in the main event. They stuffed themselves with beer and hotdogs and peanuts during the undercard matches which were lackluster according to the fans' expectations. No one was thrown through the ropes or body slammed onto the canvas. By the time of the main event, the air was thick with cigarette smoke, anticipation and perspiration.

Maletesta looked at his pocket watch after the end of the second undercard match when the lights went down. The crowd hushed momentarily. A red carpet magically unrolled itself down the aisle from the last row to ringside. Maletesta and Tal looked up the aisle and saw a man dressed as a valet, spraying the air in front of him with what appeared to be an oversized perfume bottle. He stopped at the ring, sprayed the ropes and shot a few puffs at the referee. The loud speakers erupted with the theme song "Pomp and Circumstances," and the crowd stood up and went wild, shouting, booing and applauding simultaneously.

A purple spotlight picked up Gorgeous George at the top of the aisle and he began his regal descent to the ring. Resplendent in platinum hair and a purple satin robe festooned with sequins and lace, he strode down the aisle, waving to his fans, who screamed in response. As he passed each row, he pulled gold bobbie pins out of his hair and threw them into the audience. The fans fell over each other trying to catch them.

Maletesta burst into laughter, but Tal remained scowling slightly, embarrassed by the spectacle. She turned to her father, who bent down to hear her over the din, and shouted into his right ear, "Dad, this is crazy, like crazy, like nuts."

Gorgeous George stopped at ringside and paused to make his entrance into the ring. In the opposite corner, Lord James "Tally Ho" Blears stood, calm and disdainful. Gorgeous George paid no attention to Blears. Instead, he turned and bowed to the crowd, who booed heartily again. As he completed his bow, he saw Tal standing in front of her seat on the aisle. Smiling, he strode over to her, handed her a gold bobbie pin, and said, "for you, my lovely." Tal stammered a polite thank you and Gorgeous George climbed into the ring.

Lord Blears, George's opponent, was noble and sufficiently long suffering during the event. At every opportunity, George pulled a dirty trick. He was known in the trade as a heel, a bad guy. When the referee turned his back, which was often, George took off: a kidney punch, a gouge, a low blow. Lord Blears groaned and staggered to the canvas. When the ref challenged George, he broadly exclaimed his innocence as the crowd howled "foul" to the apparently deaf referee. And so it continued through the match with foot stomps, scissor holds, illegal grabs and body slams by the triumphant and posturing Gorgeous George. Maletesta and Tal got caught up in the unfolding drama, yelling at the ref at each dirty deed and cheering Lord Blears as he took his lumps from the heel. Suddenly, with only a few minutes to go in the match, the seemingly hapless victim gathered up new energy and went on the attack. Lord Blears came roaring up from the mat, charged into the ropes, and rebounded with a flying kick that knocked George down. Then he picked up the groggy George and helicoptered him as the fans screamed.

"Finish him off, finish him off!" the fat man next to Maletesta yelled, shaking his fist.

Lord Blears' theatrical timing was impeccable. At the peak of fans' screaming, he slammed Gorgeous George on the canvas and pinned him. The all-of-a-sudden alert referee did a quick count. As the applause and cheers shook the air, the lights came up a hordes of happy fans made for the aisles.

Maletesta suggested that they wait until the audience thinned out before walking up the aisle to the lobby.

"Well, what do you think? Maletesta asked. "Not so bad, huh?"

Tal held up her gold bobbie pin.

"Kind of cool, somehow, I guess," she murmured politely.

As they jostled through the crowd in the lobby, Tal noticed a man in a Tyrolean hat watching them as he leaned against a cigarette machine. He stared at them for a moment and then darted out through the crowd to the street. Tal turned abruptly and grabbed her father's elbow. Maletesta stopped and looked at his daughter quizzically.

"*Apai, alau dinga*! There's something here. Something's wrong, *apai,* I can feel it," she whispered. "I can feel it, Dad, like years ago! There was a guy over there in one of those hats with a feather in it. He was looking at us. He was staring at us, something's wrong, I know . . ."

"OK, Tal, watch yourself. Stay close."

Maletesta understood immediately. Since their early days in the jungle of Borneo, he had recognized that special quality in Talah and respected those moments when she sensed something was not quite right. He put his hand into his overcoat pocket and slipped out the .25 Bernadelli with the extension magazine, holding it against his thigh nestled in the folds of the overcoat. It was small. It was nearly invisible. He clicked off the safety.

The two of them pushed along with the crowd to the sidewalk. The fog was in again, swirling under the Winterland marquee and creating an eerie picture of blurred shapes in the street lights and headlights. The crowd was in a good mood--boisterous, half drunk and loud with a lot of pseudo wrestling moves being inexpertly applied here and there. As Maletesta and Tal neared the curb and began walking toward their car, a green Buick pulled out of a parking space across the street, executed a u-turn and drove up alongside them. The passenger side window lowered as the car approached.

"Say, fella, can you tell us how to get to Market Street," a voice called from the Buick as the car stopped beside Maletesta. Tal froze.

"Hat!" she gasped.

From the glow of the lights on the dashboard Maletesta recognized the glint of an automatic pistol rising from the speaker's lap. He quickly brought the little .25 up and snapped off six shots into the Buick's open window. The shots were so rapid that it sounded like someone tearing a sheet in half. The sixth round stove-piped in the chamber and jammed the pistol. There was a garbled yell from inside the car, and the automatic went off, burying a bullet in the dashboard. The driver punched the accelerator and the Buick shot out into the traffic with a screech of burning rubber.

"Stop thief! Stop thief!" Maletesta yelled, stuffing the Bernadelli back into his overcoat pocket.

"There they go!" Tal shouted and pointed in another direction.

The two of them ran down the sidewalk toward the block where they had parked their car alongside other people who were running from where the shots were fired. In confusion and terror, the rest of the crowd ran in different directions, adding to the general chaos. When Maletesta and Tal reached the Oldsmobile parked on Pierce, he tossed her the keys.

"You drive. Sausalito."

Tal deftly pulled the Olds out of the parking place and sped north up the hill. She hung a right on Bush and then a left on Steiner, barely getting through the intersection on the yellow. They heard police sirens somewhere behind them. Maletesta twisted in the front seat to look back and then relaxed.

"Take it easy, Tal, no one's after us. Don't break any traffic laws."

Tal slowed and eventually turned left onto Lombard and then up Doyle Drive to the Golden Gate Bridge.

"Tal, take the right lane. It's closest to the railing."

As they approached the middle of the bridge, Maletesta rolled down the window and took a breath of fresh air.

"Slow down."

The Oldsmobile dropped speed, and he tossed the Bernadelli automatic out the window and over the bridge railing.

"Thanks," he murmured after the pistol.

"Talah, I haven't heard you speak Dayak in quite awhile. Thank you, once again. Are you all right?" Maletesta asked.

"I think so, depending on what you mean by all right. Shouldn't we call the police?"

"No. Carlo. *Traditore*." Maletesta answered after a moment's thought.

"Uncle Carlo?"

"He's the only one who knew we'd be at Winterland tonight. *Merde.*"

"I don't believe it, Dad."

In silence, they rolled off the bridge and down into Sausalito. Tal pulled into the first parking lot they saw, found a space, and turned off the ignition.

"I know," her father said.

"What?"

Maletesta exhaled loudly.

"Everything just changed. Last night that could have a prowler in the back yard or a nosy teenager. Tonight, there's no benefit of the doubt. Someone just tried to kill us."

Tal began shaking uncontrollably.

Maletesta reached over and squeezed her shoulder.

"Easy, Tal; easy, honey. We just need to be on high alert now, watch ourselves. I think tonight also means that we're closer than we think to clearing up this mess."

"Sure, Dad, whatever you say."

"How about we find some pie ala mode and coffee somewhere around here?"

"I think I'd rather go home, Dad."

"OK."

THIRTY SEVEN

Steiner Street

Sunday, December 20, 1959

"I'm going the church this morning, would you like to come?"

"Excuse me?" Tal asked.

Tal was at the kitchen sink, washing up the remains from their Sunday breakfast. She had finished the plates and was starting on the pans in which she had cooked pork sausages and her father had fried scrambled eggs with garlic and curry. The radio was tuned to a generic pop music station and the songs of Ella Fitzgerald alternated with Perry Como and Pat Boone. Maletesta sat at the table reading Ralph Gleason's jazz column in the newspaper holder and smoking his third cigarette of the morning.

"I'm going to Mass today," he repeated. "Is there something wrong with that?"

"Well, Dad, it's been quite awhile, wouldn't you agree?"

"Yes, but this is Christmas week. I want to go to the 9 o'clock Mass at Saint Mary's because they have a wonderful choir. It's small and it's plain, and right now, I like the simplicity. Denise Leveratov would understand."

He took a deep drag on his cigarette and continued.

"It's just not the same feeling I get at St. Vincent's."

"I know what you mean, Dad," Tal countered. "I've been to both. They're both well-heeled congregations and almost all of them always have their eyes open to spot someone who doesn't look like them."

She immersed a frying pan into a deep bowl of soapy water like she was trying to drown it.

"Yes, I know," Maletesta agreed, "they're all too white and there's a lot of attitude, but today I'd like to hear some choir music at Mass. Or, maybe, I just *need* to hear some choir music. Maybe we both need to hear something, Tal."

Maletesta stubbed out the cigarette in the porcelain ash tray.

"You know what I mean?"

"They call it a service, Dad, not a Mass," Tal corrected, putting the final pan in the drying rack. "You wouldn't make a very good Episcopalian."

"Same difference, they just don't have a pope and their priests can get married. Other than that, it's that same old *dignum et justum est*."

Tal removed the rubber gloves and turned to him.

"Dad, what about Uncle Carlo? Did you call him?"

"Yes, but there was no answer. He told me they were going to Tahoe for the weekend, but I don't know how long his version of a 'weekend' is. I'll try again tonight, and tomorrow, and the next day. *Bastardo.*"

Tal walked over to the table and put a hand on his shoulder. He looked at her steadily.

"You don't know for sure, Dad. I can't believe Uncle Carlo would ever harm you, whether he's supposed to be a gangster or not."

"Tal, who else knew we were going to Winterland last night, huh? Nobody."

Maletesta stood up and began to pace the kitchen.

"But why?" he continued. "Why did someone try to take a shot at me? Am I on to something about these murders? I sure as hell don't know what it is they think I know!"

He waved his hand in disgust and continued.

"It all goes back to Carlo, doesn't it? Who knew we'd be at Winterland last night, huh? Nobody! Nobody except Carlo, that is. *He gave me the tickets, Tal*! He's got a lot to answer for."

"We were lucky, Dad, but I'm not sure what we should do next. Are you? Is Uncle Carlo our enemy now?"

Maletesta sighed deeply and sat down again. He looked across at his daughter, her hands folded quietly on the table. They had been through a lot together.

"I don't know, honey. Part of me just can't accept it, but who else knew we'd be there?"

The clock chimed in the living room. Maletesta stood up again.

"I'll reserve a final judgment until I talk to him, OK? Maybe there's some other explanation. Now, I'm going to clean up and head over to church. Are you coming?"

"I think I'll wait for Christmas."

The phone rang as Maletesta walked through the hall. He picked it up.

"Hello?"

"Mister Maletestoh?" A slight laugh on the other end of the phone line.

"Yeah, Cool Breeze. What's up? Are you working on Sunday?"

"Time and a half."

"We'll see. What do you have?"

"A man asking about the property at Melrose Records left a business card, and I have it right in my hand. Shall I read it to you?"

Maletesta set the phone down clipped on the shoulder clamp and placed it on his shoulder. He picked up a pencil on the small table next to the phone.

"OK, let's have it."

"The card says 'Golden Gate Investments' and in the corners, it says 'San Francisco' and 'Oakland.'"

"Is there an address or a phone number?"

"No address. Telephone number: Atwater 5-2700."

Maletesta wrote it down on the phone pad and exhaled loudly.

"Fantastic work, Mister King! Thank you very much! Good work, my friend!"

Maletesta dialed the telephone number on the card. It rang about ten times before he realized that it must an office that was closed on Sunday. He put the phone down and looked around. He assumed that Tal had gone into her room to read and was avoiding the mess of books and paper on the dining room table. He knew she would eventually get back to it. He picked up the phone again and dialed a number.

"All Saints College," the operator answered.

"Hello, this is John Maletesta and I'd like to speak with Sister Agatha, please."

"Good morning, professor Maletesta. I believe Sister Agatha is in her office. If you will hold a minute, I will connect you."

"How are you, John?" Sister Agatha asked as she picked up the phone.

"Fine. Everyone seems to be working on Sunday. Are you getting time and a half too?"

"Lord sakes, no! I just came in to get a head start on the Spring calendar, but I welcome an interruption. How is your investigation proceeding, and how is Tal?"

"She's holding up, but I don't feel like I'm making any real progress. It's like one of those magnetic puzzles for little kids, you know? All the little bits come together, and if you move it slightly, they fall apart. On top of that, Tal's problem is one thing and another is the death of a young black man who was murdered in the Fillmore last week."

"Oh dear," Sister Agatha said and crossed herself. "Are they connected?"

"I don't think so, but I have to solve both of them."

"You have a keen mind, John. I believe you will find the answers. Is there anything I can do?"

"Yes, Sister. I have a possible lead regarding on property in the City, but I need more information. Do you have any connections in City Hall, particularly in building or planning or permits, someone in those areas?"

There was a brief silence.

"I'd say my cousin Dennis is your man," Sister Agatha said. "He works in the building permits office, but he's the busybody of the family. The man is a natural bureaucrat; he loves files and filing cabinets. His wife is a meticulous housekeeper. They're very well met."

Maletesta couldn't help but laugh.

"What do you need, John?" Sister Agatha asked.

"I need any information about a company called 'Golden Gate Investments.' In particular, who owns the company and what they're up to in the Fillmore."

"Ah--up to," Sister Agatha concluded, "nefarious activity, I imagine."

"Well, I suspect that they--whoever 'they' are—are involved in some kind of shenanigans in that neighborhood, but I don't know what. I do think that somehow it's tied to a murder."

"Ah, shenanigans: a useful word. Golden Gate Investments. I will call Dennis this afternoon."

"Thank you, Sister."

Maletesta glanced at the clock in the hall and frowned. If he hurried, he had just enough time to throw on his blue blazer with the brass buttons and walk over to St. Mary's.

THIRTY EIGHT

Steiner Street

Sunday, December 20, 1959

Maletesta was scribbling urgently on his pad when he reached for a cigarette and found that the pack was empty. He crumpled it and tossed it toward the waste basket in the corner of the study. *Two points*, he thought when the pack disappeared into the receptacle. He rummaged through the desk drawers, but no cigarettes were to be found. He walked back to Tal's bedroom door and called out.

"Tal, I'm going over to Spiro's to buy some smokes."

"OK," was the muffled response.

"Don't let anyone in. Don't answer the telephone."

"OK."

"Are you working on your paper?"

"I'm thinking about it."

"Think a little harder," he said, shaking his head as he headed out the door.

It was another warm day of the drought, and the streets were quiet. On Steiner, some kids were throwing a football around and watching for traffic at the same time. When a car approached, the kids yelled "car" and retreated to the sidewalks. Maletesta waved to them as he crossed the street. He glanced at Saint Mary's and realized that he rather enjoyed his time in the church that morning. The choir as usual was uplifting. The church--more of a chapel--was small and wooden. If you were in a pew near the front, you were only about twenty feet from the choir. It was intimate and yet imposing in the grandeur of the voices of the choir. The choir was a mix of men and women: some old, some middle aged, some overweight, a few bald and one almost blind. *And yet when they sing it's as if the heavens have opened and all is right with the world.*

Nonetheless, Maletesta slipped out of the church right after communion as usual. He seemed to have an internal clock which told him it was time to leave before the service or Mass was over. Maybe it was because he was uncomfortable around the cheerful people who gathered outside the church after the Sunday morning services. Or maybe it was because he never was very comfortable with small talk, the empty chit chat of strangers thrown together for a religious rite. Particularly now in the middle of three murders and his daughter's dangerous predicament.

He dismissed his meandering thoughts about church as he walked into the corner market across the street from the church. It was owned by a Lebanese immigrant named Spiro who worked seven days a week. Spiro was a stocky man in his forties who sported a huge black mustache and had two daughters he wished were two sons.

"Good morning, mister Maletesta," Spiro said as Maletesta entered the incredibly cluttered store. "What can I get you this fine Sunday morning?"

Unlike a large store in a super market chain, the shelves of Spiro's Market were crammed with items that the neighbors actually wanted. Spiro didn't carry every brand of cereal, but he stocked the eight brands that the customers ate for breakfast. It was the same policy with such varied products as cigarettes, bar soap, furniture polish, and wine. Occasionally a stranger came in asking for a brand he didn't carry and then a bystander would witness Spiro's masterful art of successfully selling someone something they did not want. Neighbors regarded those situations as the high entertainment of the day.

"Two packs of Fatimas, Spiro. How are things going for you today?"

"Hunky dory, hunky dory. You like the words hunky dory?"

"Sure," Maletesta laughed, "hunky dory is all right."

Spiro turned to retrieve the packs from several stacks of cigarettes on the shelves behind him. A radio on the shelf near the cigarettes was broadcasting a program about growing vegetables in your back yard.

Spiro looked at the radio and scoffed.

"You can't grow things here like we did in the old country, too cold."

"Probably not," Maletesta agreed cheerfully, as he laid a dollar bill on the counter.

"Thanks, Spiro," he said as he put one of the packs in his jacket pocket. He was reaching for the other pack when the gardening program was suddenly interrupted by an announcement:

"We have a breaking story: early this morning, San Francisco police discovered an abandoned green Buick sedan with a dead body in it downtown on Stevenson Street, near Seventh and Market. Stay tuned for more details on the hour."

Maletesta stood as if paralyzed, the pack of Fatimas still in his hand.

"Are you OK, mister Maletesta?" Spiro asked, leaning over the counter to squint at his customer.

"I think so," he replied slowly, "I just need to make a phone call."

"I have my phone here."

"Thanks, I'd better go back to the house," Maletesta answered and left the store.

Talah was at the dining room table working on her paper when Maletesta came in.

"I've got to call Brennan," he announced.

"What for?" Tal asked, frowning.

"They found a green Buick this morning near Seventh and Market with a dead man in it."

"Oh my God!"

"Yes. Something's starting to add up, but I still don't know what it adds up to. One thing for certain, that green Buick turns up way too often to be a coincidence."

"How many green Buicks do you think there are in the City?"

"I have no idea, but those guys last night were in one, and witnesses said El Pilar was hit by one."

Tal bit at her lip.

"Last night."

"Hey, we were in worse situations in Borneo, remember?" he said lightly. "And the dynamic duo came through, right? How's the paper coming?"

"Dad, I'm going to lie down for a minute, OK?"

"OK, honey." He hugged her as she stood up.

"Don't worry," he murmured, "we're unstoppable, right?"

"I hope so, Dad."

Tal walked slowly down the hall to her room. Maletesta waited until she closed her door, and then he went over to the telephone in the study and called the Hall of Justice. He doubted Brennan would be in his office on Sunday, and he was right. He left a message with the switchboard, picked up some darts and hurling them at the dart board. This time all of the darts stayed on the board. The "Flower Carrier" was not in danger.

THIRTY NINE

Steiner Street

Sunday, December 20, 1959

The telephone rang in the hall, and Maletesta picked it up on the third ring. The grandfather's clock had just chimed 3 pm.

"Hello?"

"This is Brennan; I got a message that you called earlier. What do you want?"

Brennan's voice was hoarse. He was working through the weekend and he was tired. He didn't like to work on Sunday. Sunday was his day with his family: get up early, read the Sunday paper, Mass at 10 o'clock. Teach his eight year old son how to ride a bike in the Stonestown parking lot after lunch. Later, teach his fifteen year old daughter how to handle a stick shift in the very same empty lot. That's what Sundays were for: he liked them.

Brennan shook a black cough drop out of the Smith Brothers box on his desk and popped it into his mouth. He glared at the pictures of the bearded brothers. *Bums,* he thought, *look just like beatniks.*

Maletesta put the shoulder clamp on the telephone and sat down at the desk in the study with a yellow pad and the Parker.

"Have you gotten anywhere with the Sinclair murder?"

"If it's any of your business, no, I got no more information since the last time we talked about it."

"What about your case against Talah? If you still have nothing, when are you going to drop it?"

"For crap's sake, John, I've got a hell of a lot more on my plate now than that bum, Sinclair, and whoever the hell pushed him off the roof."

Brennan spit the cough drop neatly into the waste basket next to his desk. He despised the Smith Brothers and all of their products.

"Look, John, you guys on the outside, you don't get it. We live in a jungle, you know? Take this weekend. Before it even started, some guy got run over by a car in North Beach. Not an accident, you know, according to a witness, on purpose. I think it was probably a drunk, but some know-it-all witness talked to the paper, so they're all over us. You get it?

"Hey, let's back up for a minute, okay, John? Week before, this guy Yooseff gets bumped off in the Fillmore. But wait, there's not only Sinclair getting tossed off the roof in North Beach; a bookie, gets blasted right outside church . . ."

"Do you have some kind of a 'Current Crimes Sheet' on your desk, Mike?" Maletesta interrupted. "How long is it?"

"Stay with me, John, stay with me. It's been a long day."

Maletesta grunted.

"Okay, and now we come to last night: a shooting outside Winterland. Anybody see anything? Hell no, all those morons who go to wrestling matches were running for cover. Somebody saw a guy in an overcoat. How many guys you think were wearing overcoats last night? Huh? Five hundred? What do you think? How about this: we get a witness for a maybe-hit-and-run on a dark street, but not a single one for a God-damned shooting outside Winterland in a crowd! Huh? Real bright, those wrestling fans: they 'saw some guy in an overcoat.' Thanks a lot, morons."

Brennan paused to take a breath.

"You know what they said today on the TV news, huh? 'Christmas Crime Wave Cripples the City.' How do you like that: 'cripples.' Where do they get the guys who write this stuff, huh, from Batman comic books?"

Maletesta jotted "Christmas Crime Wave" near the fleur de lis growing around the upper left corner of the pad.

"Then comes this morning, Sunday," Brennan rasped. "Yuh with me, Professor?"

"Yeah, Sunday morning, today."

"Guess what? Some bum with a hangover looks into the window of car parked on Stevenson Street and sees a dead body."

Brennan was on a roll. Maletesta heard him clicking his ball point pen as he talked.

"I heard about it on the radio," Maletesta added.

"Yeah? Good for you. Did the radio say the stiff was shot six times with a .25 automatic? Who the hell carries one of those: a pimp, a whore?" Brennan paused to yawn and stopped clicking the pen. His internal motor was running down.

Maletesta interrupted.

"I once read that more people get shot by .25 automatics than any other caliber pistol."

"Really?"

"Yeah."

Brennan yawned again.

"OK, do you want anything else? I got no more on your daughter's case. And yes, she is still a suspect."

"Yeah, well, that's a lot of bullshit, Mike, and you know it."

Brennan said nothing.

"I have a question, Mike."

"Shoot. Ha, ha."

"Have you found out anything about the dead man in the car, and have your forensic guys gone over the car yet?"

"That's two questions."

"You were always better in math than me."

"Very funny, up yours. Number one, we don't have much on this guy yet. He's a white male, late thirties, five seven, a hundred and fifty pounds, cheap suit, turtleneck, one of those funny little hats with a feather in it from Switzerland or somewhere. Nothing on him: no wallet, keys, nothing. Somebody, probably the driver, grabbed all the important stuff and ran. Greyhound's down the street; buses leave all the time."

"That's it?"

"Oh, they found an empty cartridge case on the floor board with some funny writing on it, probably a Luger. Checking for prints and checking the buses, but that's going nowhere. We don't even know who we're looking for."

Maletesta swallowed to keep his voice casual.

"What kind of writing on the shell?"

"Hell, I don't know, foreign and the numbers one nine three seven. If that's a date, it's pretty old stuff if you ask me, but who knows where these hoods get their ammo?"

"How about the car?" Maletesta asked.

"Stolen in Pacific Palisades a couple of weeks ago. Phony plates. We towed it to the yard."

"They said on the radio that it was a green Buick. Is that right?"

"Wow, those radio people are really on top of it, aren't they? Yeah, it's a green Buick. What about it? You want one for Saint Patrick's Day or something? By the way, professor, your two questions are up. I gotta get back to work."

"Mike, listen to me. Tell your forensic guys to go over it for any evidence that it might be the same Buick in the Thursday night hit and run: blood, hair, clothing, I don't know what else they look for."

Brennan held the phone out in front of him and looked at it like it was a strange object and then brought it slowly back.

"What's going on, professor?" he said slowly. "What do you know about green Buicks?"

"Hey, like Will Rogers, all I know is what I read in the newspapers, and, in this case, what I heard on the radio. On Friday morning, there was a story in the *Chronicle* about a guy in North Beach being run over and killed by somebody in a green Buick on Thursday night. Today, I'm down at the corner store and the radio says a green Buick was found downtown with a body in it. It makes you wonder about how many green Buicks are in the City, or is it that same car?"

Brennan was listening intently. There was a lull in the conversation.

"You still there? I can smell wood burning," Maletesta asked, without relaying his growing excitement.

"God damn it, Maletesta, what do you know about green Buicks? Last night the only witness west of Franklin Street who wasn't deaf, dumb and blind said he saw a *green* Buick barrel-assing out Geary not long after the shots were fired at Winterland!"

"Hmmm," Maletesta murmured.

"Then on Friday," Brennan resumed, "a beat cop named Powell turned in a report about two drunks making trouble at the Forbidden City at closing time. Powell rousted them, but Powell's one of those red hots who takes notes. You know what, John? His notes say the drunks left in a green Buick!"

"Sounds like it might be the same car, doesn't it?"

"And now *you're* asking me about *green* Buicks!" Brennan continued. "Are you on to something? There's one too many coincidences here for me. What the hell do you know, mister professor, and what are you hiding? Maybe I should haul you in here as a material witness or something. You want that?"

Maletesta placed the Parker on his pad and removed the telephone clamp from his shoulder.

"I'm not sure, Mike, but if I find something, you'll be the first to know."

"That's not good enough. What do you know? Hey, John, listen: what the hell's going on with you, huh? Hello? Hello?"

The line went dead.

Brennan seized the box of Smith Brothers cough drops, crumpled it in his hand and threw it into the wastebasket as he stormed out of his office, cursing.

Maletesta opened the center drawer of the desk, and as he retrieved the cartridge case found in the alley where Yusef died, the telephone rang again.

He hesitated and then picked it up, rolling the case between his fingers.

"*Monsieur* Maletesta?" a voice with a heavy French accent asked.

"Yes."

"This is to confirm that you may expect delivery next Wednesday. This is acceptable?"

"Yes, thank you for calling"

"*Merci, monsieur.*"

Maletesta hung up silently. The cartridge case from the alley lay on the desk behind the ashtray. Leaning forward, he picked it up and flipped it around to read the head stamp again: an unrecognizable script and the numbers, "1937."

"Gotcha," he whispered.

FORTY

Sunday, December 20, 1959

Steiner Street

"At least the hero has a mustache, so he actually looks a little like one of those guys in photographs of the Old West. All the other heroes in these westerns look like insurance salesmen in cowboy hats," Maletesta quipped as Tal brought a bowl of ice cream into the living room.

She joined him on the sofa to watch yet another western on television, this one called "Lawman."

"The law man came with the sun," Tal intoned from the program's theme song. The plot was familiar, the characters were familiar, even the buildings and trees and boulders were familiar. They both jumped when the telephone rang in the hall, but Tal was the first to reach it.

"Hello," she said apprehensively.

"Tal, it's Maria," the voice answered. "I'm sorry to be calling so late. The kids were in a Christmas program at the school, and I just got back. Is your dad there?"

"Sure, hold on a minute. How was the program?"

"Super! You know, nobody's really on key but there's lots of good energy."

Maletesta levered himself out of the arm chair, walked over to the hall and took the phone from Tal who had attached the shoulder clamp.

"*Hola*, Maria."

'John, I know it's late, but I got something for you."

"Don't worry about the time: what is it?"

"I went into work this afternoon to cover for Isabella who was sick. It was super busy. We had tourists, holiday shoppers, everybody and their cousins. Son of a bitchin' bastard, I was swamped! We were all runnin', so I didn't see Henri until I finished my shift. So, I'm going out the door, and he hands me a letter and says 'this came for you yesterday,' when I was off. I stuck it in my jacket pocket and boogied out. Whew! I had to run to get the kids dressed and to the Christmas program."

Maria took a breath as if she was re-living the whole exercise.

"I just got back and looked at the letter. There's no return address, just a name in big fancy capital letters, El PILAR."

"Holy moley, what does he say?"

"I haven't opened it yet. I thought I should call you first."

"Maria, you're wonderful! Please open it."

Maletesta lit a cigarette as listened intently to the tearing of paper on the other end of the telephone.

Maria extracted a meticulously printed sheet of three-hole binder paper from the envelope and began reading:

"This letter is for the one-armed man who paid me to find out anything about the unfortunate passage of the mediocre poet, Sinclair."

"Guess he didn't think much of him," Maria interjected.

"Keep reading, please, Maria."

"I don't dig the vibe I'm picking up whilst I look around this community," Maria read. *"A shadow of evil is clouding the passage of the lamented Sinclair. I spake with multiple persons, square and cool, and something is upside down, man, inside out. A sterno drummer told me that he was also sorry for the angel. 'Alas for the poet' he said, 'and alas for the angel, he cashed in his chips.' That'd what he said. Who is the angel, I asked? Nada. Sterno boy was gone, gone, gone. Not my scene, Maria of the Spirits. Other things of note regarding paper and property: bad news, my ersatz poet Sinclair, mister Spam, not anti-materialistic after all. Bad, bad, bad. Please tell your one-armed friend to be over careful. I will see him tonight."*

"That's it," Maria said.

"OK, thanks, Maria. Can you read it again to Tal? She's very quick at note taking."

"Sure."

Tal cradled the phone and scribbled down Maria's words. She hung up and turned to her father.

"Who the heck is the angel? Is this getting spooky or what?"

Maletesta raised his eyebrows.

"I admit, it does sound like something out of the Middle Ages, but El Pilar—or whatever his name was—was not all there. You know, the light's on but nobody's home? But there must be something to it: he was afraid, and that night, somebody ran over him."

"God!"

"Yeah."

"The angel," Maletesta repeated as he sat down again in the armchair. "He cashed in his chips. Who the hell is the angel, and does it mean that he is dead or left town? Tal, will you please turn off the TV?"

The phone rang again. This time Maletesta got there first.

"John, it's Maria again. I have an idea, doll baby. Victor knows everybody in the Beach that I don't. I'll ask him if he's ever heard of anyone called 'the angel.'"

"Victor?"

"Victor Wong, the artist. I showed you one of his paintings."

"Oh yes, that superb water color! *Gracias*, Maria."

He hung up the telephone and went back into the living room.

"Dad," Tal said, "I'm going back to my paper. Would you like anything from the kitchen before I go to my room?"

"No thanks, honey, I've got to think and I need a clear head."

Maletesta sat at the Rucker Fuller desk and worked on his notes, bits of evidence and suppositions until eleven o'clock. He reviewed and re-entered rows of dates, times and places with side line entries of characters and motives. When he was finished, the end result didn't make any sense at all.

"Christ," he said to Rivera's flower carrier on the wall, "this is ridiculous. I've got a grand-standing poet who was pushed off his roof by somebody. Who pushed him? Why did they push him? Then I've got a deranged poet who was killed in a hit and run two days after I asked him to check out the poet who was pushed off the roof. Are they connected or is it a big time coincidence? Who said there are no coincidences? Huh?"

The flower carrier remained silent under his burden.

Maletesta lit another cigarette.

"Then I've got the SOB who tried to take a shot at me . . . from a *green* Buick. And, to make matters worse, I have no idea why somebody killed Cayenne's brother, but the cops find a cartridge case in the undoubtedly same damned Buick which seems exactly like the one I got from the little girl outside the alley on Buchanan! Jesus Christ!"

He went down the hall and peeked into Tal's bedroom. She was asleep. He poked around the kitchen, found the bourbon and poured himself three fingers in an empty mug that didn't quite make the after-dinner washing. He tossed back half of it when he telephone rang. Almost gagging, he ran to the hall.

"Yes?" he said tentatively. In his family, late calls usually meant that some relative was in the hospital or had died.

"John, it's Maria again. I'm very sorry to call so late, but Victor called and I thought it was important."

"Absolutely, what do you have?"

"Victor plays the horses."

"Yeah, so do I. I like Tanforan."

"Well, so does Victor, doll baby. Thing is, he only likes to bet when he can see what he's betting on. You dig? Victor has to go down to where the horses walk around and looks at them before he places a bet."

"Yes," Maletesta said tiredly, "I do understand that. The paddock. Sometimes I stand on the rail so I can watch all that mud fly when they close in on the finish line. So?"

"So Victor told me that one time somebody told him if he wanted to place a bet without going to the track, he should see 'the angel.'"

"What?" Maletesta was now wide awake.

"If-he-wanted-to-place-a-bet," Maria repeated like she was talking to a slow learner, "he should see the 'angel,' you know, a bookie."

"A bookie?"

"Yeah, in North Beach."

"Does he have a name?"

"Nope. Night-night, doll baby."

Maletesta hung up the phone and wrote down "alas for the angel" with three question marks after it. Underneath it, he wrote "bookie" and "North Beach.'

OK, so now I have someone called the 'angel' who is apparently a bookie but what the hell does it all mean? Is he connected to a beatnik poet, according to El Pilar's drummer? I doubt it. Beat poets don't hang out with local bookies. Hell, don't forget, Gianni, the damned the drummer's on sterno! Jesus, that guy's brain was in the oven. Forget it!

Maletesta strode around the living room several times and went to bed.

FORTY ONE

Mission District

Monday, December 21, 1959

"Seventeen Reasons Why."

Maletesta stared at the large sign on the roof of the furniture store through the window of the 10 Mission bus as it navigated its way out Mission Street, dodging cars, jitneys and jay-walking pedestrians. The Mission's "Miracle Mile" offered block after block of five-and-dimes like Woolworth's and Kress's, large emporiums of furniture and appliances, smaller shops with shoes and shirts. The "Miracle Mile" had its own printed supplement inserted in the local newspapers and attracted shoppers from all over the City. Maletesta's bus journey would end at the half-block long Sears Roebuck store at Mission and Army.

Maletesta had seen the Seventeen Reasons Why sign before and, like other advertising gimmicks, it fascinated him. He assumed the "why" was the directive to buy furniture in the store, but how could there be "seventeen" reasons? Surely, one of two would do: fair price, good quality. That left fifteen more reasons. Free delivery? Good terms on loans? OK, thirteen now. As the bus rumbled out Mission, his mind reeled in the murders. The same questions over and over. Why and who? And no answers.

Why is the murder of a popular beatnik poet somehow connected to the hit and run death of a hapless crank in a monk's robe? Why did El Pilar write 'paper and property' in his note? What the hell does that mean? What did he find out?

Why did someone shoot down a young black man in the Fillmore? Why did someone try to kill me? Are the guys who tried to shoot me from the green Buick the same guys who ran over El Pilar? Seems likely. Is the green Buick involved in all of them? Why? Who are these guys? More importantly, who are they working for?

Gianni, why do you say, 'a young black man in the Fillmore?' He was Cayenne's brother, for God's sake! You sound like a sociologist: his name was Yusef, and now he's dead.

Cayenne, oh God, Cayenne, Cayenne. Where are you, baby?

Maletesta's eyes welled up as the bus lurched past McCarthy's bar. Maletesta had been there a few times. They still served a cheap plate of beans at the counter in the rear of the saloon, a policy begun during the Depression. Someone said the horseshoe bar was the longest in the West Coast. Maletesta thought that it probably wasn't and he could care less as he blinked back tears.

You're a real jerk, Gianni, a real God damned jerk. You know she's gone and you don't even have a phone number for her, just Kathleen, Georgia, her mother's place. You let her down, you bastard, when she really needed you.

"The Tingler" starring Vincent Price jumped off the marquee of the New Mission theatre.

A horror movie, just like my life.

There was a line outside the theatre.

Maybe they just want to see a life more horrible than their own.

A block later, the bus passed the El Capitan which was next to Bruno's. He scowled at Bruno's, a popular restaurant next to the old Cap: Italian food, starched table cloths and framed caricatures of the City's movers and shakers plastered on the walls. Bruno's was usually full of city hall deal makers who Maletesta didn't like. This is probably where they hatched out that sleazy deal for a ball park at Candlestick point, he thought as the bus left Bruno's behind.

You do see more from a bus than from a car. You see even more when you're walking, but I didn't have time for that today. Hell, who cares anyway? I've screwed everything up. Cayenne, Christmas. God damn you, Gianni! Cayenne. I'm so sorry, baby. Cayenne: I love you.

The bus stopped, jolting him into the present. He pushed Cayenne's image away and turned his attention to the new passengers coming down the aisle, taking seats here and there: Hispanic, with a few old Irishmen in their blue suits, white shirts and red faces topped with a few tufts of white hair.

The Mission is changing, probably beginning to look more like it was before the Gold Rush. Maybe I should ask some of my more conscientious students to do a paper on poetry the clash of cultures, something like the Fillmore, maybe?

"You Italian? You look Italian. You Italian?"

Maletesta almost jumped.

The question came from a very large woman across the aisle, her ample lap supporting several bags of packages and gift wrapping paper.

"Excuse me?"

"You're Italian, right?" the woman repeated.

"Yes."

"So, you know what they used to say about the Mission? The Germans grow fruit, the Italians grow vegetables, and the Irish grow nothing."

The woman guffawed loudly, almost dropping some of her packages.

Before Maletesta could respond, the driver called out, "Army Street, next stop," so he stood up and began making his way towards the rear door. When the bus crossed Army and stopped, he jumped down to the sidewalk with all of the shoppers heading into Sears for the final sales before Christmas. Dodging around the shoppers, he crossed over to the east side of Mission and walked up the hill. He stopped outside a small store under the sign, "F. Bob Chow, Gunsmith."

Maletesta smiled and pushed through the entry door, setting off a low decibel buzzer. The two men behind the glass counters recognized him.

"Ah, Professor Maletesta," announced a middle aged man in a blue smock, "to what do we owe this honor?"

"One, I've got a question," Maletesta held up the index finger of his right hand, "and, two, I've got a request," he said, adding the middle finger to the index finger.

"Is this some kind of a television quiz show?" a voice from the room behind the counters called out.

"Hello Mister Chow," Maletesta said.

F. Bob Chow was somewhat of a legend in the competitive shooting world both as a competitor and a gunsmith who built first class pistols for high stakes matches. Personally, he held a number of championship shooting records, including thirteenth overall in the 1948 Olympics and a first for the US Navy National .45 Caliber Team in 1951. In self-described cosmopolitan San Francisco, he was virtually unknown, an anomaly outside Chinatown.

"Mister Chow?" Chow responded, "at Sharpe Park, we are John and Bob!"

"Well," replied Maletesta, "I've been a teacher for 13 years, but hardly anyone calls me 'professor' outside the school grounds. So, the only thing I can think of is titles for everyone. You know what I mean?"

Chow laughed. "Yes, John, I do. However, I have a licensing appointment downtown and I must leave you in the capable hands of William here. Please excuse me," he added as he walked by Maletesta and smiled. “We still need to go *mano a mano* on the pistol range someday soon.”

“Not likely unless I can blindfold you!” Maletesta snorted.

With a final smile, Bob Chow was gone.

“So, what can I do for you?” William asked as Maletesta approached the glass counter and display case. William was a serious bespectacled balding man in his late forties.

“I need a barker,” Maletesta replied.

“Excuse me?” William asked.

“No,” Maletesta interjected, “excuse me. It’s a term I found in an old English novel, and I thought I’d try it.”

“Ah,” William chortled, “you mean like a heater or a gat?”

“Yes, but not an automatic . . .”

A frown crossed Maletesta’s brow.

“One jammed on me recently, he clarified, “and I might even need something that I can fire in my pocket . . .”

“And ruin a good overcoat,” William completed the sentence. “Well, I’ve got just the revolver you need. It hasn’t been available until very recently.”

William stooped down behind the display case, slid back a glass door and reached over several automatic pistols and long barreled revolvers to retrieve a stubby little revolver in the front. It was nickel plated. He opened the cylinder to show that it was unloaded and then placed it on a thick cloth pad on the counter.

"Smith and Wesson Centennial," he announced. "Five shot, .38 Special, enclosed hammer, nothing to catch up in the clothing."

Maletesta picked the Centennial up from the counter and flipped the cylinder closed. He kept his finger off the trigger, shoved it in his pocket and pulled it out again. He pointed it at the floor and squeezed the trigger.

"Slick," he said and placed the pistol back on the pad. "I saw one like this after the war, but it was lighter, didn't feel as solid . . ."

"That would have been the Safety Hammerless," William interrupted, "they stopped making them about 20 years ago. They were chambered for pipsqueak calibers like the .32."

"Yeah," Maletesta remembered, "that's what Howard said. I was on my way to Borneo."

"Howard Fraley?"

"That's right. At the range. I saw him last week."

"How is the old buzzard?"

"Still firing and giving rookie shooters hell. 'Safety first.'"

"Do you listen to mysteries on the radio?" William asked abruptly.

"Not anymore," Maletesta replied. "You know, William, most of us have televisions now."

"Well, yes, of course," William frowned, "but what happens to your imagination? On television, you get the picture and the story. You just sit there and look; you do not use your imagination."

William shook his head at the enormity of it: the end of imagination.

"Anyway," he returned to the present, "this is what 'Johnny Dollar' the investigator, carries, a lemon squeezer."

"Then I guess I have to take it!" Maletesta laughed. "If it's OK for Johnny Dollar, it's OK for me. How much?"

A short while later when the paper work was complete, Maletesta took an empty cartridge case out of his pants pocket and handed it to William who looked at it quizzically.

"Do you have any idea of what kind of a hand gun fired this?" Maletesta asked.

William put a jeweler's glass in his eye and studied the case, turning it round in his fingers and squinting at the head stamp.

"I don't recognize the head stamp," William admitted, "I'm sure the '1937' is a manufacturer's date, but the other markings are anybody's guess."

"The diameter looks to me about 9 mm," Maletesta added, "but it doesn't feel like a Luger."

"No, the case is different. Hmm. Hold on just a minute."

William disappeared into the back room and after a few minutes returned with a box of empty cartridge cases in one hand and a handful of jacketed bullets in the other. He set the bullets and the box on the counter, pulled out one of the cases and laid it down next to Maletesta's evidence.

"It's definitely longer than the Luger case but the head stamp isn't like any I've seen on an American cartridge," William pronounced. "Let's try a bullet. These are 9 mm Luger."

The bullet fit perfectly into the case found in the alley off Buchanan Street.

"Definitely some kind of 9 mm," he said, "but what kind?"

Maletesta shrugged.

"You tell me."

"A mystery, I'm afraid," William sighed, "like Johnny Dollar."

A half hour later, Maletesta left Bob Chow's shop with the strange cartridge case in his pants pocket and a loaded Centennial in the deep right pocket of his duffle coat.

FORTY TWO

Mission District

Monday, December 21, 1959

After he emerged from the gun shop, Maletesta walked south on Mission Street to try to clear his head. Images of Sinclair and El Pilar danced in his mind, bobbing and weaving. He didn't even know what Yusef looked like, so a faceless young black man joined the scene. *Christ, and the bastards almost got me. And Tal, God damn them! There must be an explanation somewhere. Shit!*

Walking blindly out Mission, his mind wandered through the jungle of facts, tripping over bits of conversations Brennan, Cayenne, the phantom green Buick . . .

"An' they murdered James Connolly, the Irish Rebel!"

The croaky baritone voice rang out from a bar Maletesta was passing. A burst of clapping and hooting followed the end of the song. Maletesta smiled and stopped suddenly, shaking his head. That voice belonged only to one man: Con Buckley, Sister Agatha's rascally uncle. Eager to see the old longshoreman, Maletesta turned into Kavanaugh's bar, a favorite of the Mission District's working class.

Maletesta walked into the dark saloon, squinting from the brightness of day light. As his eyes adjusted, he discerned a group of four or five white-haired men seated at the bar and laughing.

"Is that you, Uncle Con?" he shouted to a broad shouldered man near the door. "I don't know anyone else who sings 'James Connolly' like that."

"Sure an' it's none other," the man answered loudly, "and that looks like my niece's favorite professor, Sean O'Faolain Maletesta." The man cackled at his own joke, swaying a bit on the stool.

Cornelius Buckley was a retired longshoreman who was devoted to his only niece, Sister Agatha of All Saints College. He was a widower for many years who had no children but shared a kindred spirit of non-conformism with the school president.

Maletesta smiled and put his hand out.

"It's been a long time, Uncle Con, how are you?"

Buckley downed the contents of the shot glass in his left hand and took Maletesta's in his right.

"Call Holy Cross!" he shouted.

Buckley's bar stool friends burst into laughter again. Holy Cross was the Catholic cemetery in Colma.

"You must be well," Maletesta said, "because you've been using that line for quite a long time now."

"Ah," Buckley rejoined, "will you have one, Seannie?"

"A little bit too early, thanks."

"It's never too early, see, when you don't have to go to work!"

Maletesta chuckled as he took the stool next to Buckley.

Suddenly, Buckley leaned over toward him in a conspiratorial fashion.

"John," he whispered, "I'm in a wee bit of trouble. I've got to talk to you, quiet like."

"Sure, Uncle Con, how about that table over there?"

"Fine, fine. I'll be back in a minute, lads."

As they sat down at a table by the rest rooms, someone fired up the juke box with the Dick Haymes' standard, "How Are Things in Glocca Mora?"

Buckley waved to the bartender with two fingers up which translated into two bottles of Lucky Lager and two shots of Early Times.

"On your tab is it, Connie?" the bartender asked as he put the drinks on the table.

"Sure'n as God made Sunday," Buckley replied.

The bartender shook his head and returned to the bar.

"OK, Seannie," Buckley said after the bartender left, "here's the trouble, by Christ."

He swallowed the shot of bourbon and slammed the shot glass down on the table. Then he laid a pack of Domino cigarettes on the table and gestured to Maletesta to help himself. Maletesta declined, but tossed back his shot.

"I've been supeenied to appear before the House Un American Activities Committee! Can you believe it?"

"Yes, Sister Agatha told me," Maletesta's voice jumped an octave. "The witch hunters. That's absurd!"

Buckley motioned him to lower his voice.

"Well," Buckley whispered, "I was in the Lincoln Battalion."

"So what," Maletesta said, "that was over twenty years ago!"

"I know, I know. But, you know, Seannie, the truth is, I don't know how to fight these bastards from Washington."

Buckley clasped his arthritic hands together. They were knotty and large from years of manual labor.

"I know how to fight the cops," he said, making a fist with his right hand and holding it up and cocked like a boxer, "like we did on the waterfront back in '34, an' I know how to make a Mauser rifle sing like it did in Spain in '37 . . . by Christ!"

Buckley paused and cleared his throat.

The old Irishman fell silent for one of the few times in his life, sipping his beer and seeming to study the label on the bottle. The men at the bar were laughing their heads off over a joke told by the bartender. Dean Martin followed Dick Haymes on the juke box.

Finally, Maletesta broke the silence.

"Were you in the Party, Uncle Con?"

Buckley sat straight up in his chair.

"Mister professor, that's none of your God-damned business an' nobody else's neither!"

"No, of course not," Maletesta quickly agreed, "but you'll need some kind of defense. These witch hunters are very good at character assassination. They've destroyed the careers of many people whose only fault was being on the left of Mussolini. What are you going to do?"

"I don't know, see, that's the thing! I don't know yet. One thing though: I'm not leavin' this country--I'm a citizen, by Christ--an' I ain't goin' to jail . . . the bastards!"

Maletesta reached over the table and clasped his hand over Buckley's gnarled left hand.

"Uncle Con, listen to me," he said evenly, "whatever you need, you've got it. I know an excellent criminal defense attorney. I don't know exactly how the committee works, but this attorney will be at your service in a phone call's time. There's no need for you to worry. You've done nothing wrong."

"Bastards," Buckley muttered again and looked at his empty glass. "I worked like hell for this country . . . God damn them! Don't they know that?"

Maletesta shook his head.

"Ah, to hell with it," Con decided. "Another one, Seannie?"

"No thanks. I'm in the middle of this problem Tal has with the police, and I've got a lot of work to do."

"Aggie told me about that. Box stuff! That girl wouldn't hurt anyone! Lucky thing, see, she's got you. You're smart, Seannie, I know you'll figger it out. How's that goin'?"

"I have a few more leads to follow," Maletesta answered. "You know, Uncle Con, it's like a detective story, you know, like the mysteries you brought to me when I was in the hospital years ago. Do you remember those books: Sherlock Holmes, Nero Wolfe, Dashielle Hammet? The detective gathers evidence, he interviews people, and then he draws a conclusion from all the facts he's assembled and then he solves the crime."

"Ah, like Joe Friday: 'just the facts, ma'am.'"

"Exactly. The only problem is, I've haven't been very good at it, and I have absolutely no conclusions to draw. I'm not Joe Friday."

Buckley mulled the response over.

"Whaddaya got?" he asked.

"Well," Maletesta answered, "I've got a lot of information and a cartridge case in my pocket that no one can identify."

"From a pistol or a rifle like?"

"A pistol. Bob Chow's guy couldn't make it. I found it near one of the murders."

“Let’s have a look at it, then.”

Maletesta took the shell out of his pocket and handed it to Buckley who laid it on the table and rolled it under his fingers. Then he picked it up and peered at the head stamp.

“Can’t see a damned thing in here,” he stated and got up from the table. “Let’s me an’ you go outside.”

The two men squinted as they stepped outside of the bar into the bright sunlight on Mission Street.

Buckley reached into the pocket of his hickory shirt and pulled out a pair of Woolworth’s reading glasses. He hummed as he held the cartridge case close to his eye glasses.

“Yep,” he said, continuing to hum.

“Yep, what?” Maletesta asked in an irritated voice. “Do you recognize it?”

“’Course I do,” Buckley replied, flipping the case back to Maletesta. “Seen lots of ‘em.”

“Where?” Maletesta asked, catching the case.

“Spain, where else? It’s a Largo, see, the Basques made ‘em up north. Them are Basque markin’s on the head. You see that, that ‘Gobierno de Euzkadi?’ That’s what the Basques call their country, ‘Euzakadi.’ Funny huh, 1937, same time I was over there. Aye, Largo—means long in Spanish, nine millimeter long.”

Buckley stared at his right hand, closing it slightly and seeing something that Maletesta couldn’t see.

"Archie gave me an Aster automatic an' a box o' bullets after Jarama. 'Don't put them bullets in a Luger,' he said. 'They're longer; if you mix 'em up, look out!' Long-nosed ugly thing it was, that Aster, noisy like, Christ, but powerful."

The old man cleared his throat and spat into the gutter.

"Jarama, for Chrissakes! Truth be told, Seannie, I wouldn't be here today if some lads from the IRA didn't take me under their wing! 'Keep yer damn head down, County Frisco,'" they said. "County Frisco, they called me, an' me from Cork! Ah, they were Connolly's men, a little older than the rest, like me. All gone now, God rest 'em."

He gazed blindly up Mission Street, remembering. Maletesta waited.

"Lotta good men died there, Seannie, poor devils, God rest their souls. An' at Belchite, where I lost that Aster. Franco an' his sons of bitches."

Suddenly Buckley began to laugh.

"I'll tell all that to that Johnny Bull committee comin' to the city, the bastards! They want names? Sure'n I'll give 'em names; you want old Con Buckley to name names, you bastards? Here's some names for you: Franco an' Hitler an' Mussolini an' Lindberg an' Henry Ford an' the Kind of England! Sons of bitches!"

"Uncle Con, you are a marvel!" Maletesta grinned and hugged the old man with his right arm.

"Now, now, don't you be gettin' carried away; you eye-talians do a lot more huggin' than I'm comfortable with. Must be all that hot weather down there, see. Fires up the blood."

"Thank you, Uncle Con," Maletesta said, "this is incredible! And you let me know what you want to do about the committee. The best attorney is only a phone call away, and I mean it."

"*Salud*," the old longshoreman replied headed back into Kavanaugh's. He stopped at the open door and, to the delight of his cronies inside, sang loudly again.

"Oh I left Bandon for Port Costa landin'

To work for Scanlon for a pound a day.

Goodbye to Scanlon and Port Costa landin'

I'm back to Balvourney for to stay."

Maletesta smiled at the old man retreating back into the bar and then jumped on the first inbound bus on Mission.

FORTY THREE

Cow Hollow

Monday, December 21, 1959

"Now, what the hell do you want?" Brennan growled as he grabbed the ringing telephone "It's past time for normal people to be home."

Brennan was angry as usual; he had gotten nowhere in his investigations of the sensational murders which had occurred during the past week and a half, and the chief had called him three times that day because the mayor had called the chief twice.

"You're telling me that you're normal, Mike?" Maletesta said lightly.

"I do have *two* arms, professor."

Maletesta stiffened.

"Yes. There are some benefits to being stateside in uniform . . ."

"It's not my fault that the war ended before they shipped me out!"

There was a silence on the phone, each of them waiting. Finally, Maletesta broke it.

"Did your forensics people find anything in the green Buick?"

"Maybe. Why? This is police business, professor."

Another silence.

"OK, Inspector," Maletesta slowly pronounced, "let's lay our cards on the table. I'm trying to clear my daughter and help a friend at the same time. You've got your boss on your back, because he's got the mayor on his back because the mayor's got the newspapers, radio and TV on *his* back. OK, so far?"

"Yeah, so what?"

"OK, so, money on the table, Inspector. We trade information and maybe we both get what we need. *Capisch?*"

"What do you got?"

"Oh no, Inspector Brennan, SFPD, that's not how it works."

Maletesta paused, listening to Brennan snapping that damned gum.

"There's nobody on *my* back," Maletesta said, clearing his throat, "and I *know* that you don't really have anything on my daughter. I also know that you can make life miserable for her."

Maletesta stopped and waited for the words to sink in. Then he continued.

"So I'm willing to *trade* some information about your so-called crime wave. But if you want to play cop hard ball, we can hang up right now."

Silence.

"Goodbye, Inspector Brennan," Maletesta said, lowering the phone.

"Wait!" Brennan yelled. "John, wait!"

"Yeah?"

"All right, John, you win. I'm being hammered and nothing I find makes any sense." Maletesta was sitting at the desk in the study with the extension telephone in the shoulder clamp. He looked at the items listed on the pad in front of him and picked up his pen.

"So," Maletesta began, "first, you found a cartridge case in the car. Did you find a bullet?"

Brennan hesitated.

"Uh, yeah, we did. How did you know that, John?"

"It's logical when you think about it, Mike," Maletesta explained. "If an empty shell was found in the car, then there's a good chance the gun went off inside the car. If it was fired out the window, you wouldn't have the case, right?"

"Well . . . I guess so, yeah."

"So, where did your guys find the bullet?"

"In the dashboard."

"What caliber?

"The lab guys say it's a 9 mm, but we didn't find a gun in the car. The stiff had an empty shoulder holster, but anything coulda been in the holster. By the way, we've IDed him: Robert Kalinowski from Gary, Indiana, of all places with a rap sheet longer than the toilet roll in your bathroom. Arrested last month for assault in LA, out on bail. Maybe the bullet in the dash matches the case we found, but I don't have a written report on it yet."

"OK. Here's what you should do. Tell your forensics people to compare that slug with the 9 mm bullets they took out of the body of Yusef X."

"Yusef X? The guy killed in the Fillmore? C'mon."

"Yes, the guy killed in the Fillmore."

"You know how those people behave in the Fillmore, John. There always shooting or cutting each other. That don't have nothing to do with hoods who steal cars in Pacific Palisades."

"Mike, *you're* the one who told me Yusef was killed by a *9mm* pistol. Are you going to compare the bullets or not?"

"All right, all right, if you say so," Brennan conceded, "but what would those two guys from LA be doing in the Fillmore? Buying bar-be-que?"

Maletesta wasn't listening. He checked off an item on the pad.

"Next," he continued, "did your boys find anything under the Buick's front bumper or the fenders?"

"You know, John, this 'Twenty Questions' thing is starting to piss me off," Brennan said. "If I think you know something, I can still have you hauled in for withholding evidence."

Brennan set his shoulders back in his chair and began tapping his foot under the desk. Maletesta's patience ran out.

"OK, Mike, hang up and we're done. I have no problem with that. It will be harder for me, but I'll find another way to get the information I need."

Brennan grimaced and tossed his ball point pen at the radiator which pinged when it landed. There was no one else in the office to witness this unusual show of frustration. He spoke quickly into the phone.

"No, no. Don't get temperamental on me, John. I'm stuck: it's your show."

"Good. So, what did they find?"

"Evidence that the car hit somebody. We don't know who yet."

Brennan stopped to open a new package of Black Jack. He pulled off the wrappers on two pieces and stuck the gum in his mouth. He dropped the wrappers on the top of his desk and tossed the package on a nearby desk. He was so angry he didn't even try a waste basket shot.

"I suppose *you* have an idea about that too, right, professor?" Brennan had difficulty controlling his voice.

"Maybe,' Maletesta answered. "I think you should see if anything they found matches anything on that man who was run over in North Beach last Thursday. Remember, the witness said it was a green Buick."

"There you go again with the green Buick! Jesus, there's more than one of them, you know, professor. You got a fixation or something?"

"Just check it out, please. The victim's name was El Pilar."

"El Pilar? What a lulu! Next thing you'll be telling me is to check out Laughing Sal at Playland, right?"

Maletesta did not rise to the bait. He waited.

"All right, John, I'll do that," Brennan finally agreed. "Now, what have you got for me in this trade?"

"Mike, I just gave you damn near everything I know. The whole thing is still very confusing to me. You might check to see if anyone else was shot with a 9mm recently. These guys seem to be all over the place. I have a few more details to work out, but I do need the information about the deaths of Yusef and El Pilar. Will you have the answers by tomorrow afternoon? Let's talk then. I might have more, but I don't know for sure."

"What about Toolah's poet?" Brennan asked. "Don't you have anything on him? She's not out of the woods yet, you know. It's still an open murder case. And, how do you know the hit-run stiff was named El Pilar?"

"It's time for you to go home, Brennan. Call me tomorrow afternoon."

FORTY FOUR

Steiner Street

Tuesday, December 22, 1959

"Uncle Con subpoenaed by HUAC? That's a bad joke, Dad."

"It's not a joke."

Tal sat crossways on one side of their kitchen booth, leaning back against the wall and staring at the nativity scene on religious calendar hanging on the opposite wall. Neither she nor her father felt like clearing the table awash with the remains of Tal's poached eggs and English muffins with marmalade breakfast. Maletesta laid his burning cigarette on his plate and sighed. It was a breach of his smoking etiquette, but Tal didn't say anything. She knew her father was tired and frustrated over all the developments about the murders.

The clock in the living room chimed eight times.

"I still can hardly believe it," Maletesta sighed. "Uncle Con's an old man. The Lincoln Brigade vets were blacklisted all over when they came back from Spain, but Con got his job back on the docks."

He stubbed out his cigarette on the plate.

"That's what I've always liked about the guys on the waterfront. They kowtow to nobody. I like that old *baciami il culo* attitude."

"What if he doesn't go?" Tal asked.

"We were just talking about the Hollywood Ten the other day, remember? Uncle Con doesn't have a lot of choices. The Committee can hold him in contempt or something like that. I remembered that Dashiell Hammet refused to name names and spent six months in prison. Can you imagine that, Tal? Hammet, the man who wrote the *Maltese Falcon* and *The Thin Man*, in prison for not ratting on his friends! And what would he have ratted about: that a long time ago he knew a writer who went to a meeting and expressed a political opinion? I still can't believe it."

Maletesta ran his hand through his hair several times. Tal began picking up the plates.

"Arthur Miller dissected the whole ugly process very convincingly in *The Crucible*," Maletesta added. "So, how's the paper coming?"

"It's coming; it's coming. I went down to the Periodical Room at main library yesterday to research more recent information on political machines like Tammany Hall. It's absolutely amazing all the material they have: newspapers, magazines, newsletters, you name it. I even got into the 1906 earthquake, Dad. The old photographs in the newspapers are really cool! Full front page spreads, headline two inches tall! I guess that's what they did when they didn't have TV or even radio. Pretty cool!"

"Did you find anything helpful to your thesis?"

Tal frowned.

"Well, to be honest, not really. I got distracted. I was flipping through old *Time* magazines and guess what I found?"

"Surprise me."

"OK, an article on Edward Dmytryk, the director of the new 'Blue Angel.'"

"Ha! So, back to the black list! What happened to him?" Maletesta asked, raising his eyebrows.

"It's very interesting," Tal answered. "When he was subpoenaed by the Committee in 1947, he refused to say anything about his political activities or his membership in the Communist Party, so he was blacklisted and moved to England. By the way, did you know that the Communist Party was legal until a law was passed in 1940 making it illegal?"

"No. Anything else?"

"Dmytryk eventually came back to the US, recanted his testimony and 'named names.'"

"He did?" Maletesta exclaimed. "What happened?"

"He got his job back as a director. No more black list."

'Really!"

Tal placed the plug in the sink drain and began running hot water over the plates and silverware.

"So," she said, "that's how it works, I guess. You sell your soul and you get rewarded. Hammet goes to jail; Dmytryk gets a new movie."

"Well," Maletesta said, "it also explains why the new 'Blue Angel' has a happy ending: everything nice and tidy, just like 'Leave It to Beaver.'"

"Gollee, Wally," Tal smirked.

Maletesta stood up and stretched.

"By way, Tal, I have two appointments today. I'll be back in the early afternoon . . . and I hope you'll have a draft of your report for me to read. Oh, and I need you to wrap this book before I go. Thanks."

Maletesta retrieved an old book from a bag on the bench and handed to her. She looked at the cover and then opened it to the title page.

"Wow, Dad," she exclaimed. "*Poems of Emily Dickinson,* published in 1896! Let me guess: for Sister Agatha?"

"Yes."

"Cool. Is that who you're seeing today?"

"Sister Agatha and Uncle Carlo."

She turned off the water and faced him.

"Be careful, Dad."

"I will. Sister Agatha has a quick left hook."

"You know what I mean, Dad."

"Don't worry. If you're thinking about Uncle Carlo, he's past his prime. He just doesn't know it."

"Do you still think he . . ."

"Until I learn something different, yes."

"Please be careful, Dad. Promise me," Tal pleaded.

"Don't worry, honey. Stay with our new drill: don't answer the door or the phone. If I call, I'll let it ring twice, hang up and then call again."

"OK."

Her father stopped at the door.

"I also need to pick up a few more things for Christmas, so I won't be back until around three o'clock. When you're finished here, start typing."

"You sure know how to spoil a morning."

"Start typing."

FORTY FIVE

All Saints College, Burlingame

Tuesday, December 22, 1959

Sister Agatha squinted at the two wall calendars laid side by side on the top of the desk in her office. On the left was a well-thumbed and scribbled-on 1959 issue. On the right lay its crisp and pristine 1960 counterpart. She was transferring important dates from the old to the new with a fountain pen. Periodically, she dipped the pen into a bottle and refilled it by manipulating a small lever on the side of the pen. There was a soft knock at the door, and she looked up, placing her pen on the desk next to the blotter and removing her rimless spectacles.

"Yes?" she asked.

A young nun opened the door.

"Professor Maletesta to see you, Sister."

Sister Agatha smiled and stood up.

"Please show him in, Sister. Thank you."

The young nun exited as Maletesta stepped into the room.

"What an unexpected pleasure!" Sister Agatha exclaimed, "Good morning, John."

She offered him her hand.

"Good morning, Sister," Maletesta replied, taking her hand. "I have a delivery."

"Wonderful, and I have information for you. My cousin called just ten minutes ago. Please sit down."

Sister Agatha returned to the chair behind her desk.

"Really?" Maletesta responded, taking the old side chair on the other side of the desk, "that's terrific!"

"First, I must say that you are looking quite dapper, professor Maletesta, in that new tweed jacket, leather elbow patches and buttons! I do believe that Mister Chips has come to All Saints."

"It's an early Christmas present from my mother, who loves Ronald Coleman and thinks that all teachers should look like him. Actually, she'd love it if I grew a tooth brush mustache like his! I don't have the heart to tell her I'd look like a fruit peddler without a monkey!"

"Oh, you would not," Sister Agatha replied, unable to squelch a laugh at the image.

"Do they still make organ grinders?"

"Stop it, John, I have another concern. Your jacket hangs lower on the right side because there's a bulge in the right pocket. The bulge is questionable. It looks more lethal than something you would be delivering to me."

"Uh, well, here's what I'm delivering."

Maletesta reached into his inside jacket pocket and laid a small Christmas paper-wrapped package on her desk.

"Merry Christmas, but no opening until at least Christmas Eve," he said.

"Thank you, John, and the explanation for the heavy pocket?"

"It's a new Life Insurance policy from the Robert Chow Company on Mission," he answered lightly, pulling out a pack of Fatimas. "You know, they say that you can never have too much insurance these days. Accidents happen. By the way, I thoroughly enjoyed Denise Levertov."

While he was lighting his cigarette, Sister Agatha opened a drawer, brought out the old Alcatraz ashtray and placed it on the corner of her desk. She picked up the gift wrapped package and shifted it in her hands.

Maletesta was impatient.

"What did your cousin say?"

"Lord sake, I almost forgot."

Sister Agatha placed the package back on the desk and flipped open a small spiral notebook. After a minute of thumbing pages, she found the one she wanted and read:

"Golden Gate Investments is owned by a man named Ambrose, Robert Ambrose. In the past year, Golden Gate Investments brought two houses and a beauty salon on Hayes Street. The two houses are on one side of a large apartment building and the salon is on the other side. Together the four properties take up most of that block. Let me know if your friend wants to know who owned the properties that Golden Gate Investments bought."

Sister Agatha tore the page out of the book and handed it to Maletesta.

Maletesta scanned her notes.

"Oh," Sister Agatha blurted, looking at her note book, "there's more on the next page: Dennis said that this block of Hayes is possibly in the redevelopment area."

"The redevelopment area," Maletesta repeated, frowning as he looked at the second page.

"Is Dennis' information helpful, John?"

"Sister, I thank you and your cousin from the bottom of my heart, but I'm not sure what it all means: yet."

He stuffed the notes into the inside pocket of his jacket.

"Can you please ask Dennis for the names of the owners of the property Ambrose bought and the names of the owners of the apartment building? If you find anything, can you call me tonight?"

"Certainly. What is the situation with Tal? Is she in the clear yet?"

"I think I see a light at the end of the tunnel."

Sister Agatha watched him as he headed for the door.

"Let's hope it's not a locomotive," she warned.

FORTY SIX

North Beach, San Francisco

Tuesday, December 22, 1959

The crowd at the North Star Café was thinning when Maletesta pushed through the swinging doors. Lunch hour was over for the blue collar clientele and some of their white collar counterpart were finishing up small desserts and selected liqueurs. Maletesta had eaten at the North Star many times since grammar school. It was always a special occasion when he ate lunch there with his father, Joe, who was a regular. Old men smiled at him and patted him on the head. By the time he was in college, many of those men were gone, but his father still commanded respect and the owners deferred to him when he came in for lunch with his son. Years had passed, but the culture of the North Star had not changed.

The tables were set up for family style meals with four or more. A typical table might have an iron worker, an electrician, a judge, and a loan officer from the bank, each of them waiting for a meal that changed daily. The fare was classic Italian: servings of minestrone, salad, and pasta followed by an entrée like veal cutlets, chicken cacciatore or pigs' feet. Maletesta grimaced, remembering how much his father loved pigs' feet.

The egalitarian seating policy was laid down by the Lagamarsino family, who owned the place for over twenty years. No one objected to the haphazard combination of shirt sleeves and suit coats.

Today, three days before Christmas, the windows of the North Star were draped with ancient strings of mottled tinsel accompanied by odd sized figurines of old Santas, members of the Magi, elves, angels, shepherds and miniature reindeer. Maletesta spotted his uncle at a table back next to the wall under a window with vividly sprayed pine cones on the sill. It was not in the restaurant's usual operation that Carlo Manzone could have his own table for two.

Maletesta wondered about this set up as he navigated through the tables and the customers. He looked over at the owner, Ernie Lagamarsino, at the bar and laughed. Ernie was wearing a WWII gas mask topped with a Santa Claus hat. Maletesta gave Ernie a wave of dismissal and Ernie responded with a one finger salute.

Eventually, Maletesta arrived at his uncle's table. Carlo had a glass tumbler of red wine and a simple plate of lettuce, tomatoes and peppers in front of him. A set of oil and vinegar bottles stood ready next to the wall.

"So, *Gianni*, what will you have?" Carlo asked cheerfully as he pushed his fork into the salad.

"When did you start coming here?" Maletesta asked

"Hardly ever: too many working stiffs like your father hang out in this place. And I don't care if he sits with judges. Judges are for sale like everyone else."

Maletesta pulled out a chair and sat down.

"Give me one reason why I shouldn't beat the crap out of you right now, *traditore*."

Carlo stopped mid meal and slowly laid his fork back on the plate. He sat back in his chair and placed his hands on his thighs.

"What do you mean, *Gianni*?" his eyes now half closed. "Speak carefully, *Gianni*, I wouldn't throw the *traditore* word around too easy."

Maletesta leaned across the table and looked directly into Carlo's eyes.

"You know exactly what I mean, Carlo, *zio mio,"* Maletesta said. As he spoke, he picked up the bottle of vinegar and began sprinkling it on Manzone's salad. "You gave me two tickets to Winterland for Saturday night. Someone tried to kill me outside Winterland. And they might have hit Tal too." He took a breath and shook more vinegar onto the salad. "You are the only one who knew we'd be there. *Capisci, figlio di puttana?*"

The blood drained from Manzone's face and lines of perspiration rolled down his forehead as his hands gripped his thighs tighter and tighter. The muscles in his jaw vibrated as he chewed hard on nothing. He took several deep breaths.

"Jesus Christ, *Gianni*! On my mother's heartbeat, I swear I would never do you any harm! Who the hell do you think I am? And who the hell are you to talk to your own uncle like this? In the old country you wouldn't . . ."

Maletesta was silent.

"*Gianni*, would I murder my own flesh and blood?" Manzone repeated.

Manzone's face flushed with color. His hands became fists, coiling and uncoiling on his thighs under the table. Two watchful waiters sauntered over toward the table.

Maletesta slowly replaced the vinegar bottle back next to the olive oil.

"All right, *zio*, if that's the truth, then who tried to kill me?"

"Look what you did to my salad, *stupido*! Come in here, making accusations, calling me a traitor . . ."

"I'll buy you another salad," Maletesta said, turning in his chair. "Hey Ernie, another salad over here, please, for the rabbit." He picked up Manzone's plate and set it on the empty table next to them. "There, you happy now, *zio*? So, I'll ask again, *who tried to kill me?* It was not an accident; it was a professional hit: Tal saw a guy watching us in the lobby. The same guy who was the shooter. . . ."

"I was in Tahoe."

"Yeah, so what? Don't give me that 'I was in Tahoe' bullshit, Carlo," Maletesta sneered. "Who knew I would be at Winterland, huh? Who told some hood from a green Buick to watch for me in the lobby, huh? I want some answers, Carlo, and I want them now. *These bastards could have hit Tal!* Do you hear me? They could have hit my daughter! If I'm supposed to believe that you weren't part of it, then you'd better come up with a better answer than "I was in Tahoe!'"

Maletesta leaned so far forward that he was less than a foot from his uncle's face.

"I'll give you twenty four hours, *zio*, to prove you weren't part of it. And if I don't get anything, I'm coming after you, blood or no blood."

A wide-eyed waiter arrived with another salad and placed it in front of Manzone.

"*Mangia*," Maletesta said, pushing the plate toward Manzone.

"Don't you threaten me, *Gianni*," Manzone spat back at him. "You don't give Carlo Manzone any hours for anything, you punk! You get that? Who the hell do you think you are, huh, who the hell do you think you are?"

Customers at nearby tables glanced in the direction of the raised voices, recognized a noisy dispute in a typical Italian family and went back to their meals.

Maletesta said nothing.

"You be careful, *Gianni*! I told you, I don't know nothin' about it!"

Maletesta stood up.

"One more thing, *zio*. Who's 'the angel?'"

"What?"

"You *owe* me, *zio*. One more time: who's 'the angel'? He's supposed to be a bookmaker in North Beach. Who is he? You know: a-n-g-e-l, angel, like on top of the Christmas tree?"

"Why?"

"Because you fucking owe me, period."

Manzone scowled and glared at the moldy Santas on the window shelf.

"I'm still here, *zio*."

"D'Angelo," Manzone finally muttered, "the angel. Somebody popped him a couple of weeks ago outside St Peter and Paul's," Carlo pointed his index finger like a pistol. "Nobody knows why. Outside hit."

Maletesta waited.

"They say he was coming out of confession. He goes right to heaven, eh?" Manzone snickered and turned his cold eyes on Maletesta.

"That's all you get, *Gianni*."

"Not quite, *zio*. *You* still got twenty four hours," Maletesta snapped and stormed out of the North Star, knocking a few chairs awry as he crossed the dining room.

FORTY SEVEN

Steiner Street

Wednesday, December 23, 1959

Tal was wrapping Christmas presents on the dining room table when her father looked into the room. He had overslept and was still in his pajamas and bathrobe.

"Good morning, Dad!" Tal chirped as she curled ribbons around a package with an old butter knife.

Maletesta frowned, rubbing his neck.

"I guess so," he mumbled and started for the kitchen.

"Did you sleep well?" she asked after the retreating figure.

Before Maletesta answered, the door ball rang, reverberating through the flat. It rang again. Tal started toward the door. Maletesta raised his palm toward her.

"Hold it, honey. Stay back there," Maletesta said quietly.

Tal halted where she was. Maletesta pulled the nickel-plated Smith and Wesson Centennial out of his bathrobe pocket and walked slowly to the front door, holding the revolver by his side. He looked through the keyhole and saw no one on the porch. He waited for a moment and looked again. *Nothing.*

"Tal, come over here a minute and stay by the other side of the door jamb."

Tal tiptoed over to the door as directed, and her father positioned himself on the opposite side.

"Reach over here and grab the knob," Maletesta whispered, and Tal slid silently half way across the door to grasp the knob.

"When I say 'now,' pull it open fast, but stay behind it."

She nodded as Maletesta brought the pistol up to his waist.

"Now!"

Tal jerked the door open.

Maletesta darted half way out the door, quickly pointing the snub-nosed revolver first to the left and then to the right. There was no one on the porch or on the stairs. He glanced down at the sidewalk and saw two of his elderly neighbors coming up the street with their elderly dog. None of them took any notice of him as he clumsily shoved the Centennial into to his bathrobe pocket and jumped back inside the doorway. As he did, he noticed a white envelope sticking out from under the door mat. He picked it up quickly, and Tal closed the door behind him.

Back in the dining room, Maletesta held the envelope down on the table as Tal nervously ran a letter opener under its seam. He extracted the single white page inside, unfolded it and spread it on the table. The message was barely legible, apparently typed on an ancient typewriter long in need of a new ribbon.

"Someone had a big mouth on the hand ball court. Somebody else had big nosy ears on the very same court. Tomorrow those ears won't hear nothing, no more."

They both scanned the note and Maletesta read it aloud. Neither of them said anything. They stood at the dining room table, digesting the meaning of the message in the letter which could be from no one other than Uncle Carlo. The clock chimed the half hour. Tal shuddered. Her father picked up the letter, crumpled it, walked into the study and tossed it into a wastebasket. When he returned to the dining room, Tal still stood silently in front of the table.

"It can't be from Uncle Carlo," Tal whispered. "Can it?"

"God!" Maletesta suddenly exclaimed, "what a melodramatic family! If this is from Carlo, he's been watching too many gangster movies. All this tough guy talk, Jesus! What's that expression: life imitates art? Or is it art imitates life?"

Tal stared at him with glistening eyes.

"Hey," Maletesta said, "aren't you and your friends going for a bike ride today?"

"Yeah, I'm riding to Sausalito with Ray and Antoinette. Don't worry about lunch, Dad; we'll get something over there."

"Ray from the movies?"

"Yeah, Ray from the movies. He's cool. He thought the Blue Angel was corny too, 'like Walt Disney,' he said."

"Hmmm, bright guy," Maletesta mused. "Where does he go to school?"

"He doesn't," Tal replied. "He graduated from Galileo High last year. He lives in North Beach."

"Oh no, a young beatnik," Maletesta raised his eyebrows as in shocked.

"No, Dad, he's actually taken the exam for the Fire Department but will probably go in the service first. Is that enough information for Professor Ann Landers?"

"OK, OK. Well, you still need a lot of energy for riding a bike that far, to Sausalito for crying out loud! Tal, you know that you need to hold up the reputation of the Maletesta Family, you know, *la famiglia* Maletesta!"

Tal cocked her head and squinted at him.

"I haven't heard of the famous bike-riding *la famiglia* Maletesta, Dad. Where are you going with this?"

"You need a solid breakfast, Tal, my daughter, for such a ride! Let's you and me hustle over to California Street and get one of those hearty breakfasts at Miz Brown's. And—you know--it's almost Christmas, and we need to get into the swing of things. I haven't even finished my shopping. Hang on while I get dressed."

She forced a smile at him, understanding what he was doing.

"I'll be ready in a jiff, honey," he continued, heading down the hall.

The jiff turned out to be about twenty minutes as usual. Over the years, he had perfected the use of a button loop to button his shirts, a sock darning ball to help pull his socks on, and a long shoe horn for his shoes, but switching to an electric razor brought the real breakthrough: no more difficult lathering, no more clumsy blade changes, no more missed patches of beard, and no more nicks and cuts.

Maletesta pulled on a bulky sweater that morning and slipped the Smith and Wesson Centennial into his waist band before he met Tal at the door.

"Miz Brown's, here we come!" he announced as he took the front stairs two at a time.

FORTY EIGHT

Steiner Street

Wednesday, December 23, 1959

"This is like a Sherlock Holmes story," Tal sputtered, waving her arms and coughing at the smoke. "Aren't you taking this a little too far, Dad, filling the room with smoke? I mean, holy cow, you should have one of those long-stemmed pipes and a fancy smoking jacket or whatever they call those things. Where's Doctor Watson?"

Maletesta continued pacing around the living room. He stubbed a half-smoked cigarette in the standing ashtray next to the bookcase and lit another one. Tal squeezed her eyes shut.

"That's very funny, Tal. You can be Watson is you like, but I'm missing something, aside from the fact that Brennan didn't call this afternoon. Remember, he said he'd call . . ."

"Well, I think you told him to call . . . "

"Ehhhh . . ."

"Did you eat anything since I left this morning?"

"No."

Dad, it's almost six."

"I'm not hungry. If *you're* hungry, we can call the Flying Chicken. I'm not cooking tonight."

"I had a BLT in Sausalito."

After Tal left to go biking with her friends that morning, Maletesta corrected term papers in the study for several hours. Around two o'clock, a crew from Goodwill cleared out the garage below the flat. The garage was filled with old furniture left behind by people long gone from the building, covered with sheets that were growing mold. Some of the chairs and dressers were valuable, but Maletesta wanted the space available for a four o'clock delivery, so if there was any money to be made on the furniture, he hoped the charitable organization would make the best of it. The delivery at four o'clock was on time, and he locked the garage after it. Then he went up to the flat to review the whole crazy situation that was laid at his feet.

He stopped pacing and looked directly at his daughter.

"Something doesn't add up, but I can't put my finger on it. Something somebody said not that long ago."

"About the beat poets?"

"No. It's something I heard."

"At the barber shop?"

"No. I've got to re-trace my steps over the past couple of weeks," he said, stopping by the arm chair.

Tal dramatically coughed again and sat on the couch, folding her legs under her.

"I don't know," she said, "it seems like you were in a lot of places, that pool hall, North Beach, the school, Aquatic Park, grandpa and grandma's, the Sharpe Park range . . ."

"That's it!" Maletesta exclaimed, "Sharpe Park! Tal, I love you, in case you didn't know!"

"I know," Tal replied blandly. As her father rushed to the telephone in the hall, she rushed to open the windows and empty the ash trays.

Maletesta dialed a number and held the phone tight against his head. He counted five rings on the other end of the phone before someone picked it up.

"Hello?" a slightly cautious voice answered.

"Howard? It's John Maletesta, are you in the middle of dinner?"

"Hell no, John. I thought you was this windows replacement company that keeps callin' me. Nothin' wrong with my windows, the just need a little paint, not something made of 'luminum!" he snorted. "Anyway, me and the missus don't eat til seven. How the hell are yuh?"

"I'm fine, Howard, but I don't have a lot of time. Do you remember that conversation we had the last time I was down at the range?"

"Uh, jeez, John, which one?"

"About those two kids with the Civil War rifle."

"Oh, yeah, the Stromeyer boys. Yeah, what about 'em?"

"I need to know what happened to their father. Didn't you tell me that the newspaper said he "jumped or fell" out of a hotel window in Los Angeles?"

"Well, yeah. As I recall, he went down to LA for his business. Next thing you know, he fell out the window of a big hotel." Howard paused. "John, it was a damn shame. He was an OK fella, to my way of thinkin'. Not much into shootin' or huntin' but wanted his boys to learn it. He was a vet like you."

Howard cleared his throat. Maletesta waited.

"Yeah, real damn shame, that was," Howard continued, "and that's what the papers said, damn their eyes, that it coulda been a suicide."

"You didn't think so?"

"Nah, too much goin' for him. Loved his kids. Fella like that don't jump out a window. Great Caesar's ghost, he was with the 101st Airborne in the Bulge! Jump out a window? Nah."

"OK, Howard, thanks. I'll be down there next month. I hope you and Mrs. Fraley have a Merry Christmas!"

"And you, John, and your young 'un!"

"Oh," Maletesta said, "one more thing. What kind of business was Stromeyer in?"

"He had an iron works, somewhere down on Bay Street."

"Bay Street? Thanks." Maletesta made a note of the pad.

Maletesta walked slowly back into the living room and sat in his over-stuffed chair with the floral pattern. Tal looked up from her book.

"Did you find out anything?"

"Yes," he said tentatively. "I think so. I'd like to run some ideas by you."

Tal put the book down on one of the sofa cushions.

"That was Howard Fraley," Maletesta began. "The last time down the range, Howard introduced me to two teenagers whose father died in LA last summer. Thing is, he fell out of a hotel window, or should we posit "pushed out?" It's very similar to Jean Paul's murder, and we now know that a Buick stolen in Los Angeles was involved in El Pilar's murder and that someone inside it tried to shoot at us. Is that too tenuous a connection?"

"No, I don't think so, but what in the heck does it mean?"

"I don't know . . . yet. I'll be in the study for a while with my yellow pads. Can you get back to your paper tonight?"

"Almost finished."

The conversation over, Maletesta went back into the study and sat down at the old desk. He switched on the goose neck lamp, lit a cigarette and placed it in the ashtray. As the smoke arose into the light, he picked up his pen and began flipping through the pages of the pad, making a note here, scratching out something there. Every once in a while, he tore out a page and left it on the top of the desk. At 10 o'clock, Tal peeked in the doorway and saw him asleep in the leather chair next to the desk. She turned out the light and continued down the hall to bedroom.

The ringing sounded far way. Church bells? No, Maletesta's brain told him, the ringing is insistent and church bells are merely time keepers. They inform your duty. *If you blow it, it's your afterlife. No, Gianni, the ringing is the telephone and it won't stop until you answer it.*

Maletesta's eyes blinked open at the clock on the night stand: twenty five minutes after twelve. *What the hell?* He jumped out of the chair and stumbled toward the telephone in the hall.

"Hello?" Maletesta said into the phone.

"Maletesta?"

"Yes."

"Osceola King."

"Ah, mister King. It must be very important to call at this time of the night."

"It is. I have something for you, hot off the press as the newspapers say."

"OK."

"The last time we met, I told you that the people making the inquiries about the leases and the deeds over here in the Fillmore are from a company called 'Golden Gate Investments.'

"That's right. I haven't been able to get in touch with anyone from the number you gave me. Apparently, they don't answer the phone."

"Golden Gate Investments is a front for a man named Ambrose."

"OK, Cool Breeze," Maletesta interrupted, "thanks, but I already found that out."

"You're one smart professor, Mister Maletesta! So you already know that Golden Gate Investments is owned by Ambrose. Do you know what else he owns?"

Maletesta hesitated.

"Uh, no."

"A major share in a company called 'Pacific Iron Works.' My sources tell me he's married to the sister of the owner who recently passed away."

Maletesta stepped back and almost dropped the phone. Then he collected himself and asked the question.

"Is that Pacific Iron Works on Bay Street?" he asked carefully.

"That's right, 227 Bay."

"Thank you, Cool Breeze! Thank you, Mister King!" Maletesta blurted into the phone. "This is incredible. This is amazing. Great work! Where shall I send the check?"

"Oh no, no, no, John," King laughed. "This is a cash operation. Where can you meet me or where can I pick it up?"

"Well, let's see. I'll be home tomorrow morning. Can you come by here?"

"You got it, man, and I'll have some bonus information coming in by the time I arrive. Knock you out. I'll be there at ten o'clock tomorrow."

"You know where I live?"

"Of course I do--that's my business."

FORTY NINE

Steiner Street, San Francisco

Thursday, December 24, 1959

The doorbell rang while Maletesta was sorting Christmas cards on the table in the living room. Tal wanted to display them on a string across the mantel of the fireplace; he wanted to stash them in a wicker basket on the floor next to the tree. The morning newspaper was scattered around the table along with wrapping paper, labels and scotch tape. Tal was in the shower.

Maletesta sauntered over to the door with a scowl on his face. It was way too early for Osceola King. He looked through the peep hole and saw Inspector Michael Brennan. He did not open the door.

The bell rang again. And again.

"What the hell do you want?" Maletesta yelled through the heavy door. "Do you have a warrant?"

"No, I don't have warrant. So what? We need to talk!" Brennan yelled back.

Maletesta opened the door slightly with his right foot rooted to the bottom of the door.

"You were supposed to call me yesterday. Did you forget our deal? What do you want to talk about now?" he asked.

"Bullets and Buicks," Brennan answered.

"What about my daughter, Talah?"

"She's off the hook. We got new information."

"On the level, Brennan?"

"Yeah."

"Just a minute," Maletesta said, closing the door. He turned to Tal who was standing behind him, dripping wet in a robe and frowning.

"Dad, I don't want to see that man again. I'm going into my room until he leaves."

"OK, honey. He won't be here very long."

Maletesta opened the door and Brennan pushed himself into the hallway. Maletesta took note of the haggard look on Brennan's unshaven face and the wrinkled condition of his suit. *Looks like he slept in his suit.* He directed him to the living room where Brennan slumped down on the sofa.

"What do you mean, 'off the hook'?" Maletesta asked as he positioned himself in the armchair.

Brennan waved a hand of dismissal.

"We got found a neighbor of Sinclair's who is both a night owl and a busybody, huh? She looks out the window every time she hears a squeak: you know the type? She heard something the night he went off the roof and looked out the window. What do you think she saw? Two guys running from Sinclair's entry way and jumping into a car. She thinks it was a dark Buick, probably green, a God-damned *green* Buick! Probably the same one you wanted for Saint Patrick's Day."

Brennan yawned and sank further down into the sofa, his eyelids closing.

Maletesta picked up a pack of cigarettes on the end table next to his chair and shook one out. Slowly and deliberately he lit it with the Zippo and loudly snapped the lighter shut. Brennan flinched and opened his eyes.

"What?"

"Why don't you stop playing these chicken-shit little games, Mike? First, when did you find out about the nosy neighbor? Yesterday?"

"Uh . . ."

"Last week? Last week, right?"

"Uh, yeah."

"Last week!"

Brennan stuck his chin out.

"So what?"

"Last week. Last week! And now you want *me* to help *you*?"

Brennan twisted around on the sofa and tried to straighten up his rumpled coat.

"You don't get it, John. I got people on my back. I need to . . ."

"Bullshit, Mike, and you know it."

Maletesta stood up and walked over to the grandfather's clock near the fire place. He watched the pendulum swing from one side to the other. An image floated into his memory of the second hand of his watch ticking as his severed arm lay on the ground twenty five years ago. He shivered and shook his head to dislodge the memory. He turned back to Brennan.

"What did you find out about the bullets?"

"They match," Brennan mumbled.

"What's that? A little louder, please."

"They match!"

"“They match.' Is that what you said?"

"Yeah."

"So the bullet in the dashboard matches the bullets taken out of Yusef X? Right?"

"Yeah."

Maletesta stubbed out his cigarette in the standing ashtray near the grandfather's clock and pulled open the curtains on the windows that looked out onto Steiner. It was another clear day in this year of the drought.

"Did you find anything more about the stuff on the bumper of the car?" he asked, continuing to look out the window.

"Another match."

"Explain that, please."

Brennan hauled himself out of the sofa and stomped over to where Maletesta was standing by the window. He was taller than Maletesta and tried to do his towering act, a technique he used to intimidate suspects. Maletesta shook his head, returned to the arm chair and sat down.

"Mike," he said, "cut the crap."

Brennan's shoulders drooped.

"All right," he confessed. "Everything matches, professor. God damn it! The blood and threads found on the bumper of the Buick match the clothes on the guy called El Pilar. And the bullet in the Buick's dashboard matches the one they took out of that Black guy in the Fillmore."

"The Black guy had a name, Brennan. His name was Yusef X."

Brennan shrugged.

Maletesta took a deep breath. Brennan trudged back to the sofa and sat down sullenly, like a school boy in detention. Maletesta was in no hurry to ask the next question. He cleared his throat.

"I asked you to check on anyone else who was shot with a nine millimeter recently. Did you do that?"

"Yeah."

"Jesus Christ, Brennan! What did you find out?"

"A bookie named D'Angelo was shot with the same gun," Brennan mumbled.

Maletesta pounced.

"So Yusef was shot with a nine millimeter that was not a nine millimeter Luger, right?"

"Yeah."

"And a bookie named D'Angelo was shot with the same gun?"

"Yeah."

"And a bullet from the same gun was found in the dashboard of the Buick on Stevenson?"

Brennan squirmed on the sofa. He was not happy with the direction this interview had taken and he was looking for a way out. He reached into his inside coat pocket, looking for his Blackjack gum but then remembered he had thrown the package out. He bent over to tie one of his shoes. Maletesta walked over the sofa and placed his right foot on Brennan's shoe.

"What the hell!" Brennan screeched, "you've got no right . . ."

"Shut up and listen to me! I can hang you out to dry, and you know it. The bullet in the dashboard of the Buick is from the same pistol that killed Yusef X in the Fillmore and a bookie named D'Angelo in North Beach: right, Brennan?"

Brennan looked up.

"Right."

"A 9mm *Long*, not a Luger," Maletesta continued, removing his foot from Brennan's shoe, "probably fired from an Astra automatic pistol. Spanish. You know what, Brennan? I found another casing for that pistol."

"You did? Where?" Brennan asked sarcastically.

"In the alley where Yusef was killed. The same alley where your cops were too God damned busy to investigate! A kid found it. It has the same markings as the one you found in the car. The foreign language is Basque."

Maletesta was now pacing the room.

"Back to the Buick," Maletesta turned and almost shouted at Brennan.

"The Buick you found on Stevenson is the same Buick your all-of-a-sudden witness saw leaving Sinclair's entry way on Bannam Alley right after he was killed. Isn't that right, Brennan?"

Brennan felt sick and began looking around the room. His instincts told him he should leave, but his legs would not support him.

"Right, Brennan?" Maletesta repeated.

"Yeah, that's what we think."

"And that's the same Buick that ran over El Pilar, right?"

Brennan did not answer.

"Right, Brennan?" Maletesta shouted. "The Buick and the gun, a Spanish automatic, involved in all the killings, right? God damn it, Brennan! Four killings: D'Angelo, Sinclair, Yusef and El Pilar. Same killers, right, Brennan?"

"Five killings," Brennan corrected, "if you count the body of the hood in the Buick."

"Nobody gives a damn about that punk, Brennan," Maletesta countered, "maybe his partner shot him before he hot-footed it to the bus station or where ever. Thieves fall out."

"Maybe," Brennan scowled.

"Let's go over the facts again, Brennan: four people killed by two guys from LA who used a Spanish pistol and a Buick, right? Right, Brennan?"

Maletesta took a few deep breaths to control himself.

"And you knew my daughter was innocent all along, didn't you, you bastard!"

"I don't have to listen to this," Brennan said and stood up.

"You know where the door is, *brutto stronzo*," Maletesta answered and stomped out of the living room.

FIFTY

Steiner Street, San Francisco

Thursday, December 24, 1959

A few minutes after Brennan stomped out banging the front door, the telephone rang. Maletesta picked it up in the hall.

"Is the coast clear now?"

"What do you mean?" Maletesta answered.

"Mister Maletesta, I'm in the phone booth down on the corner," Osceola King said, "a sharp dressed man just walked out of your house. He looked a little raggedy, but he was a cop. You got any more in there?"

"No. How do you know he was a cop?"

"Please."

"OK, all right. Yeah, the coast is clear." Maletesta put the phone back on the receiver and went over to open the front door.

"You're a careful man, Mister King," he said as King entered the house.

"That's right, and in my business, a careful man is a live man, not a dead man."

"Please, have a seat," Maletesta said, gesturing toward the living room. "Would you like some coffee or a drink? It's Christmas Eve, my friend."

Osceola King sat in the Louis XIV chair.

"In a European chair that is as uncomfortable as this one, John, I believe I deserve a Cointreau."

"It was a wedding gift from my mother's cousin Sofia," Maletesta laughed as he opened the liquor cabinet in the corner, "and she'd be angry if I tossed it out. You didn't trifle with her."

"I understand that," King laughed. "My old granny was like that: she kept pistols all over the house. If someone sneaked in through the bathroom window, she could shoot him from the living room."

Maletesta poured the liqueur into two small crystal glasses, handed one of them to King and then sat down on the end of the sofa.

"*Salute*," Maletesta said raising his glass.

"Bottoms up," King replied.

They set their glasses down on the glass coffee table between them.

"So, Cool Breeze, what's the 'bonus information' you found?"

King reached inside his suit coat and retrieved a folded sheet of paper. He placed the paper on his knee and slowly unfolded it. Then he pulled out an ancient pince nez and carefully positioned it on his nose.

Maletesta waited, understanding that the presentation was an important part of the program. King cleared his throat and looked at Maletesta.

"This is a copy of a Will," King stated, "which spells out who gets what on the demise of the owner of a business on Bay Street called Pacific Iron Works."

Maletesta whistled sharply.

"Yes, Maletesta first name John," King smiled, "I told you I had bonus information."

"So," he adjusted the pince nez and continued, "it says that Cynthia Ambrose--born Cynthia Stromeyer—will get a forty-nine percent interest in the business. It also says that, if her brother, David Stromeyer, who also has forty-nine percent, should die before she does, she gets to assume complete control of the business."

Maletesta raised his eyebrows.

"Why does Cynthia—who's obviously Robert Ambrose's wife—get complete control? She and her brother have equal shares."

"Because," King answered, "in the event of David's death, Cynthia gets control of Harold's two per cent."

"Harold?" Maletesta asked.

"Harold is their father, Harold Stromeyer, who owned the whole enchilada at the time the will was made."

"Unbelievable! And there's nothing to David's family?"

"Apparently not," King answered, looking up over the top of his odd eyeware.

King pulled another piece of paper out of his pocket and held it up.

"It says here that said business was sold last October."

Stunned, Maletesta's mind reeled. *There it is; there it is.*

"Jesus! Where did you find this paper?"

King raised both hands in feigned surrender.

"Oh no, John, that information is what they call a trade secret. I have associates who are true artists, masters of manipulation of mechanical devices. I would never betray their art. Their success is their reward. They live for the deed of accomplishment, you see."

Maletesta lit a cigarette and slowly smiled.

"OK, I will accept that, Cool Breeze, and the artistry of your friends. I'll be right back."

A few minutes later, Maletesta returned to the living room with an envelope in his hand.

"One hitch I see," King said, "is that you hired me to uncover a reason for the death of one Yusef X. I'm not sure how all of this information helps to solve *that* problem."

"I think poor Yusef got too close to an ugly master plan to buy property in the Fillmore ahead of development. We're almost onto that, and your information gives us a source and a reason."

"I see."

"So, my extremely helpful friend, how do we settle this on Christmas Eve? You have done really incredible work. Give me a number."

"I'll give you a number, John, but first, I will give you some free advice: if you have an attorney, never leave anything important in his office."

"Ah," Maletesta nodded. "How about that number?"

"Five hundred."

"Let's call it nine hundred fifty and done," Maletesta replied, spreading the bills from the envelope out on the glass coffee table.

"You are one righteous man, John Maletesta," Osceola King said as he picked up the bills and headed toward the front door, "I hope we can do business again. My very best wishes for you and yours in this holiday season, or as my friend Charles Brown would sing, 'Merry Christmas, Baby.'"

FIFTY ONE

Thursday, December 24, 1959

Steiner Street

Nat "King" Cole crooned from the radio in the living room about chestnuts roasting when the phone rang. Tal was in her bedroom where Maletesta hoped she was working diligently on her paper. Earlier they talked about going to Midnight Mass, but that was several hours away. Maletesta sat at his desk in the study absent-mindedly listening to Cole while he doodled on a pad.

"Hello," he said flatly, picking up the extension phone on his desk.

"That's not a very jolly voice, John, for the eve before our Savior was born."

"Good evening, Sister Agatha. The good news is that, according to the police, Tal is in the clear."

"Thank God."

"The bad news is that the other pieces of the puzzle have not come together. We haven't found a murderer . . . it's been a long day."

"Yes, well, I'm sorry about that, but I have some information which will probably make it longer," Sister Agatha said. "My cousin Dennis called with the information you requested about the properties on Hayes Street."

"Holy moley! What is it, Sister?"

Maletesta could hear a muffled conversation at the other end of the telephone.

"Just a minute, John," Sister Agatha said, "we apparently have a disagreement with the choir master about where the family members of the choir will be seated tonight."

"What?"

""I'll be right there, Sister Thomasina," Sister Agatha called to an unseen person on the other end of the phone. "John, I'll call you later."

"Wait! Hello, hello?"

Maletesta banged down the phone. He bounced his pen off the pad and stomped out of the room. He stopped abruptly in the hall and retraced his steps back into the study. He pulled a small black board and an easel out from behind the file cabinet in the corner and set them up next to the door. He rummaged through the desk drawer for a piece of white chalk and, referring to his yellow pad, drew four boxes across the board. He made one slightly bigger than the other three. He sat down at the desk and admired his work, a slight smile on his face.

The phone rang and he picked it up on the first ring.

"Sister Agatha?"

"Yes, John, and I apologize for the delay. The choirmaster, to put it mildly, is a bit of a stickler for medieval rules regarding the order of seating during High Mass. He is quite excellent with the choir, so we make allowances for his foibles."

Maletesta coughed.

"Now, I have the names of the owners of the apartment building on Hayes Street, but Dennis told me something else that may interest you."

"OK . . ."

"Dennis confirmed that there is a City project called 'Redevelopment' which plans to knock down many of the buildings in the Fillmore District and replace them with new buildings . . ."

"No," Maletesta interrupted, "I heard something about that, but I can't believe it will ever happen. It's crazy!"

"As I was saying, Dennis told me it's called 'urban renewal.'

"Still seems unlikely to me. How about the names of the property owners?"

As Sister Agatha spoke, Maletesta exhaled loudly, scribbling the names on a pad.

"I hope this information helps you solve your puzzle, John."

"I think the pieces just came together, Sister," Maletesta replied. "If I had a tail, it would be wagging. Thank you and Merry, Merry, Merry Christmas!"

Sister Agatha hung up laughing.

"Tal!" Maletesta shouted.

Tal came running into the study, her eyes wide with apprehension.

"I'm sorry," her father apologized, "there's no need to be frightened. Sister Agatha just gave us the last two pieces in the puzzle."

"What do you mean?"

"Look," Maletesta said, motioning her over to the desk and tapping his index finger on the yellow pad. "It all comes together now."

"OK," she said tentatively, leaning over her father's shoulder as he began ticking off a list on the page which was titled, "Facts."

"First," he began, "we have our facts. We have that green Buick everywhere. A neighbor saw in on Bannam Alley the night that Sinclair was killed . . ."

"Jean Paul, Dad, please."

Maletesta squeezed her hand.

"Yes, Jean Paul Sinclair, "Maletesta murmured, as he moved his finger down the list. "Then we saw that Buick outside Winterland when those two hoods tried to shoot me.

We also learned from police forensics know that it's the same Buick that ran over El Pilar."

Maletesta paused, taking a deep breath and letting it out slowly.

"Then we have the bullet in the Buick found on Stevenson. It's an unusual 9mm cartridge, often confused with a Luger but actually from a Spanish pistol. The police found a bullet in the dashboard. The cops don't know how it got there, but we do: outside Winterland, I saw the gun coming up and fired first."

"Yes," Tal sighed.

Maletesta flipped over to the next page.

"Bullets. The cartridge case I bought from the little girl near the alley where Yusef was murdered was unusual: I didn't recognize it, Bob Chow's guy didn't recognize it, Brennan could care less. But Uncle Con recognized it: he came across it in Spain. So we had an odd gun and cartridge which might link all the shootings together, and I asked Brennan to check out all the recent shootings which involved a 9mm bullet. He did, reluctantly, and found another shooting."

"The 'Angel,'" Tal shuddered, "that poor man who was murdered two weeks ago."

"Unfortunately, yes," her father answered. "The murders of Jean Paul Sinclair, Yusef X, El Pilar, and D'Angelo are inextricably connected by the Buick or the bullets."

"Dad, this is really awful, but why? It doesn't make any sense!"

"Now it does," Maletesta replied, walking over to the black board, "thanks to Sister Agatha's cousin."

"So what are the boxes?"

"These boxes represent four properties on Hayes Street in the Fillmore," pointing to the boxes on the board. Maletesta picked up the chalk and crossed out two smaller boxes on one side of a larger box and another small box on the other side.

"We know that Golden Gate Investments bought these three buildings earlier this year."

"OK."

"Here's our working hypothesis, Tal," Maletesta explained. "Why hasn't the buyer of the buildings on either side not bought the large building in the middle? The answer has to be that whoever owns that building—which turns out to be a rather large apartment building—does not want to sell it."

"Yes," Tal agreed, "if it's valuable property, the owners were probably holding out for a better offer. That makes sense, but how do all these transactions fit into the mess we're in?"

Maletesta faced his daughter.

"Because the owners of the apartment building in question are Florindo "Frankie" D'Angelo and Paul Seiberling, known locally as Jean Paul Sinclair."

Tal blinked in disbelief.

"No."

"Unfortunately, yes," her father clarified, "the bookie called 'the Angel' and Jean-Paul Sinclair the poet owned a large apartment building on Hayes. I think it cost them their lives."

Tal sunk into the leather chair.

Neither of them spoke for a few moments as the information sank in. Maletesta tossed the chalk onto the desk. Tal stared at the boxes on the black board, her eyes filling with tears.

"Dad, what you're saying is that two people were murdered because they owned an apartment building," she whispered.

"That's what it looks like. Whoever hired the killers would then own that entire block on Hayes, assuming the survivors would sell it."

Tal shook her head.

"We don't know that."

"No, we don't, but we do know from Sister Agatha's cousin that Hayes Street is probably in the redevelopment area, and a real estate guy in the barbershop said the that redevelopment means big money for the owners of the property in that area. I'd guess there wouldn't be a problem in the sale of the apartment house, given the extraordinary means used to get it. Actually, it's not unlike the schemes of your Tammany Hall politician . . ."

"Plunkitt. But, Dad, this is the work of a psychopath; Plunkitt was just a crook."

"Yes, the only similarity is that someone finds out big public money is coming into some area and gets there first. Unfortunately," Maletesta clarified, "I think it cost three more people their lives: Yusef, El Pilar, and probably the owner of Pacific Iron Works, David Stromeyer."

"My God! This is the work of a mad man! Who would do this kind of thing? And why would someone want to do this?"

Maletesta turned over a few more pages on his pad and glanced at his notes.

"Well," he began, "we do know that Yusef was asking questions all over the Fillmore about people buying out the residents. Someone thought he was a threat. Maybe he was warning people. We'll never know. El Pilar was investigating Sinclair's death for me. He obviously uncovered something."

Maletesta picked Tal's scribbled notes from Maria's phone call off the desk and read them quickly.

"It seems to me that El Pillar's note made two important points. He talked about 'other things of note regarding paper and property' and 'alas for the Angel.'"

"'Alas for the angel,'" Tal repeated.

Maletesta shook out a Fatima and lit it. He closed the lighter quietly, laid it on the corner of the desk and turned to face Tal.

"I think that Stromeyer was the first victim of Golden Gate Investments. His accidental death in Los Angeles last summer was exactly like Sinclair's and the Buick was stolen in Pacific Palisades, not far from there. It has to be the same two hit men."

"But, can we prove any of this, Dad? It seems like a lot of suppositions because the killings were almost done by like, remote control. You know what I mean?"

"I am afraid that you are absolutely correct."

Maletesta stood up and stubbed out the cigarette.

"However, as far as the police are concerned, at the least, you are in the clear. They have enough circumstantial evidence that the hoods from LA killed Sinclair, Yusef, D'Angelo, and El Pilar. However, the trail back to Golden Gate Investments stops right there."

Tal suddenly stood up and shook herself.

"You know, Dad, it's Christmas Eve and we're deep in this really ugly thing. I mean, really ugly. It's just too much for Christmas. I feel like we should go to midnight Mass or something, anywhere."

"You're right, Tal, let's get the hell out of here. Get your coat. Oh, and I want to give you your present when we get back."

Tal raised an eyebrow, confused.

"You're saying *present*, as in just one?"

"Yeah, just one. Get your coat. I don't want to stand. All the Christmas and Easter Catholics will be there."

"Like us."

"Get your coat."

FIFTY TWO

Steiner Street, San Francisco

December 25, 1959

Maletesta presented a strange sight hovered over the stove with his new Sherlock Holmes deer stalker cap on his head, smoking a curved calabash pipe. He was engrossed in making one of his breakfast specialties: scrambled eggs with garlic and oregano, sautéed onions and parmesan cheese. He gently turned over the eggs in the frying pan with a spatula as Tal entered the kitchen. Italian sausages warmed on a smaller pan on one of the back burners.

"Dad, I can't believe what's in the garage," she whispered, "my own car, a brand new Renault. I don't know what to say or how to thank you enough!"

Tal hugged her father, giggling.

"Red is fantastic!"

"Not red," Maletesta corrected, "*rouge corail.*"

"Whatever you say, Dad. I can't believe it! My own car!"

Tal stood back and studied her father.

"My oh my, aren't you the picture of Sherlock Holmes!"

Maletesta put down the spatula and took the pipe out of his mouth.

"Elementary, my dear Talah. This is a wonderful Christmas present! Regarding the car, Doctor Talah, it is time for you to be doing your own driving, and I just couldn't resist the TV commercial boasting of a car with a 'city' horn and a 'country' horn. The absurdity of it seemed to fit us."

The telephone rang and Tal answered it in the hall.

"Merry Christmas!" she said as she picked up the telephone.

"*Buon Natale*!"

"Oh yeah, '*Buon Natale*.' Is that you, grandpa?"

"No. Tell your father: page two in today's paper. No more problems."

"OK, but what is this about? Hello? Hello?"

There was no answer and then a dial tone. Shaken, Tal hung up the phone and returned to the kitchen.

"Who was on the phone?" her father asked, frowning at the eggs as he turned them.

"I'm not sure. It was a man who spoke Italian, but not grandpa. He said '*buon natale*' and then said 'tell your father page two in today's paper. No more problems."

Maletesta laid the spatula on the side of the stove and turned off the gas burner.

"Uncle Carlo?"

"Maybe. I haven't heard his voice in a long time."

"Will you get the paper, please, Tal?"

Tal went outside and picked the newspaper off the stairs. She separated the front section and placed the rest of the paper on the table in the hall. Back in the kitchen, she dropped the front section like it was a rattlesnake. She waited as her father sat down and turned over the front page. There was a one column wide headline at the top of the page announcing "*Body Found in the Bay*," followed by a short paragraph.

"*Last night the body of a middle aged man was found floating near Pier 45 by longshoremen coming off their shift*," Maletesta read aloud. *"Police said the man was well dressed but had no identification on him, and they suspect foul play. More details will be announced as the investigation continues."*

Maletesta scanned the rest of the page, tapping his fingers on the table. Tal leaned over his shoulder, reading. The two of them quickly scanned articles about the dry weather with a map of normal rainfall in the Bay Area, another about a warehouse fire in San Jose, and a large ad for after-Christmas sales at the Emporium. There was no doubt that the telephone reference was to the body in the Bay.

"Is this the 'ears won't hear nothing, no more,' Dad?"

Maletesta hesitated.

"I'm not sure, Tal, but I think that we are seeing some kind of rough justice."

Tal walked into the living room and stared out of the window on Steiner Street. Maletesta came up behind her and put his arm around her, hugging her close. They said nothing for several minutes.

"Talah," Maletesta finally murmured.

"What?"

"It's over, honey. It's finally over."

"Dad, it's Christmas; it's Christmas Day! Is this how we celebrate the beautiful day of Christmas? Did Uncle Carlo kill that man?"

Tal turned to her father.

"Is this how we celebrate? How can we live like this? How?"

"Let's walk," her father said.

They left their breakfast half cooked on the stove in the kitchen, walked out the front door and down Steiner Street to the Marina Greens. Then they walked west through Crissy Field out to Fort Point. They paused to watch pelicans fly over them and dive into the Bay, fishing. Maletesta handed his daughter his handkerchief to wipe tears away. Sail boats flitted through the Gate and back. A few dog walkers and an MP in a jeep passed them. When they reached Fort Point, they walked back holding hands.

Not a word passed between them.

FIFTY THREE

Ingleside, San Francisco

December 25, 1959

"Pop, you said you'd tell me what you've heard on Bay Street about Pacific Iron Works after dinner. I'm ready."

Maletesta and his father sat at the table in the dining room of the Borica Street house. Dinner dishes had disappeared, and they were drinking strong Italian coffee from delicate cups with violets on them, part of the "fine china" set that Joe gave Guilia for their fortieth wedding anniversary. The handle of the cup was too small for his big iron-worker fingers, so he grasped the whole cup in his hand. Joe thought that the set was too pretentious, but he shared his wife's irritation when Mrs. Sodini--who lived across the street--inspected the underside of one of the plates to confirm that it was not made in Japan.

Maletesta lit a cigarette as Joe took a sip of coffee and then carefully set the cup back in its dainty saucer.

"Me and Peanut Harris had a drink on the corner after work yesterday," Joe started.

"The other Bimbo's," his son interrupted, "still going strong?"

"Yeah. Anyway, like I was saying, Peanut is still pissed off about the sale of Pacific Iron. He was a shop steward there for 12 years. I still can't believe it. Peanut said that Stromeyer was an OK guy: a pretty good boss, the kinda guy who looks after his men. You know, if he's not goin' out to lunch, he has it in the shop with his men."

Joe picked up the cup again but stopped it midair to point his index finger at his son.

"Now, the sister," he scoffed, "she's a whole different number. Nose in the air all the time, never goes in the shop . . . too dirty for her, I guess, Peanut thinks. Her brother ran everything, did all the work, the estimatin', the buyin', runnin' the projects, the whole ball of wax, Peanut says. Big problem for the sister, he says, she married a guy with what you call 'big ideas.' Wanted to be a big shot, but didn't wanna do no work. So, Peanut says, the guy became a real-a-tor. Sittin' on houses, waitin' for the money to find him."

Joe set the cup down again and picked up a slice of Monterey Jack from the plate of fruit and cheese in the middle of the table. Maletesta put his cigarette in an ashtray and forked a piece of pineapple. He smiled toward the kitchen where his mother and Tal were singing a rousing version of "Angels We Have Heard On High" as they washed the dishes. Tal was the only one Guilia would let near her fine china during cleanup.

"That would be Robert Ambrose."

"Yeah, that's the name, Ambrose, a real-a-tor. Guy's also kind of a health nut, Peanut says, plays hand ball, rides one those bikes that don't go nowhere."

Maletesta laughed.

"Peanut told me that he heard there was a problem with the will after the old man died, but he didn't have no details . . ."

"That's right," Maletesta clarified, "the father set it up so that his daughter got complete control if anything happened to his son. His son's family would not have control."

Joe scowled, thinking about it.

"What a bastard, huh? His son's bustin' his balls makin' money for the place, and he does a deal like that. Jealous, maybe. It happens."

"Jealous?"

"Sure, Gianni, you know some people don't want their kids to be better than them. Kinda stupid idea, really. It ain't the way it's 'sposed to be, goes against nature, I think. I mean, you're smarter than me, right? You got to college."

Maletesta shrugged uncomfortably.

"So the old man dies and Stromeyer finds out," Maletesta said, "that Ambrose--his brother in law--now has a big piece of Pacific Iron with his wife's forty nine per cent and the father's two per cent. He couldn't have been happy about that."

"No," Joe agreed, "Peanut says Stromeyer told him he was gonna challenge the will, say the old man was nuts or somethin' like that."

"Did he?"

"Poor guy never got the chance. Peanut said he went down to LA to bid on a job and fell outta the window of his hotel. It was in the papers. Poor guy. Then they sold it."

"Did Peanut know if Stromeyer's widow objected to the sale of the business?"

"No, no, no, no. Peanut says the widow didn't know nothin' about the business. They told her it was a good deal, but she didn't know no better. She didn't have no choice, anyway, did she?"

Maletesta lit a cigarette.

"Maybe the sister's husband needed the money for somethin'," Joe added, "you know, like to pay off a bet or somethin' else? Maybe that's why they sold."

"Yes," Maletesta agreed, "I think he had his eye on some property in the Fillmore."

"I don't know nothin' about that," Joe answered.

The door between the kitchen and the dining room swung open and Tal carried a cup of tea to the table. Guilia stayed in the kitchen, humming and making herself busy in order to avoid conversations between her husband and her son because they often ended in arguments. Maletesta smiled at his daughter. Tal glanced at her father. She knew that sometimes he needed to talk to grandpa alone.

“Tal, grandpa’s been telling me about Pacific Iron Works.”

Tal sat down opposite her father and looked directly into his eyes.

“Dad,” she said, “I really don’t want to talk about this anymore. Can’t we talk about something else? What are you working on in the basement, Grandpa?”

Joe Maletesta brightened.

“A stool,” he whispered, “a stool for your grandma outta maple, she loves the color of that wood.”

“When will it be finished?” Tal asked

“On Little Christmas; it’s a surprise.”

“What’s this about Little Christmas?” Guilia asked as she came through the swing door from the kitchen.

Maletesta jumped in.

“A friend of mine from Spain calls it ‘Three Kings’ Day.’”

“Well, she’s wrong,” his mother announced. “Father Casey read the gospel today at Mass, and he said they were wise men. Besides, you ever hear of wise kings? Not much.”

They all chuckled and finished clearing the table. A short while later, Maletesta and Tal drove back to Steiner Street in her new Renault.

FIFTY FOUR

Steiner Street, San Francisco

December 25, 1959

Maletesta walked around the living room of the flat, periodically pausing at the Christmas tree to adjust ornaments. He moved a shiny globe from one branch to another, stepped away from the tree to inspect his handiwork and then moved the ornament back to its original branch. It didn't matter now. Christmas was over, but by tradition, the tree could not be taken down until the sixth of January. The tree was drying out, so he sprayed it with a water bottle and then went back to moving the ornaments around.

"Does it really matter?" he muttered to himself.

Talah was curled up on the couch with her shoes off.

"What?" she yawned.

"Oh, nothing," he answered, "just thinking out loud."

A few silent minutes went by. Maletesta fiddled with some more with the ornaments and wandered went over to the window and glanced out on Steiner Street. He didn't find what he was hoping to find, so he went back to the tree and moved another ornament.

"Dad, that's the second time you moved that silver ornament with the red band."

He turned to her.

"Tal, will you give me a ride to the airport tomorrow?"

"Sure," she answered, "where are you going?"

"Kathleen, Georgia."

Tal sat up slowly, smiling.

"Cool, Dad. Really, really cool."

AFTERWORD

The Fillmore . . . No More

In 1948, the power brokers of San Francisco designated the Fillmore District as a “blight” neighborhood which needed to be removed before the City could prosper in the future. Euphemistically called “Urban Renewal,” the destruction of the Fillmore by the Redevelopment Agency moved into high gear in 1964 when 60 more square blocks were added for demolition. Homes and small businesses crumbled and collapsed under the wrecking ball and the bulldozer as the residents were driven out of their neighborhood. An influential white business organization called SPUR (San Francisco Planning and Urban Renewal) crowed about the physical attack on the Fillmore community in a report stating that it was vital for the City’s growth for the population to “move closer to ‘standard white Anglo Saxon characteristics.”

By the mid-1970’s, the destruction of the Fillmore was complete. The once vibrant Black neighborhood was left looking like a bombed out city in an old World War II newsreel. The Redevelopment Agency gave 883 “certificates” to Black-owned businesses, promising preference for renting or buying other Redevelopment property in the City and the right to return to the neighborhood from which they’d been evicted. Only 39 of those business certificates actually found new locations.

Another 4,719 certificates were given to families in the Fillmore, but only 1,099 families were put into new homes. Somehow, the Agency lost contact with 3,620 families and 744 businesses which held certificates of preference.

Across the country, the white establishment continued to sell these demolition projects to the white public as "Urban Renewal." James Baldwin more accurately defined it as "Negro Removal."

The House Un-American Activities Committee

The HUAC began its reign of terror on freedom of thought and freedom of association in 1938. In May, 1960 after two decades of riding rough shod over the Bill of Rights, the Committee descended on San Francisco in full showboat mode to ferret out "subversives" as defined by the right wing nuts on the committee. These hearings were a complete disaster for the publicity-conscious Committee. The Committee tried to restrict public participation in the hearings by issuing special invitational tickets, but hundreds of free speech protestors shut down the hearings in acts of civil disobedience. In a dress rehearsal of a technique used in the South a few years later against Black citizens demanding their right to vote, San Francisco police turned high pressure hoses on the demonstrators to blast them down the steps of City Hall.

The HUAC never held another hearing outside of the safe confines of Washington, DC.

Milton Keynes UK
Ingram Content Group UK Ltd.
UKHW040036281223
435071UK00007B/589

9 781647 189808